Clio rose from her seat, lifted a file bigger than my head from where it sat on the floor. "Would you like to parse through Hades's forms regarding the deaths of Fated Ones?"

"Fated Ones?" I asked.

"The heroes and artists, scientists and makers that we inspire, the ones whose fates are tied to the well-being of the world and its people," Clio said.

Taking a deep breath, I asked one last question. "If the gods quit, then why didn't you . . . I mean we. Why didn't we quit?"

Clio sat down again. She lifted a brownie to her lips and nibbled at a corner before answering me. "The muses, you mean. We've decided to stick it out. The humans need us. Without us, the world is a much duller place."

Also available from Chantel Acevedo
Muse Squad: The Mystery of the Tenth

MUSE SQUAD

SQUAD

The Cassandra Curse

CHANTEL ACEVEDO

BALZER + BRAY

An Imprint of HarperCollins*Publishers*

Balzer + Bray is an imprint of HarperCollins Publishers.

Muse Squad: The Cassandra Curse
Copyright © 2020 by Chantel Acevedo
All rights reserved. Printed in the United States of America.
No part of this book may be used or reproduced in any manner whatsoever without
written permission except in the case of brief quotations embodied in critical
articles and reviews. For information address HarperCollins Children's Books, a
division of HarperCollins Publishers, 195 Broadway, New York, NY 10007.
www.harpercollinschildrens.com

Library of Congress Cataloging-in-Publication Data

Names: Acevedo, Chantel, author.

Title: The Cassandra Curse / Chantel Acevedo.

Description: First edition. | New York, NY : Balzer + Bray, an imprint
    HarperCollins Publishers, [2020] | Series: Muse Squad | Audience: Ages 8–12.
    | Audience: Grades 4-6. | Summary: "When a young Cuban American girl
    discovers that she's one of the nine muses of Greek mythology, she must use her
    newfound powers to help a brilliant classmate who is destined to save humanity"
    —Provided by publisher.

Identifiers: LCCN 2019035448 | ISBN 9780062947703 (pbk.)

Subjects: CYAC: Muses (Greek deities)—Fiction. | Goddesses, Greek—Fiction. |
    Magic—Fiction. | Mythology, Greek—Fiction. | Cuban Americans—Fiction.

Classification: LCC PZ7.A1733 Cas 2020 | DDC [Fic]—dc23

LC record available at https://lccn.loc.gov/2019035448

Typography by Joel Tippie
21 22 23 24 25   PC/BRR   10 9 8 7 6 5 4 3 2 1

First paperback edition, 2021

For Penelope, Mary-Blair, Jaina, and Vanessa.
Thank you for being my muses.

Launch out on this story, Muse, daughter of Zeus,
start from where you will—sing for our time, too.

Homer's The Odyssey, Book I
Emily Wilson, translator

Chapter 1
THE PROBLEM WITH HEIGHTS

"JORDAN!!"

I shouted so loudly it felt like I'd swallowed the steel wool my mom uses to scrub the sink. Beside me, my best friend, Raquel Falcón, was red as a stop sign and screaming her head off, too.

We couldn't help ourselves. There, onstage and in the flesh, was superstar singer Jordan Miguel, and he had just pointed straight at us and blown us each a kiss.

Raquel and I had won front-row tickets on Y-100's "Guess That Sound" contest. We called in and guessed the noise correctly—restaurant chopsticks breaking apart. Now we were at the concert, and Jordan Miguel had made actual eye contact with us.

"Raqui!" I squealed, clinging to my best friend's arm.

"I know!" she shouted back, her eyes locked onto Jordan

Miguel as he danced up and down the stage. He sang all his hits, and we knew every word. By the time the arena lights finally came back on, we'd lost our voices. Then we went to go spend all our money on concert T-shirts.

My phone rang while we were in line for the shirts. I dug it out of my pocket. "It's probably my mom," I said to Raquel before looking down.

I must have made a face at the screen, because Raquel's eyes widened. I mouthed the words *my dad* to Raquel, and she nodded.

"Hello?" I answered the call.

"Callie, mi niña! How was the concert?"

"Fun," I said. Papi lives in New York City with my step-mother, Laura.

"Guess what?" Papi asked. It was hard to hear him over the people shouting their souvenir orders. I thrust my money into Raquel's hands and she bought our T-shirts while I talked with my dad.

"Guess what?" he asked again.

"Chicken butt," I said, rhyming with him like I always did.

Papi laughed. "You're going to have a baby brother or sister soon!" he announced the way the DJ said, "You've just won tickets to the Jordan Miguel concert!" Except it wasn't anything like that.

"Oh," I replied. I curled my fingers tighter and tighter around my cell phone as he talked. "Are you happy, Callie?

Aren't you happy?" Papi asked me.

I didn't know if I was happy or not. I already had brothers—older twin brothers, to be specific—and they were as annoying as allergies. Why did Papi have to call now, anyway, on the best night of my life? I shouldn't have been surprised. His timing was always bad.

Papi married Laura a year ago, and six months after the wedding, they moved over a thousand miles away. We hadn't seen him since he left. When he lived with us, Papi was always tired. I'd like to think that he wasn't tired of us, that that's not the reason he left. Add a new baby to the equation and, well, if the universe ever invented a better way to tire out a grown-up, I don't know what it is.

I try not to think about that at all.

"I'm happy, Papi," I said.

"You okay?" he asked. "You sound funny."

"I lost my voice at the concert," I said quickly.

"Ah. I remember those days. Well, big sister, we'll talk soon. Laura sends her love."

"Love you, Papi."

"Love you, kiddo," he said.

Just as I ended the call, Raquel appeared with T-shirts in hand, holding them up like trophies. "Jordan Migueeeeeeel," she said for the billionth time that night.

Outside, my mom and Raquel's mom were waiting for us. It had been pouring rain, but they'd stayed under an umbrella the whole concert. In the period between when the music ended and when we exited the building, Mami had texted me five times. Her last text read: Did you hear from your dad?

I texted back Yep, and I was grateful that she left it at that.

We rode the Metrorail back home, fighting the crowds of concertgoers to get on and find seats. It was an elevated train, and we watched through the windows as Miami zipped by. The rain had cleared up, and the city was all shiny and wet. Raquel leaned her head on my shoulder. "I'd give anything to be onstage like that," she said, her voice scratchy.

"Not me. Having all those eyes pinned on you? No thanks," I said.

Raquel laughed, and put on her concert T-shirt over her tank top. On the front, Jordan Miguel was standing in a spotlight, with giant wings sprouting from his shoulder blades like an angel. On the back, the cities and venues of his tour were listed, with Miami right at the very end.

I slipped my shirt on over my clothes too, but Raquel had gotten me a size too small. "Sorry. They ran out of size large, so I got you a medium. It looks good," she said.

I smoothed the shirt down. It was too tight across my stomach. "No, it doesn't. But I'm still wearing it," I said. The tag on Raquel's shirt was sticking out. Size small. I tucked it in for her and tried not to think about how well her shirt fit compared to mine.

Raquel hummed sleepily. She was my best friend in the world and had been since the third grade, when one of our classmates, Violet Prado, had decided to play superheroes at recess. Violet claimed the role of Wonder Woman, named her best friends, Alain Riche and Max Pascal, Superman and Batman, then pointed at me and Raquel and said, "You two losers have to be civilians. We may or may not decide to save you." Raquel and I stomped off and sat in the shade for the rest of recess.

"They're the worst," I'd said.

Raquel had agreed. "We can be better best friends than they are," she'd said.

"Deal," I'd said, and we shook on it.

The rest was bestie history.

The train rumbled on, stopping every so often to pick up or drop off passengers. At every station, handfuls of people loaded on, while only a few got off. The train was very full. I nudged Raquel in the ribs when an elderly couple walked on and made eye contact with me. We stood and gave them our seats. The lady tried to give us strawberry candies from her purse to thank us, but we declined.

"Please have some," she insisted.

"They're delicious," her husband added.

"No thanks," Raquel and I both said at the same time.

"Don't be shy," the woman said, and tried putting a piece of candy in my hand. Alarmed, I jerked out of reach.

"Honestly, no thanks," I said, walking away.

We took a spot near one of the doors. It was late, and the city twinkled like it was lit with a million birthday candles. Someone at the front of the car was playing a Jordan Miguel song on their phone, and Raquel and I bopped to it where we stood.

It was the perfect night.

That is, until we heard a loud crack and a *whoosh*. My hair blew into my face. The train car rattled. Raquel's nails dug into my arm, and I heard my mother scream, "Ay!"

The door at our backs had flown open thirty feet in the air. My stomach felt like it dropped just as far. I lost my balance and reached out to grab Raquel's arm.

Raquel cried out and her knees buckled. She didn't do heights. Even climbing the stairs at school she held on to the handrail harder than she had to.

"Callie, move, move, move," Raquel shouted, pushing hard toward the center of the train, but we couldn't get very far from the open door. One shove in the other direction and we would go flying.

Our moms were on their feet, trying to reach us, but the crowds were thick and everybody was panicking, including me. US 1 rushed by beneath us. Did this train always go *this* fast?

"Oh no, oh no," Raquel kept saying every time someone pushed us closer to the door. I couldn't catch my breath. When I looked at my mom, her face was frozen in a way I had seen once before—the day my tia Annie died. Her funeral had been the first one I'd ever been to. Walking up to her coffin was the scariest thing I'd done. Later, Raquel told me it was the bravest. But on the train, I didn't feel very brave at all, with the roar of the traffic below and the rush of air at my neck.

My hands started tingling so hard they went numb, and tears blurred my vision. Raquel had wrapped both arms around my chest, making it hard for me to breathe.

"Callie, make it stop," she kept saying hoarsely.

I reached out to try to push the door back in place, my hand feeling like it was being jabbed by a million pins for some reason, but Raquel grabbed my arm and yelped in my ear. "You'll fall!" she shouted, pulling me as far as she could into the train.

"Make up your mind!" I said. The truth was, I was terrified, too. The car gave a great jolt, and a few people toppled over, pushing us closer to the open door. I heard a baby crying somewhere inside the car, and tears sprang to my own eyes. Raquel and I weren't the only ones in danger. *All* these people were.

The top of my head started to buzz, as if a swarm of bees had decided to build their hive in my hair. "What the—" I started to say, but was choked off when Raquel squeezed me even tighter. I felt funny. Off. Like when a cold is coming on, or a sneeze, or like the seconds between when the lights went off at the concert and Jordan Miguel appeared onstage.

It felt like I was on the edge of something happening.

A murmur grew around us, as suddenly people in the

car stopped shouting and started planning. Just then, the adults standing near us began linking arms, anchoring one another, as if they'd all had the same idea at once. "Cuidado," one man called. "We've got this!" a woman yelled. A man in nurse scrubs, secured by a chain of people behind him, reached out and grabbed the edge of the door, sliding it closed at last. The whoosh of outside air died immediately.

For a moment, there was silence. The feeling came back to my hands and the top of my head.

Then everyone in the train car cheered, just as we pulled into the next station.

"¡Afuera!" my mom shouted, and we left the train and waited for the following one. On the next train, we took seats as far as we could from the doors.

"I'm sorry I was such a chicken," Raquel finally said when we got off the train.

"You weren't!" I said.

"Heights freak me out," Raquel said, her voice catching a little.

"It really was scary. All those people, though. A train full of heroes. Who would have ever guessed?" I said.

"Right? That part was cool." She was quiet for a moment, then her eyes came to rest on my too-tight T-shirt. "Jordan Miguel, Callie! How awesome was that?"

I squealed. "I'll never forget it. Ever," I said. Then we hugged goodbye.

Chapter 2
THE PIRATE AND THE SNOWMAN

My mom kept kissing the top of my head as we made our way into the house, and I know what she was worrying over—that I could have ended up somewhere on US 1, flat as a pancake. I wasn't thinking about it on the train, but now, with my feet on firm ground, I couldn't stop imagining myself in free fall.

"I'm okay, Mami," I lied. I couldn't stop trembling.

"I know," she said, but she understood the truth. She looked at me for a little longer than necessary. "Bueno. Go to sleep. Have sweet dreams, mi amor," she said at last.

Not gonna lie, my legs were shaking as I pulled on my pajamas. The twins were awake and softly talking in the bedroom next door. Mami wanted me to go to sleep, but I knew I couldn't just yet. The boys would distract me from what had happened, probably by irritating me. That would help get my mind off things.

They weren't identical twins. Mario had brown, wavy hair, like mine. But he was skinny, and his eyes weren't dark brown. They were green like the ocean on a stormy day. Fernando looked more like me—with baby fat around the middle and big brown eyes that Mami called "color café." All three of us had inherited our mother's nose, which had a little bump in the middle, the inability to touch our toes without lots of stretching first, and a tiny mole just above the knuckle of our left pinkie finger.

Gently, I pushed the door to their room open. Half the room was painted yellow, and in one corner was a huge, rusty anchor. That was Fernando's side. He liked trolling the junkyard and bringing home the weirdest things he could find. His treasures, he called them. When Fernando was younger, he used to say he wanted to be a pirate when he grew up.

The other side of the room was painted sky blue. There were pictures of snowcapped mountains on the walls, a beat-up pair of skis over the closet (another of Fernando's junkyard finds), and bookshelves that were neat and dust-free. Mario's side. Even though we'd never seen snow, when he was little Mario used to say he wanted to be a snowman.

An actual *snowman*.

It was ridiculous, even for a little kid, and we still teased him about it.

They'd just turned sixteen that September and they hadn't talked about pirates and snowmen in a long time. I wondered what they whispered about now, always a little jealous that I wasn't in on the conversation.

They were sitting on their beds (yellow bedspread for Fernando, blue for Mario), and chucking balled-up pieces of paper at one another as they chatted. I felt left out at the sight. They always had each other. Meanwhile, I was all alone next door. "Hey," I said, interrupting. They both turned at once and each threw a ball of paper at me.

"Nope. Out of our room," Mario said.

"What he said," Fernando added.

"Come on, guys. I almost died tonight," I said. Fernando laughed and waved me off. Mario narrowed his eyes at me. "Really. Ask Mami. One of the Metrorail doors opened up and Raquel and I nearly fell out."

"Seriously?" Mario asked.

"Come here," Fernando said, and scooted over to make room for me. He slung a heavy arm around my shoulders and dumped a couple of paper balls in my lap. "Aim for his nose. He hates that," he said.

"At least she can throw," Mario taunted.

"A compliment?" I asked in surprise. "I should almost fall to my death more often." Then Fernando pushed me clean off the bed. I dropped like a sack of rocks.

"Better?" he asked.

Laughing, I kicked at his shins, but he dodged my feet.

"Shh, Mami thinks we're asleep," Mario said, and we quieted down.

It was good to be in their room, even if I'd just been dumped onto the floor. At least it wasn't lonely. My legs had stopped shaking, but something else was bugging me.

"Did you talk to Papi?" I asked quietly.

My brothers nodded. Fernando swiped at his nose. Mario started to scan his bookshelves, as if he were going to pull a book down and start reading right then.

"What a mess," Fernando said at last.

"Nothing's been right since Tia Annie died," I said.

"I think we're supposed to be happy about the baby," Mario said.

"I'm not," Fernando mumbled.

"Me neither," I said.

Mario sighed. He always seemed older to me, though Fernando would point out that Mario was actually ten minutes *younger* than him.

"I'm not mad. Just surprised is all," Mario said.

"Yeah," Fernando and I both said at once.

We were all quiet for a moment. Then the paper ball war started again, the three of us getting louder and louder until Mami pounded on the door.

"Calliope Maria! Fernando Luis! Mario Ignacio! GO TO SLEEP!"

We stopped and fell silent. "Dang," Fernando whispered. "She used all our names."

"You'd better go," Mario said.

I got to my feet, gave my brothers a wave, and wandered into the hallway. My room was dark, but my mom had turned down my bed and set a glass of water on my nightstand. The events of the night seemed very far away now. Papi, the Metrorail, even Jordan Miguel, were all starting to feel like a dream.

I rubbed my hands together. That numb sensation had gone away. I touched my head. Not tingling anymore. It had been the strangest feeling, almost like I was coming down with a flu or something. Then it had stopped as soon as we were safe.

I slid into bed and soon realized I was gripping my bedsheets, as if a strong wind might blow me away. *Relax, Callie,* I told myself. I loosened my fingers, tucked the blanket under my chin, and concentrated on the mattress against my back, nice and firm, until I fell asleep.

Chapter 3
I Make Things Weird

The next thing I knew, I was looking out on a green field that ended, strikingly, at the edge of a vast body of water. It wasn't an ocean, I knew that much being from Miami. Maybe it was a river? If so, it was a big one. My heart thundered away.

I didn't have a clue how I had gotten there.

I spun a few times, trying to get my bearings, when I remembered. I had been sleeping. In my room. But where was I now?

The cola-dark water in the distance sparkled. One corner of the sky glowed, as if a spotlight had been pointed at it like some kind of dream Bat-Signal.

The earth rumbled beneath my feet. One by one, small hills ruptured the earth and white ostrich eggs popped out. Except they weren't ostrich eggs—they were white heads, white faces, then necks and torsos; hips, legs, and feet. Statues. Giant statues, each taller than my school. There were nine of them. All women. They glimmered in the light, their faces restful. Slowly, as if they might shatter if they moved too quickly, the statues turned to face me.

So I did what any intelligent eleven-year-old would do in that situation.

I bolted.

Where to? I had no idea, but I ran harder than the time my brothers caught two flying cockroaches off the fruit trees in our backyard and released them in my room. I ran until I was in the water. My feet were wet, my pajamas were soaked. I turned around and those statues were still staring at me. They looked . . . amused. As if my little show of running had delighted them.

"You're dreaming," a voice said behind me. I turned and saw my tia Annie. Seeing her made me feel funny, like having the wind blow your homework into the street and then watching it get run over by a car. When a thing like that happens, you can't believe your eyes. But I was dreaming. Tia Annie had just reminded me.

"I know," I told her. She was in the water too, bald, and wearing her hospital gown. I couldn't look at her straight. When I was very little, I used to call Tia Annie my best friend. She was the kind of grown-up who didn't mind playing with a kid, didn't mind endless rounds of board games or hide-and-seek. When she got sick, she was too tired for all that. Not the same kind of tired as my papi. She was scary-tired. But, even so, she was still my tia Annie. No, I couldn't look at her in that gown, in the water, talking to me in this strange and too-brightly-lit place. My throat clamped tight looking at her. It felt like I was at her funeral all over again, trying not to cry so much that I gave myself a headache. I needed this dream to end.

"Sometimes, dreams are portents. Do you know what the word 'portent' means?" she asked.

I shook my head. Tia Annie wrung out the bottom of her gown and tsked before answering me. "It means a dream that can tell you what's coming."

This time, I stared my aunt in the face. "You mean to tell me killer statues are coming for me?"

Tia Annie pursed her lips. "There's a message you're meant to receive, but your dream brain, the one you control, is making this, um . . ." She searched for the word. "Weird. You're making it weird, Callie."

"You're telling me I'm weird?" It stung a little to hear her say it.

"I'm telling you to let go," Tia Annie said. I looked at the statues again. Each of the women held an object. One gripped a frowning mask, another a flute. One held a globe aloft, as if she were studying it, while another balanced a trumpet on the palm of her hand, another a golden arrow. I saw another mask, and two harp-like instruments.

I took a deep breath. "So what does this dream portent?"

"Portend, you mean. 'Portent' is the noun. 'Portend' is the verb." Tia Annie had been an English teacher, and old habits died hard, I guess.

"What does this," I said, waving at the statue, "portend?"

"Can't tell you. You'll have to wait and see," she said, and then, just like that, I was awake and in my bed. I touched my feet, expecting to find them wet, but they weren't, of course.

The dream was just a dream, and it confirmed what I sort of knew about myself—weird things always happen to me, and maybe I'm the reason why.

Chapter 4
RAQUEL HITS A HIGH NOTE

The next morning, groggy and out of sorts, I went to the bathroom, washed up, and checked the mirror. A zit had sprouted on my forehead overnight. My uniform shirt was wrinkled. I pinched a roll near my waist, sucked in my breath to flatten it out. I felt crummy for a moment, then remembered *not falling to my death* the night before and felt better.

Perspective, I told myself.

At breakfast, Mario and Fernando took the last of the good cereal and left me with granola, and I was so tired, I didn't care. Why did weird dreams have to be so exhausting, anyway?

"¿Qué te sientes?" my mom asked over breakfast.

"Strange dreams. It's nothing," I said.

My mother narrowed her eyes at us. She took a bite of

her buttered Cuban bread and a sip of her café con leche. Then she cleared her throat. "I know that your father's news may have left you a bit shaken."

"Shook, Ma," Fernando said.

"And we aren't. Shook, I mean," Mario added.

I glanced at him, and he kicked me under the table.

My mom continued. "He won't love you any less because there's a new baby on the way," she said, though it didn't seem like her heart was in it. The news was hard on her, too, I knew. It wasn't like Mami had kicked Papi out, after all. He left us.

"We know, Mami," I said. "We've got this."

"Yep," Mario said. "Worry not, dear Mother." He raised his spoon like a sword when he said it.

If I had a knack for making things weird, then my brothers had a gift.

Mami took another bite of her bread, another sip of coffee. "Okay, you three. If you need to talk about it—"

"No talking. More eating," Fernando said, slurping his cereal. Honestly, that could be his motto. He could get a tattoo with "No talking. More eating" across his chest and nobody in the family would be surprised.

My school, Miami Palms Middle, serves free breakfast in the cafetorium every morning. Today it was silver dollar pancakes, and I got in line for some, even though I'd already eaten at home. Because who can resist tiny pancakes?

I slipped in line behind Violet Prado, Max Pascal, and Alain Riche, who were just as irritating as they'd been in the third grade. Max and Alain were two of the most popular boys in school. Violet was popular, too, and Cuban-American like me. We'd been in classes together since kindergarten, but she didn't seem to like me very much, or have very many actual friends besides Max and Alain. Violet was in the choir at church, and participated in a local theater, and she told anyone within earshot that she was going to be famous someday. Alain was the class clown, always cutting up, with a smile so charming the teachers let him get away with anything. Max was tall and athletic, and got really good grades.

I kept my eyes on my cell phone as the line shuffled forward, hoping not to draw their attention. I'd almost made it to the front when Violet turned around, pulled my phone out of my hand, and clicked the button that showed the home screen.

"Aw, isn't that cute," she said as her eyes locked on the selfie of me and Raquel. "A perfect ten."

Max and Alain laughed, and Alain said something to Max in Haitian Creole.

"Um. Thanks?" I said, and held my hand out for my phone.

Violet plunked the phone down hard on my palm. "Get it? A perfect ten," she said, and formed a zero with one hand and a one with the other.

I didn't get it.

"Hey!" Raquel called out from the front of the cafetorium, waving wildly at me to save her a space in line.

"There's the one," Violet said, and now I understood. Slender, elegant Raquel was shaped like the one. And me—round and zit-faced—was the zero.

"Grow up," I said.

Violet rolled her eyes. She, Max, and Alain loaded their trays with pancakes and walked off together, laughing.

Raquel made her way to me, cutting in front of half the line. "Sorry, sorry," she kept saying.

Our science teacher, Ms. Rinse, shouted at Raquel from across the cafetorium. "No cutting in line, young lady."

Violet, Max, and Alain snickered loudly.

"I'm suddenly not hungry," I said, my eyes following Violet and her crew.

"Don't let her get to you," Raquel said, loading up a tray for me. "Come on. My manager needs her strength."

I laughed, took the tray from Raquel, and left the line in search of a table. "Your manager?"

"Sure. I'll need one when I'm on Broadway," Raquel said. After classes were over, she was going to audition for the lead role of Belle in our school's musical rendition of *Beauty and the Beast*. Actually, I'd been the one to sign her up. I faked her handwriting on the sign-up sheet, putting her name just underneath Violet's. Raquel didn't talk to me for three days afterward, but then I caught her singing the opening bars of Belle's first song. Raquel was a great singer, though she didn't believe it.

She'd put on some rosy lip gloss that morning, and a set of press-on nails, which she clicked against the table as I ate.

"I thought you'd be nervous," I said through a mouthful of pancakes.

Raquel was thoughtful as she chewed. "Me too. Maybe I got it out of my system on the Metrorail? That was so scary."

"Speaking of scary," I began, then I told her about my dad and the new baby.

"I don't know. I've always wanted a baby brother or sister," Raquel said.

I tapped my spork onto my tray. "It's just that we never see him. A new baby makes it harder to get away. Airline tickets aren't cheap, and neither are diapers, I think, and . . ."

"Maybe don't overthink it just yet," Raquel said.

"Coming from you? The number one overthinker on the planet?"

"Liar," Raquel said, laughing.

I got up to put my tray away just as the first-period bell rang. "Come on. Ms. Rinse will kill us if we're late to science," I said.

"Don't exaggerate, Cal. She won't *kill* us. Maim us, maybe," Raquel said.

"You're right. Ms. Rinse is not the murdering type," I said. "Now Ms. Fovos on the other hand." We both looked to the front of the cafetorium, where Ms. Fovos stood, glaring at all the students. A pad of detention slips stuck out from her pocket, and she had a pen tucked behind each ear, ready to give out detentions with both hands if necessary.

Raquel pretended to shiver at the sight of her.

"Let's go," I said, and the two of us walked quickly past her.

"Uniforms!" she screeched at us, and we tucked our uniform shirts into our skorts rapidly before she could write out a detention.

I sighed. Weird dreams. Violet, Max, and Alain being rude. Having to see Ms. Fovos first thing. Some mornings were just plain stressful.

Raquel really *is* an overthinker, but I do my best to help. Sometimes, that means I have to lie to her. I don't lie often, but when I do, I make sure it's at least a helpful lie.

"Raquel Falcón," I said, "you're the best singer at Miami Palms Middle School. You are basically a Venezuelan Beyoncé."

Raquel knew it was a lie. We were sitting in the cafetorium before the auditions. Whatever confidence she'd had that morning had evaporated.

"That's it. I'm not auditioning," Raquel said. She twirled a pencil over her fingers like a tiny majorette's baton. As she did so, she groaned.

"I thought you said you weren't nervous."

"I am now," she said.

"Don't be."

"I'm not. It was the pizza at lunch. I'm lactose intolerant," Raquel said.

"Since when are you lactose intolerant? You snarf down cheesy arepas like you need them to live," I said.

Raquel stopped twirling the pencil. "Callie. I can't do it. Violet Prado is going to wipe the floor with me."

Raquel was *not exactly* the best singer at Miami Palms Middle, and we both knew it. She was good, though. Really good. But so was Violet. Maybe Violet *was* going to wipe the floor with her. But Violet was also kind of a jerk. Besides being a talented singer, Raquel was kind, patient, and a good friend—everything Violet wasn't. She deserved that part.

Raquel covered her face with shaky hands.

"Look at me," I said, taking hold of Raquel's shoulders. "You are Raquel Falcón. You're on the honor roll every quarter, you're a starter on the volleyball team. You know all the lyrics to at least four Sondheim musicals, and—"

"But, Callie—"

"*And*," I said, putting my hand across her mouth to shush her, "aaaaand, you have a really sweet voice. You will be Belle. Belle will be you. Everyone else out there is just a beast. Get it?"

Raquel blinked a few times but still had a startled look on her face. *Well, I tried,* I told myself.

The cafetorium was packed with kids from the after-school program noisily playing board games in the back of the room, while the theater kids amassed up front, lounging on the stage, sitting at tables and either poring over lyrics or scrolling through their phones. Other kids had shown up just to watch. Over at a nearby table, the class triplets, two girls and a boy, were drawing on one another's arms with markers as they waited for the auditions to start. They'd recently moved to Miami from Tampa and walked around school with coffee mugs, like grown-ups on a break at work. They each had a name that began with *L*—Letty, Lisa, and Leo. Max and Alain were thumb-wrestling at another table, while four eighth-grade girls bobbed their heads in time to the music blaring from their headphones.

An inflatable turkey, the kind people put up on their lawns for Thanksgiving, wobbled in one corner of the room under a rush of air from the AC. It was the Tuesday before Thanksgiving break. You could feel that familiar buzz among the students—vacation loomed. The drama teacher, Mr. Gomez, stood next to the turkey. He wore suspenders over his big belly, his frizzy white hair was uncombed, and he held a red pen in his mouth, even as he spoke.

"Belle auditions first," he barked. "Then Gaston. Princesses and villains, in that order, LINE UP!" he shouted. The pen trembled in his mouth like a twig in the breeze. The inflatable turkey wobbled some more.

"You've got this," I said to Raquel, giving her arm a little squeeze.

She nodded, her cheeks pale.

"No, you definitely *don't* got this." I felt a shove. "Move, hippo," a voice growled in my ear, and I watched as Violet, carrying a huge garment bag, pushed Raquel out of the way.

"Don't listen to her. You aren't fat," Raquel whispered to me, letting Violet sashay past her onto the stage.

My feelings were stinging a little, but I took a deep breath. Then I turned to my best friend. "Nope, this isn't about me. Just ignore her and do your thing." Raquel nodded and followed in Violet's wake, her arms crossed over her stomach.

"She's awful," a little voice squeaked beside me. It was Maya Rivero. We were both in the sixth grade, but she wasn't like anyone I had ever known. Tiny as a fourth grader, Maya wore her long hair in two thin plaits every day, the part down the middle of her head so straight and tight that it seemed to glow in the fluorescent lights of the cafetorium. Her mouth was full of very crooked teeth, covered in braces. A metal contraption against the roof of her mouth flashed whenever she talked, and it gave her a slight lisp. "ItTH for my narrow upper archTH," she told me one day during class. Today she was wearing a denim jumper over her uniform shirt, a flagrant abuse of the uniform rules, which no teacher ever called her on.

That was because Maya Rivero was a genius.

She could have skipped middle school altogether, but she didn't want to miss out on any "developmental social milestones." At least, that's what she told my science class on the first day of school, when we had to introduce ourselves. Everyone else sat at their desk while they talked about their favorite color, or the sport they played, or what they did over the summer. Not Maya. She stood up, her rainbow backpack still on, her hands on her waist in a "hero pose." She told us that she wanted to go to Space Camp, but that she couldn't afford the trip, and that a never-before-seen species of lizard had moved into her backyard ("Probably an invasive species," she said, except she pronounced it "invaTHive THpeeTHees"), that she loved orca whales, and that they were in danger of extinction thanks to global warming. Then she started to sob, right there in front of everyone, using a pigtail to wipe her eyes. Our homeroom and science teacher, Ms. Rinse, had to tell her to sit down. Twice.

It was a *scene*.

Speaking of scenes, I asked her, "So, Maya, are you auditioning?"

"I'm auditioning for the narrator," Maya said.

"Oh," I said. "I didn't know this play had one."

Maya then began to *narrate*, Once-Upon-a-Timing with gusto, her hands dramatically moving through the air, as if she were doing a hula.

"Okay, Maya," I said, but she kept going. "Maya. *Maya. Okay.* You're . . . you're great. You can stop practicing now."

Maya froze, her eyes on the stage. The entire cafetorium had gone silent.

There stood Violet in a yellow gown. It was off the shoulders and embroidered in gold thread. The stage lights bounced off the dress, which sparkled when Violet turned around.

"We were supposed to bring costumes?" Maya asked nobody in particular.

Mr. Gomez clapped his big hands. He has one of those loud claps, the kind of applause that makes my ears feel as if I've gone too far with a Q-tip. "Brava, Violet!" he said, before hearing a single note.

"Merci," Violet said, curtseying. "Belle was French, so I'll say it again, MERCI, MONSIEUR GOMEZ!"

A couple of groans from the afterschool kids snapped Mr. Gomez out of it. "Okay, Violet. Sing your song," he said, and sat down beside me. He pressed Play on his phone, the music started, and Violet sang.

I hate to admit it, but Violet really does have a nice voice. It's the kind of voice you expect from a princess—lilting and nonthreatening. It's a voice that's nothing like her personality.

Halfway through the song, Maya tapped Mr. Gomez on the shoulder, asking, "Can the narrator audition be next? I have a SAP meeting." He ignored her. Maya glanced at her watch. "I suppose I can be a few minutes late to SAP," she whispered, except she pronounced it "THAP." Then, she sat back down again.

"Sap?" I asked. What kind of club calls itself Sap, I ask you?

"Scientists Are People," Maya said very seriously. "It's

an anti-science world, Callie. We're fighting a good fight."

"Oh. Right. Of course," I said.

Violet was curtsying again, her song finished. It was Raquel's turn next. Violet faced the wings of the stage and said, "You can all go home now," before relinquishing the spotlight.

"Come on, Raqui!" I shouted, jumping up and down. Mr. Gomez gave me a look, so I sat again.

Raquel emerged from the shadows slowly. I watched as Violet passed Raquel. Violet's yellow-slippered foot reached out to trip Raquel, who fell in slow motion, her hip hitting the stage floor first, her face crumpling.

Don't cry, don't cry, don't cry, I said in my head, because Raquel was close to bawling, I could tell. Lazily, Mr. Gomez asked, "Are you okay?" from where he sat. Raquel sat up and dusted off her legs and butt. She blinked pathetically, looking like a lost kitten with a double eye infection.

That was my best friend up there. She was bombing her audition in a big way and here I was, powerless to help. I was so mad, my skin started to buzz, like I might explode.

Suddenly, Maya stood and shouted, "Fight the good fight, Raquel!" Everyone turned to look at her—quiet, mousy Maya, with bared teeth and her hand raised in a fist. My mouth dropped open, making me look like a stunned fish.

Everyone got quiet. Violet snickered.

"It's our SAP rallying cry," Maya whispered, sitting down.

Raquel was on her feet again, eyes dry. She set her jaw and took a deep breath. In the wings, Violet was swishing her voluminous dress skirt back and forth, mouthing the word *loser* in Raquel's direction, in time with her dress swishing.

Lo-ser, *swish-swish*, lo-ser, *swish-swish*.

That's when IT happened. The more Violet swished, the stronger the feeling got, too—every single strand of hair on my ponytail lifted up a little bit, sort of like when someone rubs a balloon on your head and the static electricity makes your hair go all frizzy. Like that, but more. My fingertips and toes tingled, too, like when your limbs fall asleep. And finally—this is the worst part—I wanted to cry. My throat felt thick and my eyes prickled. I hate crying.

All those sensations surprised me at first, but then I remembered that I'd felt this on the Metrorail. Maybe the feelings were a reaction to fear? Except this time, I wasn't afraid. I was angry at Violet for having tripped Raquel. I shook my hands to try to get some feeling back into them.

Then, *boom*. All those feelings went away at once, as if they'd been washed off somehow. I looked up and Raquel was suddenly . . . beautiful. I mean, she's always been my beautiful best friend, with long dark curls and big brown eyes, and freckles on her nose. But this was different. She was glowing a little. Her cheeks were pink. Her lips looked like she'd just refreshed her lip gloss. She was . . . taller. How could that be? And when she opened her mouth to sing . . .

"You're an angel!" Mr. Gomez shouted. In his excitement, he fist-pumped the air, accidentally punching the inflatable turkey, which folded in half with a whoosh before filling up again.

The afterschoolers went quiet, dropping their board games and leaving their homework behind. They surged forward, hugging the stage like fans at a concert. Raquel sang and sang. Maya, beside me, was transfixed. Even Violet leaned against a wall and gazed dreamily at Raquel, who was, at the moment, utterly stealing the lead role right out from under her.

What was happening? My scalp tingled again, just a little this time. The prickling in my eyes started up again. I touched my fingertips and found that they were numb once more. Raquel went for the high note of the song, which she lengthened and stretched as if the music were Play-Doh. Louder and louder she sang, the note rising, rising.

I don't remember what happened after that, because my world turned black, and when I woke up, I was somewhere familiar—and a little frightening.

Chapter 5
A VISIT FROM HISTORY

Douglas Hospital is actually just down the street from where I live in Miami, off Calle Ocho in Little Havana. So it was a pretty convenient place to end up with a head injury.

Mr. Gomez told my mom that Raquel's high note shattered the light fixture above my head, and that the whole contraption came crashing down right on me, knocking me out, and that it was Maya Rivero who applied pressure to the gash on my forehead to stem the bleeding.

That's about the gist of what I knew. When I woke up, my mom was there, still in her dental hygienist scrubs. Mario and Fernando were standing in the doorway. Mario was clutching Scumby, my teddy bear. Fernando had my phone and charger.

Mami rushed toward me as soon as I opened my eyes. She touched my face gently, and called me "mi amor," and "sweetheart," and "mi niña," which was all well and good, but ow, my head hurt.

"Fifteen stitches," my mom announced. Then her cell phone rang. It was Papi. "Toma," she said, handing me the phone.

"Callie girl, what happened?" he asked.

"Hi, Papi. Freak accident," I said, my voice low. My brothers were watching me. I gestured silently to the phone, and they shook their heads, as if to say, "No, we don't want to talk to him."

"Do I need to go down there? Speak with the principal about the condition of that school?" he asked, his own voice rising.

"No, Papi. It's fine. I'm fine," I said. In the background I could hear my stepmother, Laura, asking how I felt.

"My head hurts," I said.

"You poor thing," Laura said when she got on the phone, then added, "Feel better, muñeca." She always called me that—a doll. Honestly, I didn't know how I felt about it, though sometimes, when she said it, I imagined Laura picking me up and putting me on a shelf to gather dust. We said goodbye and hung up. I handed the phone back to my mom.

My brothers stepped forward. "Here's Scumby," Mario said, handing me the tattered bear that I'd had since I was a baby. "Now you look as beat up as he does," he said, patting my knee.

"Your phone, dummy," Fernando said. I clicked it on and noticed that he'd made my screensaver a picture of himself flexing a muscle, but that he'd also charged it for me.

Everyone stayed through dinnertime—my brothers breaking off to bring fast food for us. We were crowded in there, and one of the nurses kept telling us all to be quiet, but it was no use.

We were a big Cuban family, and we weren't loud.

That's just how we talked.

My head started feeling better after I ate a cheeseburger and a milkshake. When a doctor showed up to tell me I could go home in the morning, my mood improved even more.

My brothers finally left the hospital after sunset. My mom stayed with me. A nurse rolled in a cot for her, with a pillow and blanket. We turned down the lights. She watched television, while I texted Raquel.

Hey.

Are you okay?

Concussion. Your audition nearly killed me.
What happened to you?

I don't know! It was so crazy.
I've never sung like that. I've never FELT like that.

Me neither.

???

Nothing. Just a weird feeling before your audition. My skin got tingly.

Hmm. I felt confident. Like, SUPER CONFIDENT. Like I could do anything, say anything, and it would be okay. Better than okay. It would be PERFECT.

I knew you had it in you!

I didn't.

Hey, are you . . . taller now?

It took a minute for Raquel to text me back. I figured she was measuring herself.

Callie. What in the world happened to me today?

I take that as a yes.

I'm an inch taller. Pretty sure my hair is longer too. What is this? Mega Puberty?

I didn't text back for a while. The truth was, Raquel wasn't "super confident" about much. She got excellent grades, yes, but she was afraid of roller coasters, nervous about ordering pizza delivery on the phone, and honestly, had never, ever sung like that before. And people didn't just sprout an inch in the blink of an eye. I couldn't help but think of that tingly sensation—my hair, my fingers and toes, and the lump in my throat—I'd felt it all before IT, whatever IT was, began. I remembered my dream with Tía Annie and those statues. Maybe they were trying to portend IT.

My head was throbbing again, so I slowly made my way to the bathroom and took a peek beneath the bandage. It was gruesome now, but I knew it wouldn't be so bad once it healed. The scar would lie right alongside my hairline. Aside from the stitches, I was still the same Callie, though. Whatever had affected Raquel had made no change in me.

When I came out of the bathroom, my mom was asleep, lightly snoring. I turned off the TV and lay in bed, my phone charging beside me. Raquel had texted while I'd been in the bathroom.

Goodnight, Cal. Thanks for cheering me on. I'm sorry about your head. Love you, bestie.

I thought of something my mom always said. *Callie, you are loved, and if you're loved, you'll be okay.* Something weird was definitely going on, but Mami was right. Everything would be okay.

This is what I told myself when I closed my eyes for ten seconds.

I was woken up with a nudge by a tall doctor with white hair and golden eyes. Her name tag read DR. CLIO ZAZAS, and she was flashing a light at my face.

"Calliope?" the doctor said.

"Nobody calls me that. It's Callie," I said, squinting like crazy at the light.

"I'm Clio. Everyone calls me that," she said, tucking away her small flashlight. Tiny golden trumpets dangled from her ears. They glimmered, even though the light in the room was dim.

My mother stirred. "Oh, Doctor. Is everything all righ—" She stopped. No, it was more like she *froze*. Her hand stayed in the air in greeting, her mouth stuck mid-speech. My scalp was tingling again.

"What happened?" I shrieked.

"Shush," Clio said. "Scoot over." And when I didn't budge, she moved me with her hip and plopped into bed beside me. She smelled like brownies.

"What's wrong with my mom?" I yelled.

"Are you always this loud?" Clio asked.

That shut me up. "What did you do to her?" I said, in a whisper this time. I was leaning far away from the woman now, too scared to move.

"I've relegated your mother to history. She's now in the time before this. Just a little before. And only temporarily," she said, chuckling to herself. "Get it? Temporarily? The Latin root 'tempus,' meaning time? Oh, never mind."

My mouth must have hung open. I had no idea what Clio was talking about. I was in the presence of some sort of witch and my mind had gone utterly blank.

Clio sighed. "They don't teach you anything at school anymore. All the new muses need so much *remedial* study. Listen carefully, Calliope, you—"

"Callie," I said.

Clio took a deep breath. She smoothed her white hair with her hand. "Callie. I am Clio, Muse of history. Do you know what a muse is?"

Clio was looking at me skeptically, but I actually did know. "My mom has a small statue of a muse on her dresser back home. She told me once that she was a goddess of inspiration."

"Yes, that's right. There are nine muses."

"N-nine?" I stuttered, my head swimming. Nine muses, nine statues, was I dreaming again?

"Yes, nine. I'm one. And so are you, Callie."

I laughed outright. "I'm not a goddess, and I'm not inspiring anyone," I said.

"Is that so?" Clio asked, and then, my phone started to buzz. It was Raquel. I answered it.

"CALLIE!" she screamed into her phone. "I'm dying. I'M DYING, CALLIE."

"Oh my God, what's happening? Call nine-one-one!" I said, panicked. I'd gripped Clio's forearm, forgetting all about my pounding head, this muse business, my dreams, my frozen mother.

Raquel laughed. "No, not literally. I'm dying because someone uploaded a video of my audition and it has, like, two thousand views already."

"*What!* How?"

"This is how people get famous, right?" Raquel asked. I put her on speakerphone and searched for her video. There it was. Raquel singing her head off. The views counter ticked up and up even as I watched.

"Raquel, I'm watching it now. Do . . . do you see me when I—?" I started to ask.

"No, the video cuts out before you got hurt. Hey, Cal, gotta go, I've got another call," she said, then hung up on me.

Clio was smiling without showing her teeth.

"I . . . I did that?"

"You did that. You inspired her."

"All I did was give her a pep talk," I said.

Clio shook her head. "That bit was important, yes. But you did more than that. You brought forth Raquel's hero within. The star you always see in her? You just made it easier for others to see and hear it, too."

I thought of my tingling scalp, and my numb fingers and toes, and ugh, that crying feeling. "I didn't do it on purpose," I muttered.

"No. But you'll learn how," Clio said. She touched the top of my head, and there was the tingling again, lighter this time, but everywhere.

"The people on the Metrorail? When the doors were closed?"

"Now you're understanding."

"Actually, I don't understand any of this," I said, and Clio nodded, unsurprised.

"When you are ready to know more," she said, "go to the place where you always find the answers."

"What does that—"

"Oh, and dress warmly," Clio added. She got up from the bed and walked to the door. The moment her foot crossed the threshold of my room, my mother unfroze.

Mami was blinking rapidly. She smacked her lips, which had gone dry. "I must have had a dream," she said, confused and sleepy. "You okay, Callie?"

"Yeah," I said. "Goodnight."

"Buenas noches, mi amor," she said, and fell back asleep at once.

I rubbed my head softly, wiggled my toes. The shadows in the room seemed to lengthen, and I decided that it was time to put this day behind me. I closed my eyes, but the path to sleep was longer and steeper than it had ever been, and I didn't really nod off until the dawn turned rosy.

Chapter 6
A GREAT (AND BY GREAT I MEAN BIG) BED

I was home the next day by lunchtime. It was Wednesday, and I had the rest of the week off for Thanksgiving ahead of me. Plenty of time for the swelling on my forehead—the one that made me look like a messed-up unicorn—to go away. While my mother made me some "welcome home/ get well arroz con pollo," I went to "the place where you always find the answers."

The internet.

I got 3,360,000 hits on "the Muses" in 0.85 seconds.

And none of them were very useful.

I learned that I actually shared a name with one of the muses—Calliope, Muse of epic poetry—which, whatever, what did that even mean? She certainly wasn't the Muse of getting your best friend famous on social media, which is apparently what I'd done.

There was Clio, Muse of history, represented in statues and paintings, in mosaics and even in that Disney movie about Hercules. None of the Clios looked like the one who had come to visit me. Where was her toga? Her elaborate hairdo? What about the other muses? Could I expect visits from them too, like the Ghosts of Christmas Past, Present, and Future?

I watched television for a bit, and tried texting Raquel, but she didn't answer. *What gives,* I thought. School was out for Thanksgiving. What could she be doing, anyway? And why wasn't she here, visiting me? After all, I was injured because of her voice. Or maybe, if Clio was right, it was because of me.

I got up to stretch my legs, and ended up in my mom's room. It smelled like her vanilla perfume in there. Her bed was always made, her dresser cluttered with picture frames. There, between my first-grade photo and Fernando's soccer team photo, was Calliope herself.

She was a nine-inch alabaster statue. I'd played with it a thousand times when I was little. I picked it up. She was all white, her face full-cheeked and peaceful. In one hand she held a scroll, and in the other, a small stick of some sort. An ancient kind of pen, maybe? Her robes were long and flowy, and the toes of her right foot peeked out from under them. I had a horrifying thought as I looked at it—what if the statue looked back like the one in the dream did? I put the statue down at once and turned it around.

"Your aunt gave her to me when you were born," my mom said just behind me, adjusting the statue so that it faced forward again.

"Oh," I said, startled. We didn't speak of Tia Annie very often, because it always made my mother cry. She'd been very beautiful and kind, and besides being an English teacher, she was also a poet.

My brain went *click*.

"Calliope is the Muse of epic poetry! No wonder Tia Annie liked her," I said, thinking of the slender volume of poems my mother kept at her bedside, the only book anyone in the family had ever written. She'd titled it *Tycho,* which I didn't even know how to pronounce. But we were all proud anyway. Tia Annie had dedicated it to my mother and to me: *To my sister, who inspires me more than she will ever know, and to my niece. May she read this and find her way.*

I'd read the book once, but they were poems about flowers and dogs, the sea and children, and none of them rhymed. I didn't get it.

My mother started to cry a little, but only quietly, the way a person does when grief has been around a long time and they've become used to it.

"Sí, your tia loved this muse," she said, and kissed the top of my head. "She named you. Hence the statue." Then my mother did what she always does when she starts to cry. She made a joke. "How'd I get stuck with a name like Gertrudis, anyway?"

"Aw, Trudy, what's in a name anyhow?" I said, giving my mom a big hug, which she returned.

I hadn't known that Tia Annie had named me after Calliope, the muse.

"Hmm, you always make me feel better, just like your tia Annie did." She smoothed my hair. "You look tired, mi niña. Try and take a nap, hmm?" Mami said.

"Okay," I told her, then went back to my room and closed the door behind me.

I wasn't sleepy.

I was sad. Confused. I was sure that I had hallucinated all of it—the dreams, the tingly feeling, Clio. This was . . . a lot. I started to breathe really quickly and felt a touch of panic. I'd felt this way before—the night Papi left us, when Tia Annie died, when my dad introduced us to Laura and it felt like he was leaving us for a second time, telling us he was moving to New York. That one time my brothers dressed like zombies for Halloween and snuck into my room at night, or when I put my foot into my shoe only to discover a baby lizard inside.

I took a deep breath and crawled under my bed.

Don't judge me.

The darkness always helped my breathing slow, my heart rate to stabilize. Even the dust bunnies helped ground me. "Clear your mind, Callie," I said to myself. "The answers will come if you only think," I whispered, then started breathing in through my nose and out through my mouth.

One breath.

Two breaths.

When I felt better, I opened my eyes.

The bed seemed to have . . . dropped. The bottom of it scraped my belly. The light in the room was strange and off somehow. I touched the floor, which felt different, too. Everything smelled different. I looked to my left, and the place where my room should have been was gone. Instead, there was dark paneling and glass cases full of strange objects. It was dim, and thick windows in the distance with wavy glass in them let in the grayest light from outside, where there were . . .

Tall buildings. With chimneys.

I turned to the right, my heart racing again. More paneling. More glass cases. Freezing in my tank top and pj shorts, I crawled out from what appeared to be the biggest bed in the world. Seriously, ten people could sleep in it comfortably. It had four huge wooden posters that held up a wooden canopy trimmed in red and gold, like a Hogwarts bed grown out of control.

"This isn't real," I said out loud. "It's my pain meds." I touched my head. "Yes, still very much injured and recovering," I said, squeezing back under the bed and closing my eyes. "Go away, huge bed. Just go away."

I waited in the silence, shivering in the cold. I counted to one hundred. Then, slowly, I opened my eyes again.

A pair of green eyes were looking back at me.

"No way! You got the Great Bed of Ware!" shouted a vibrantly dressed white girl lying next to me, her face only two inches from mine.

For the second time in three days, I thought I was going to die. *That's it then,* I thought. *There I go.*

But I didn't die. Instead, I screamed and rolled out from under the bed and far away from the smiling girl with the bright red hair and English accent.

"Where am I?" I yelled at her. She had popped up on her side of the bed and was dusting herself off.

"The Great ruddy Bed of Ware, you lucky girl!" she said, clapping her hands together.

"You already said that. Where am I and . . . and the bed? Where are we?" I was shivering so hard now that the words came out half formed.

The girl's face grew still. "Of course. I'm so sorry. Come with me, it will all be clear soon."

I let her take me by the hand, because honestly, what other option did I have? We were in a museum. A huge museum. The ceilings were coffered and painted in vivid colors. Around us were maps, and cups, and swords, and suits of armor. She led me to a small room with a series of cloaks hung up on pegs. I was shaking and it made her whole arm tremble, too.

She handed me one in green velvet. "They're a bit stinky. The kids come in here and play dress-up with them. But they'll do against the cold, yeah?"

Sliding my arms into the cloak, I felt instantly better.

"Who are you?" I asked.

"Right. Thalia. Eleven years old. From right here in London. Kensington girl," she said, putting her hands on her hips as she spoke. Thalia talked fast, and my brain struggled a bit to keep up. "My dad's a barrister, my mum's a surgeon, so we can afford it, but my grandparents on both sides were Suffolk farmers, so we aren't posh, not really," Thalia said, and would keep on saying if I hadn't interrupted her.

"Did you say London? Are we in—"

"London, yes! Welcome!" Thalia said, then crushed me in a hug.

"Ow, my head!"

"Oops. Sorry. We heard about that," she said, peering at my bandage.

"We? You heard about my head? Did you say London? I . . . I need to sit down," I said, and dropped straight onto the floor, my cloak pooling around me.

Thalia sat beside me. "I should show you the ropes," she said.

"I'd like that. I'm so confused. Is this about Clio? Muse stuff? My dreams? Do you know about my dreams? Are *you* a dream?" I asked, but Thalia was ignoring me, instead rummaging through the pockets in her coat.

Finally, she drew out a long bit of twine tied up in a knot. "The ropes, get it?"

I decided that I had, indeed, died, and had gone straight to Annoying Girl Hell.

"I'm going back under that gigantic bed," I said, crawling away on all fours.

"No, don't leave yet! I've messed it up. I always do," she said, tugging on my cloak. When I turned to look at her, Thalia seemed sad and serious. "I'm Thalia, Muse of comedy. At your service," she said with a bow of her head.

I stared at her for a full ten seconds, which is a long time to stare at a person without saying a word. If you don't believe me, try it sometime.

Then I got up and ran away from her.

"Come back!" Thalia cried.

You've made it weird again, I told myself. *Wake up from this stupid dream right now,* I commanded, and pinched my arm hard. No dice. I was still in the museum. There was a sign pointing to a set of elevators. We were on the third floor, in the British Galleries, apparently. I passed dresses so wide that the women who wore them must have entered doors sideways. I passed models of castles made from balsa wood. I passed glossy furniture inlaid with mother-of-pearl, and knights standing at attention.

The whole time, Thalia was racing behind me. "Please come back!" she shouted. "I'll tell you my best joke! I'll buy you a pastry from the café! I'll introduce you to the queen!"

"Go away! You're just a dream. Go away," I shouted

back, and nearly ran right into the giant bed. "Finally," I muttered, and slid underneath.

The last thing I saw before closing my eyes was a pair of pink sneakers, upon which someone had drawn smiling faces with a permanent marker. *Home*, I thought, my mother's face filling my memory.

When I opened my eyes, I was, indeed, back home again. I took a deep, shaky breath. I was tingling all over, I was starving, and I was sweating. But mainly, I was sick of these too-vivid dreams. I touched my head. Maybe it was the pain medication after all. Were hallucinations one of the side effects? I vowed to stop taking it, no matter how much my head hurt.

I pulled myself out from under my bed, stood, and dusted myself off, only to find Mario and Fernando sitting on my bed, playing cards.

"Our little sister likes to hide under her bed. How weird is that?" Mario asked.

Fernando answered, "The weirdest."

"No," I said. "You have your own room. Get out."

"But yours is so pink," Mario said, gesturing to the walls that had been the same color since I was two. "And so Jordan Miguel-y," he said, making kissing faces at the posters on my walls.

"And clean," Fernando added. "Our room is gross."

"Because you're pigs," I said. "Out."

Mario gathered the cards while Fernando picked his

nose then wiped his finger on my bedspread, maintaining eye contact with me the whole time.

"OUT!" I screamed, which made my head throb.

"Fine, fine," Mario and Fernando said at once, a twin thing they did often. Then, at the door to my room, they both turned and said, "Where'd you get that robe?"

I looked down. I was wearing the cloak that Thalia had given me.

The one from the museum.

In London.

I glanced back at my bed. My knees shook. I tore off the robe and chucked it across the room.

"Hey, you don't want it?" Fernando asked, and immediately draped the thing over his head. "Phew, this stinks," he mumbled, but off he went, with who knows what plans for the robe, while Mario followed, shaking his head.

Trembling all over, I picked up my phone and texted Raquel.

Raqui. Something strange is happening.

I waited for her to answer, but she never did. I texted again with an annoyed HELLO?? but again, there was no response. Frustrated, I plugged my phone into the charger, stomped off to the living room, and distracted myself with an hour of reality TV.

+ + +

By dinnertime, I'd decided that I'd hallucinated the whole thing. I told my mom that my head didn't hurt anymore, even though it actually did, just to avoid taking any pain meds. Just when I'd convinced myself that there was no such thing as muses, Raquel texted me.

> Sorry I didn't answer earlier. Everything is bananas.

> Tell me about it.

> I'm going to send an audition tape to America's Next Star. That video online has a lot of likes. A LOT.

> It has to mean something, right?

> My cousins are coming over with their guitars tomorrow afternoon and we're going to record a song and send it.

> What do you think? Bananas, right?

YES, DO IT! I wrote back, sending her a thumbs-up emoji, a kissy-face one, and a banana one.

I waited a few minutes until Raquel finally texted:

> Can't talk now. Gotta go. I need to practice!

This wasn't like Raquel. I'd had to sign her up for *Beauty and the Beast* auditions, after all. Maybe the audition had unlocked her confidence. That must have been it. Her new faith in herself had nothing to do with anything muse related, I told myself.

But later that night, when Fernando came out of the shower, he was wearing the cloak from the museum. He gave me a thumbs-up when he saw me staring at him. The panicky feeling started in my chest again, so I went to bed early, determined to forget about it all by morning.

My eyes wouldn't shut, though.

If you sleep, you dream. And if you dream, you make it weird, I told myself.

Then a voice inside my head asked: *What if it wasn't a dream?*

Chapter 7
THE MUSE SQUAD

Sitting up in bed, I made a mental list of everything that had happened lately.

1. I almost fell thirty feet to my death after the Jordan Miguel concert.
2. My dad and stepmom were having a new baby.
3. I might have accidentally turned my best friend into a pop star.
4. Some random lady claiming to be a muse stopped time and told me I was kind of a goddess.
5. I crawled under my bed, closed my eyes, and was transported to London.

Either I was completely losing my mind, or something huge and magical was happening. But why would a huge and magical thing happen to a kid like me? I was living in a one-bathroom house with a bad roof that leaked during storms. My parents were divorced. I wasn't super smart, or athletic. I was chubby, and my hair was frizzy, and I didn't wear cool clothes. I couldn't even touch my toes. Me? Magical? It made zero sense.

There was, however, only one way to find out if I'd imagined things or not. But first, I pinched myself hard. Definitely awake. I hadn't taken any medicine since this morning even though my head was pounding.

"Callie, go. Be brave," I said, giving myself a pep talk out loud. And you know? It worked. I felt a little braver as I crawled under the bed, a little more courageous as I closed my eyes.

When I opened them, there were the pink sneakers and the hand-drawn happy faces. And there was Thalia.

"You're back! Brilliant!" she said, reaching out to grab my hand.

Okay. I'm doing this, I thought. *And I won't make it weird.*

I took Thalia's hand, which she'd been holding out for me patiently, and I rose to my feet. "I'm Callie. I guess I'm a muse, too? That's what Clio said," I told her, though it all sounded like a question.

"You certainly are. This is the Victoria and Albert Museum—Muse Headquarters," Thalia said, opening her arms as if to show it all off at once. Then she stopped and frowned at my bare arms and legs, covered in goose bumps. "What happened to your cloak? You really ought to bring it back," Thalia said, scrunching up her nose. "And come better prepared next time," she added, pointing to my tank top, shorts, and flip-flops. "It's November in London, for goodness' sake. Damp and cold, that's all we get over here. Don't want to catch a chill." I followed her back to the dress-up room, and she handed me another, even stinkier cloak.

"Warm and appropriately dressed," I said. "Where to next?" I was still riddled with doubts, but I was intent on following this girl, this dream, this . . . whatever this was . . . to its logical conclusion.

Thalia smiled in relief at my apparent enthusiasm. "Come on, we'll head to the Tea Room. It's an entrance point, too. I'll show you and we can grab a bite to eat. The Tea Room is not as terrific as the Great Bed of Ware, mind you. Honestly, everyone will be so jealous of you they'll eat their hair! But it is really nice, and maybe you're hungry?"

"I'm never not hungry," I said, and felt my cheeks go hot. Thalia grinned.

"You're funny! I love the funny ones. Come on," she said, and I followed her out.

We went down a set of wide marble stairs. At the base were a pair of busts, one on each side.

"Muses, like us," Thalia explained, then tipped an imaginary hat in their direction and said, "Ladies," as if she were a gentleman in a movie.

"Tell me about the bed. You called it my 'entrance point'?" I asked. If this wasn't all a dream, and I wasn't sure about that, I'd need to know precisely how to get out.

Thalia leaned against a statue of a girl resting on a slab of marble, the sculpture's fine marble hands crossed on her chest, her eyes closed. "The Great Bed of Ware is from the 1500s, I think. Used to be in a famous inn. Really just a quirky bit of furniture, but so fun and silly. It's everyone's favorite thing to see here, and that's because people like to laugh."

"But how does it work?" I asked.

Thalia thought for a minute. "Well," she said, and twirled a long red strand of hair for a second. "It's a bed, so you lie down on it, and cover up, and count sheep or something." There was a glimmer of mischief in her eyes that I was starting to recognize.

"Muse of comedy, I get it," I said. "Now tell me. How do entrance points work?"

"Come on, I'll show you," Thalia said, then took my hand and pulled me to the end of the hall. To our left was the biggest gift shop I'd ever seen, full of paintings and jewelry and toys. To the right were a set of glass doors. Outside was a courtyard dominated by an oval pool surrounded by pale pink tile. It was shallow, I could tell. The perimeter of the courtyard was bordered by low, leafy bushes. "Watch this," she said.

Thalia stepped into the pool, sneakers and all. At its deepest, it only reached her mid-calf. She turned to look at me, waved, and sank into the water. I gasped aloud. She was gone! I chucked my flip-flops and waded in to get a closer look. The water was ice-cold. When I got to the center of the pool, the water began to lift and part, and out popped Thalia again, her red hair glistening. Dripping and shivering, she stepped out of the pool, muttering about the cold, and I followed. Then, just like that, she was dry.

"That was amazing," I said.

"It really is. Takes me right back to the tub in our flat. My parents think I'm the cleanest girl in London 'cause I take baths at lots of random times." Thalia checked her watch. "Come on. Let's go meet the others."

She led me around the pool and through glass doors into the Tea Room, which was the most beautiful café I'd ever seen. Every inch of the walls was covered in mosaic tiles, and hanging from the ceiling was a massive glittery chandelier. Thalia put her hands on my shoulders and turned me around to face the fireplace, which was taller than I was.

"In three, two, one," Thalia said.

Just like that, two feet popped down from inside the chimney, wiggled a bit, then landed onto the flat, clean grate at the bottom. A tall black girl emerged from the fireplace, stepping out with a hop. She was wearing a NASA hoodie and spotless, cream-colored jeans.

I closed my mouth, which had been hanging open. "Like Santa Claus," I whispered.

"Well spotted," Thalia said. Then she said, "Nia! You're right on time."

"I always am," the girl said. She stopped short when she noticed me. "New person?" she asked.

I nodded, and Thalia supplied the answer. "Callie's her name. Guess her entrance point. Go on."

Nia pursed her lips. "Let me guess. You come out from behind one of the tapestries on the first floor. The one with the unicorn. You look like the type."

I didn't know whether to be offended or not, but before I could say a word, Thalia blurted, "The Great Bed of Ware!"

"Oh, come on!" Nia said. "Not fair at all." Then, she turned to me. "I'll have you know that I have to sneak into the fireplace back home every time I want to come here. You know how hard it is to do it when my dad isn't looking? He was in the CIA. It's not easy. Thank goodness this fireplace doesn't get used, and the one at home is gas, because if I ever get soot on one of my outfits—"

"So that's how it works," I interrupted. "I go under the bed at home, and poof, I'm under the Great Bed here?"

Thalia and Nia grew serious. "But it isn't a game. You have to focus on your destination. You have to calculate the time difference. We're only allowed here when the visitors are gone for the day. Or when we're summoned. You can't just come whenever. And you can't leave the museum," Nia said.

"There are heaps of rules," Thalia added.

Nia thrust out her hand. "Muse of science here. I'm obsessed with NASA's space program, zombie movies, and make the best grilled cheese sandwiches in Chicago. Basically, I'm the nerd of the group."

"We're all nerds, frankly," Thalia said.

"I'm not dreaming, right? This isn't a dream?" I asked, and the girls shook their heads. It was all feeling more real by the minute. "What about Clio? Is she here?" I asked.

"She comes in through the library," Nia said. "*Also* better than a fireplace."

"At least you aren't Mela," Thalia said. "Poor thing enters through a supply closet."

We heard a clatter, like a million brooms had fallen somewhere.

"There she is," Nia and Thalia said at the same time. I followed them through the gift shop and waited underneath a colorful glass sculpture that dangled from the very high ceiling. We were in the center of the museum, surrounded by balconies.

I assumed the girl that was coming toward us was Mela. She was an Indian girl about my height, and she wore her hair in a long black braid over her shoulder. Headphones dangled around her neck. "Do you know what time it is in New Delhi?" she asked. Her voice was musical, but quiet.

"Two in the morning," Nia said without hesitation.

"Well. Yes," Mela said a little sadly, as if Nia had ruined something for her. "You are correct." She reached me and shook my hand. I was struck by her formality, as well as her pajamas, which were hot pink with yellow trim. "Muse of tragedy," she said, announcing herself.

"Don't let her fool you, she can laugh with the best of us," Thalia said. Mela smiled softly at that.

"Why has Clio summoned us today? Is it for her?" Mela asked, pointing at me.

Nia and Thalia both nodded. "We're the welcoming committee," Nia said. "This is Callie."

Thalia wrapped her arms around her chest, as if she were trying to stop herself from combusting. "When was the last time the Muse Squad had four—*four*—kids on it? It's usually all grown-ups all the time. But not this time." Then she started to sing, "It's a new dawn! It's a new day! It's—"

"Control yourself, for the love," Nia said, shaking her head.

"Muse Squad?" I asked.

Nia rolled her eyes. "She made it up. Nobody calls us that."

"Muse Squad is a brilliant team name," Thalia said, stamping her foot. I noticed that she was still smiling. It would take a lot to get this girl angry, I thought.

Mela scowled a little in Thalia's direction. But then she

gently took my hand. "Welcome, Callie, Muse of the epic poem."

I must have frowned. It sounded so . . . boring. Muses of science, of comedy, and even of tragedy, seemed infinitely cooler than . . . whatever I was supposed to be.

Nia and Thalia looked at each other, seeming to communicate without saying a word.

"You're more important than you think," Mela said. "Come on. We'll let Clio explain it."

I let her lead me, followed by the others. Around us, moonlight poured in from windows. We stepped in puddles of light, then slipped back into darkness, back and forth, until we reached Clio's door.

Chapter 8
BRACELETS AND BROWNIES

"So, the V and A?" I asked as we stood before a set of huge wooden doors with the museum's logo on them.

"The Victoria and Albert Museum, named after Queen Victoria and her husband, Prince Consort Albert. She adored him, and when he died, she built a huge, and I mean ridiculously huge, golden statue in his honor. It's in Kensington Park. I'll show you sometime. But for now," Thalia said, stopping mid-sentence and knocking on the door twice, "we've got work to do."

The doors creaked open, revealing a two-story library. On the lower floor were rows of glossy wooden desks, each with two chairs and two green lamps. Arched windows lined one side of the library. Wine-colored books lined the other side. In a distant corner, an iron spiral staircase led to the second floor.

"Follow me," Mela said. I noticed she was still wearing fuzzy slippers. They were pink, too, and shaped like kittens.

I pointed at the slippers and whispered to Nia, "This is the Muse of tragedy?"

Nia shook her head, then said very quietly, "She loves cats. Me, I'm allergic."

We followed Mela up the spiral stairs. At the top was a white door with a brass handle. Again, Thalia knocked. Again, the door swung open on its own. A sweet smell poured from the dark space beyond, almost as if we were going in through the back door of a bakery.

I remembered that Clio had smelled like brownies at the hospital. I never did get that bite to eat in the Tea Room that Thalia promised.

"Come in, girls," a familiar voice called.

We stepped into a tight hallway, which opened up to the right into an office lit by two stained-glass lamps on either side of a glass-topped desk. Behind the desk was Clio. She didn't have on doctor's scrubs anymore, but instead wore a white suit. Her trumpet earrings still dangled from her ears. On her desk were reams of paper, books, half-worn pencils, and a plate topped with, you guessed it, brownies.

On a mirrored tray was a charm bracelet with only one charm on it—a tiny golden book. It glittered in the office light.

"A gift," Clio said, motioning toward it.

"For me?" The bracelet looked familiar, but I couldn't quite place it.

"The book is your symbol," she said, her fingers twirling one of her trumpet earrings. "And the bracelet is how I call you back to headquarters when I need you. You'll find it gets quite warm."

"Ruddy hot," Thalia said, showing off a ring with a smiling theater mask on it. Mela held out her left hand. There was the frowning mask on her finger. I noticed that she'd drawn a similar mask on her headphones, one for each ear.

Nia drew out a long golden necklace from within her hoodie. At the end was a globe. She gave it a spin. "It's how we knew to come tonight, to welcome you," she said.

"Take it," Clio said, waiting for me to reach out. I pondered the bracelet, the room, and the people in it for a long moment. If this was a dream, then it didn't matter if I took the bracelet, or tossed it out of a window, or set fire to the library. But if it wasn't . . .

"This seems like a . . ." I struggled for the words. "A commitment," I said at last.

Clio pushed back her chair, which slid with a swooshing sound. She walked over to a filing cabinet and opened the third door, then she pulled out a plain manila folder, stuffed with paper, which she laid on the desk. Inside was an eight-by-ten photograph of a group of people standing on the steps of a huge building. It was Christmastime in the picture—a tree was lit up in sparkling lights just behind the group in the lobby of the building.

"This is the V and A just outside," Clio explained. "Look closely."

I lifted the photograph. There, on one end, was Clio. She was wearing an ugly Christmas sweater with an embroidered reindeer hoisting a wineglass in his hoof. I counted eight other women—all grown-ups.

"Closer," Clio said.

"Okay." I looked at them each carefully. One seemed very old and was sitting in a chair. Her sweater was all sequins, with no particular design on it. Another had a walking cane, which she had decorated with a string of colorful lights. Then I spotted what Clio meant for me to see. I made a little sound—half whimper, half gasp.

"Muses aren't inherited roles, and yet here you are." Clio paused, her eyes watering a little. "We miss her, very much."

There was Tia Annie, before she got sick. Her hair was long, curly, and a color some people called "dirty blond." But she didn't look dirty at all. She had a Santa hat on her head. She was a tiny woman, standing in the center of it all, her hands on the very old woman's shoulders.

"You're related to Annie Martinez?" Nia asked.

"She's a legend," Mela said.

"So many heroes," Thalia whispered.

I put down the photograph. "I don't understand. Why was Tia Annie here? Does my mom know?"

Clio settled into her chair and motioned for me to sit, but I shook my head.

"Nope, not sitting. Just talk. Lay it all out," I said. I wrapped the cloak tightly around me and fought back tears. I wouldn't cry here, I wouldn't.

The other girls didn't sit either. Nia slipped her arm through the crook of mine. Thalia and Mela stood close by, too. It felt comforting, as if they were on my side. But a part of me doubted them, doubted everything.

"Your aunt was the Muse of epic poetry, like you. Don't scrunch your nose at me, Callie. The Muse of epic poetry is not really about poetry at all. It's about heroes."

"I don't get it," I said. Comedy, tragedy, science, and even poetry—these were things I understood, sort of. But heroes? What could I possibly have to do with that?

Clio went on. "All the epic poems of old tell us the stories of heroes—heroes who lived and fought and, sometimes, saved the world. But heroes haven't gone extinct. They are among us, and they need their muses. And the Muse of epic poetry is the first muse, the oldest muse, daughter of Zeus, the one who gathered the original nine together, the one who saw a need in the world. And no, your mother does not know. We must keep it that way."

"Why?" I asked. I didn't like keeping secrets from my mom.

Clio smiled gently. "Annie wanted to tell her too, you know. But eventually she came to understand that concealing our identities is part of the job, that it keeps us and our loved ones safe."

Next, Clio pulled a small book out from her desk. She

opened it, revealing picture after picture. "Odysseus, Aeneas, Nefertiti, George Washington, Toussaint L'Ouverture, José Martí, Rosa Parks—and these are only the ones you've heard of. The muses, all of them, inspired these men and women to reach the heroes within. As the Muse of epic poetry, you're the most powerful of all, because what you inspire is courage. Daring. Compassion."

I was quiet, of course. You don't learn about a sudden and great responsibility and just up and accept it. At least, you shouldn't. That's something my mom always taught me—you don't have to say yes to anything right away. She also taught me that "No" is a complete sentence. But I wasn't ready to say no just yet.

"I need to think about it."

"Of course," Clio said. "But take the bracelet. It's not binding. You can always give it back."

Slowly, I reached out. I picked up the bracelet. I'd expected to feel a surge of . . . something. Energy, warmth, a magical breeze to whip through the museum and blow through my hair. I got nothing.

"You sure it works?" I asked.

"Positive," Clio said. "Annie wore it for many years while in service."

"Oh," I said. Of course! That's why the bracelet had looked familiar! I slipped it on, struggled with the catch for a second, then managed to get it secure. It fit perfectly. Just over Clio's head, a small golden clock chimed. I had been gone almost an hour.

Mela nudged me with her elbow. "You're worried some-one will miss you at home, yes?"

I nodded. "If my mom wakes up and can't find me—" I stopped. I could only imagine the scene. Cops up and down the street. Helicopters, even, if she could manage it.

"No worries," Thalia said, gesturing to Clio. "She's got it handled."

"Quite right," Clio said. "You'll find that hardly any time at all has passed for you back home. I can't hold this moment indefinitely, however, so off you go." Clio gathered the folder and the book, and put them away. "The girls will escort you to your entry point. The Great Bed, eh? Not too shabby. We'll call you soon."

I turned to leave.

"No popping over here without a call from me first, understand?" Clio added. "For all you know the Prince of Wales himself could be here for a visit and there you go, emerging from under the Great Bed of Ware like some sort of fairy or troll. Can't have that," she said, a look of horror on her face.

"Right," I said.

"Oh, and put the cloak back on the hook in the dress-up room, please," Clio added.

"Of course," I said. "Anything else?"

But Clio was now scribbling in a notebook with one hand and eating a brownie with the other.

Mela cleared her throat. "Pardon me. Clio?"

Clio looked up midscribble. She arched one eyebrow.

"My entrance point," Mela said, lifting her chin in the air.

Clio closed her eyes and said, "Ah, yes. The paperwork on that has been brutal. So sorry about the mix-up. You may use the unicorn tapestry on the first floor from now on. It's linked to the curtains in the parlor of your home."

Nia snorted at the mention of the tapestry.

Mela smiled for the first time since I'd met her. "See?" she said, turning to face me. "The supply closet was temporary. Just a matter of paperwork."

"Hold up," I said, laying my hands upon Clio's desk. "Paperwork? To who? Where do you send it? Mount Olympus?" I could feel my heart clamping tight as my mind buzzed with possibilities. "Are there gods? Is my dad actually Zeus or something? Because that would suc—"

"Stop," Clio said forcefully. "If you must know, the gods of old have . . . semiretired, so to speak. Humans stopped building them temples, quit writing epic poems with the gods in them. Thus the gods got grumpy, and they quit. Kind of."

I felt like my brain was going to explode. All those gods and goddesses I'd learned about in elementary school were . . . real? "So, like, Athena?"

"Real."

"Poseidon."

Clio sighed. "Very real. He likes paperwork a lot." Her

- 69 -

mouth tightened into a grim line.

I cracked my knuckles out of nervousness. "Um, that underworld one. That guy?"

Mela sucked in air behind me. "Hades," she whispered.

"Yep. Hades. Him?"

Clio rose from her seat, lifted a file bigger than my head from where it sat on the floor. "Would you like to parse through Hades's forms regarding the deaths of Fated Ones?"

"Fated Ones?" I asked.

"The heroes and artists, scientists and makers that we inspire, the ones whose fates are tied to the well-being of the world and its people," Clio said.

Taking a deep breath, I asked one last question. "If the gods quit, then why didn't you . . . I mean we. Why didn't we quit?"

Clio sat down again. She lifted a brownie to her lips and nibbled at a corner before answering me. "The muses, you mean. We've decided to stick it out. The humans need us. Without us, the world is a much duller place." Clio smoothed her hands over a file folder. "There are others still about. Demigods. Minor deities."

"Like nymphs?" Nia asked, and Clio nodded.

"Satyrs? I always liked those," Thalia said.

"Here and there," Clio answered.

"Mr. Tumnus! Yes!" Thalia said.

Mela touched Thalia's arm. "We've talked about this, Thalia. Narnia isn't real."

"But, Mela," Thalia whined.

I remembered what I'd learned in school about the gods. They were sometimes petty, but super powerful. And sometimes, there were monsters to fight, too.

"What about the bad guys? The monsters and stuff?" I asked.

Clio nodded. "A fair few of those are still around, too," she said quietly.

I leaned against Clio's desk, feeling suddenly a little light-headed. Mela patted my shoulder kindly. When I spoke, my voice was a little shaky. "How come I've never seen any of these beings?"

Clio arched an eyebrow at me. "You haven't been paying attention. You'll learn to do that, too. Paying attention is everything. Paying attention will let you know what's an invention, and what isn't." Clio straightened up the files on her desk before continuing. "Bureaucracy, well, that's a monstrous invention, indeed. One of the gods' own making, and they require it. It's how they keep tabs. It's how they tell themselves they are still making a difference."

Mela sucked in another loud breath and Clio clucked her tongue. "Oh, Mela, don't be so tragic. The gods stopped interfering in any substantial way years ago. We are perfectly free to say what we want. Understood?"

Mela nodded. Thalia opened her mouth to say something, but Clio stopped her with a terse "Don't push it, you," and Thalia snapped her lips shut.

"You do the paperwork, the muses make the magic, and the gods eat bonbons on Mount Olympus," I said, trying not to glance at the brownies on Clio's desk.

"A-plus, Callie," Clio said.

I had one more question. "So my parents are—"

"Your parents are the people they've always been. I know what you're wondering. We aren't sure how Annie's muse magic transferred to you. Maybe it was a coincidence," Clio said, but her face seemed to say that she didn't believe a word of that. "For now, I have paperwork to attend to," Clio finished.

"Okay, but—" I started to say. "If Tia Annie was a muse, then how come she died?" I asked this last bit in a whisper. It still hurt to say it out loud.

Clio's face softened a little. She reached out and took my hand. "Our powers are immortal, but we are mortal. Don't take unnecessary risks, any of you. You need to take care of yourselves because the world needs you, okay?"

I nodded, my eyes stinging. I hadn't realized I'd been holding out hope that Tia Annie was actually alive out there, somewhere.

"Any other questions?" Clio added in a way that told me that there would be no other questions, at least not today. I felt Nia's hands on my shoulders as she turned me toward the door, and the others followed me out.

"Her sugar crashes must be epic," I said aloud outside Clio's office. Thalia, Nia, and Mela led me back to the

Great Bed with ease. Would I ever learn how to navigate the museum this easily? Would I even be coming back?

"See you soon," Thalia said, giving me a hug. Mela shook my hand. Nia thumped my back.

I crawled under the Great Bed. Outside, the dawn light was warming the gallery now, brightening the space. I closed my eyes, thought of home, and that was enough.

When I opened them, I was back under my small, dusty bed, which was not Great, but was definitely Good Enough. I was still wearing the dress-up cloak, which really was a bit stinky, and now that I was back in Miami, was way too warm to wear. I shoved it into a ball and put it under my bed. The dark house was just as I'd left it.

Chapter 9
BESTIE WOES

The next day was Thanksgiving. We didn't have any big dinner plans. My mom had ordered some sliced turkey and sides from a restaurant on Calle Ocho. It was just the four of us, after all. I tried hard not to think about Thanksgiving back when Papi was home, and we would go to big parties at his cousin's house.

I'd worn the bracelet to bed. It didn't do anything special—only glimmered there against my skin. But it was tangible proof that I hadn't imagined things.

It was Mario who recognized it at breakfast. "Hey, that was Tia Annie's," he said, grabbing my wrist.

Fernando muttered his agreement through a mouth filled with cornflakes.

"¿Qué?" Mami asked. Then she looked at me and the bracelet. "Where did you find that? I looked everywhere for it."

"In my music box," I blurted. "I hadn't opened it in ages, and there it was." I couldn't exactly explain that I magically traveled to England via my bed, that I'd inherited powers that I didn't understand or know how to tap, and by the way, Mom, your beloved sister had them, too.

So I lied.

My mother swallowed hard, trying not to cry. "Did she ever tell you the story of the bracelet?" Mami asked. I shook my head. "Back when we were little girls in Cuba, about your age, Annie took to hiding inside an old abandoned armoire outside, between the apartment buildings. She said she found the bracelet inside, and she never took it off again." My mom was smiling a little now, the way she sometimes did when she thought of her old life in Cuba, her little-girl life that she left behind when she was thirteen. I imagined my aunt at eleven, stepping gingerly into the puddles of light at the V and A, thinking about Cuba seemingly a million miles away.

"Tia Annie must have left this bracelet for you," my mom said, breaking my reverie. "Bueno, mi amor, take care of it." She rifled through the junk drawer and found a bottle of superglue. She let a few drops fall onto the clasp of the bracelet. "Just in case," she said. Then she patted the bandage on my head. "Feels better?" she asked, and I nodded.

I wondered what Clio would think of the glue, then pushed her out of my mind. Like she'd said, nothing was binding. I didn't have to be a muse if I didn't want to be.

My phone buzzed beside me. Raquel! I picked it up, almost toppling my glass of orange juice.

"Hey!" I said. "I've been texting you." I had tried all morning, and nada.

Raquel sounded a little out of breath. I could hear the rush of cars outside through the phone. "I know! Sorry! I'm coming over, if that's okay."

"Of course," I said.

Bestie time was exactly what I needed to get my mind off this muse stuff. Besides, I missed Raquel. While I waited for her to come over, I debated whether or not to tell her about everything that had happened. By the time she got there, I knew I was going to spill the beans. Clio could get mad or whatever, but I needed to talk to *somebody*.

"Happy Thanksgiving!" she said, giving me a hug as soon as she arrived.

"No time to talk turkey," I said, and we ran to my room.

"I have something to tell you." I twirled the bracelet on my arm nervously.

"I have something to tell you," she said at the same time.

"You first," we both said, then fell onto my bed laughing.

Raquel whipped out her phone, opened up her photos, and showed me a screengrab of an email.

Dear Raquel,

Thank you for submitting your video audition, which we have received and viewed with excitement.

Congratulations are in order!

You have been selected to audition on camera for *America's Next Star.* Attached are important documents you need to review before accepting the audition. Please be in touch with your response.

Sincerely,
Joanne Montgomery
Executive Assistant
America's Next Star

I felt Raquel's finger on my chin, pushing up gently and closing my mouth. I hadn't realized the whole "my jaw dropped open" thing happened in real life. But it totally did.

"I know!" Raquel squealed before I could say another word.

"Tell me you already said yes!"

Raquel nodded, her brown curls bobbing up and down. She held her breath, then blurted, "I'm going this weekend!"

"What? So soon?" For a moment I thought, *This is*

bananas. But then I remembered that I had recently been magically transported to another country. Maybe everything was going to be bananas from now on.

"Yep. They're paying for the airplane tickets and everything," Raquel said. She stood up and paced my room, hugging herself. As she did, she babbled a bit, something she always did when she was excited. She talked about how nice the producer sounded on the phone, what song she would sing, and on and on.

I didn't listen very carefully. My mind kept latching onto other things—the museum, the other muses, what Clio had said about Tia Annie, and that day in the cafetorium. My fingers wandered to the bandage on my head. Then Raquel said something that snapped me out of it.

"Like, I've earned this, you know?"

She'd been staring into a mirror as she said it, smoothing her hands down her dress. It was as if Clio had frozen time. There Raquel stood, slender and gorgeous. Her curls rippled down her back. Her dress was new. In fact, I could still see the little plastic strand that once held a price tag jutting out from a seam in her waist. Her hands—was that a gel manicure? Those weren't cheap. I glanced at her toes. Painted, too. In the mirror's reflection I could see myself behind Raquel, sitting cross-legged on my bed. My mouth was a little open. My hair hung limply. My T-shirt had a stain on it from breakfast. We really did make a perfect ten, she and I. Raquel was number one, and I was a total zero.

"How so?" I blurted out. I almost didn't realize I'd said it.

"Oh," Raquel said, turning to look at me. "I mean practice. Hard work. The usual," she said, a question in her voice.

I fiddled with the bracelet on my wrist. "You don't think what happened in the cafetorium that day was, you know, strange?"

Raquel bit her lip. "I *do* think so. It was . . . magic."

"Exactly," I said, feeling myself brightening. I wasn't sure I could tell Raquel everything about the muses, but just maybe—

"It was the magic that's been inside of me all along, Cal. The producer on the phone said I have 'it.' IT!" she said, and twirled twice before looking at herself in the mirror again.

"Oh," I said, deflating. That's what I'd called my muse magic in my head when it happened—IT. But obviously, Raquel meant something else.

"But don't you think this is all a bit, I don't know, sudden?" I asked. Didn't she question any of it? Did she wonder at all why her voice was so much better than it was before?

Raquel pursed her lips and her left eyebrow popped up. "A little support would be cool," she said icily.

I rolled my eyes. "*Of course* I support you. I'm your biggest fan," I said, and forced a smile.

Raquel relaxed, then plopped on my bed again. "You'll find your 'IT,' I know you will," she whispered, as if she'd seen something other than extreme irritation on my face. "You had something to tell me, right?"

My throat tightened. I couldn't tell her anything. Raquel was only seeing . . . Raquel at the moment. And when she looked at me, what did she see? Her talentless, fatherless friend, that's what.

"Nah," I said. "No news at all."

"But you said—"

"Leave it. My head hurts, Raquel. I think I need to take a nap."

Raquel's face softened and she frowned a little. "Oh my gosh, of course." She gave me a gentle hug. "See you soon, and feel better. Maybe you can help me pack!" she said cheerily, and bounced out of my room.

All I wanted was to be alone, but as soon as she left, my phone buzzed again. It was Papi.

"Hey, kiddo," he said.

"Hey."

"¿Qué pasa?"

"Nothing!" I said, trying to sound a little more upbeat. The last thing I wanted was to have Papi asking questions. Unlike Mami, he always asked too many, or he jumped to conclusions about what he thought was upsetting me.

"Is it about the baby?" he asked softly.

Oh.

That.

"No, not that," I said. With all the muse stuff happening, and Raquel acting so differently, I had forgotten about the baby. But now that Papi mentioned it, I guess I'd been worrying about it all along.

"The new baby won't change anything," my dad said. He'd dropped his voice to a whisper, and I wondered if Laura was within earshot.

"When I came along, I changed things, didn't I?"

My dad laughed a little. "You did, kiddo. You rocked our world."

"See?"

"But us? You, me, and the twins? That won't change. Maybe you guys can come up to New York this summer. How about that?" Papi asked.

I'd never been to New York. "Sounds like fun," I said. "As long as I don't have to change diapers."

"I don't do negotiations," Papi said with a laugh. "You'll love it here."

He asked about the twins, and I asked how Laura was feeling ("Pukey" was the answer), and then we hung up. I didn't know if I'd love New York, or spending time in a cramped walk-up with my dad, stepmom, new sibling, and brothers. In fact, I was sure I wouldn't like it at all.

I clicked on my messages, and saw a new one from Raquel. It was a GIF of Jordan Miguel blowing a kiss to a camera. Another message came in—a selfie of Raquel making a kissy face, too. Sending a kissy-face selfie back to her felt like a lie, as did sending a heart emoji. Instead, I left my phone on my bed, and went to get a snack.

That afternoon, when everyone thought I was napping, I slid under my bed, closed my eyes, and let the muse magic take me to headquarters. Clio had said not to come unannounced, but whatever. If breaking a rule meant not being a muse, then maybe that wasn't a bad thing. After all, what had this magic accomplished anyway? A head wound and a best friend who was acting . . . differently.

Because Raquel did feel different to me.

The old Raquel would have understood what I meant about the suddenness of all this, and she wouldn't have gotten gel manicures, and she wouldn't have fallen for it if a stranger on the phone, producer or not, told her she had "IT."

Then again, maybe Raquel wasn't the problem after all.

Maybe I was the one who was different now.

The museum was quiet. I glanced at a clock. Just past closing time. I'd looked at a map of the V and A online, trying to memorize the layout, so I sort of knew where to go. Sort of. It was a big place. I found my way to Clio's office. I hesitated before knocking, and when I did, it sounded as if the whole museum could have heard me.

There was no answer. The door opened a bit. I took a deep breath and peeked inside. Clio's office was empty. A blue plate sprinkled with brownie crumbs sat atop a stack of files. I stepped in. The first folder underneath the plate was the one she'd shown me, the one with the picture of the muses. I pulled it out gently, sat in Clio's chair.

I opened the folder. The group picture on the steps of the museum stared back at me. There were other photos, too, and newspaper clippings. One after another, the articles described people doing miraculous, wonderful things—saving a village's water supply in Mozambique, establishing a dog rescue in Paris, a young woman who lifted a car off her dad when it had dropped on him during a tire change, a young man who jumped onto subway tracks to save a stranger, teens on spring break who saved a woman from drowning, and on and on.

"That would be the hero file. They were her students. All of them," Clio said from the door to her office.

I sputtered, trying to apologize, stood, and the file fell to the floor, the clippings fluttering down after it. "I'm sorry. Clio, I'm sorry. I just, I had to get away," I said.

"Headquarters is not a vacation spot, and my office is not your personal library," Clio said. "Now sit."

I plopped back down onto Clio's chair. She took the seat opposite me. Today, Clio was wearing a sweater and dark jeans, but somehow managed to make it look professional. Her white hair was loose and coiled around her shoulders. Reading glasses hung from a chain around her neck. Her cheeks were flushed, though, and she looked worried. She held a large bronze key in her hand—the old-fashioned kind. When she saw me notice it, she put it in her back pocket.

"As I said, all those heroes were her students."

"Who are we talking about?"

Clio narrowed her eyes at me. "You can't possibly be this dense."

I exhaled. "Tia Annie. But how?"

"Online classes. Poetry workshops here and there. She got to know people, stayed in touch, inspired them to be their best selves. She mentored people far and wide. She was—" Clio stopped, her eyes shining. "She was the best of us."

"Right," I said shakily. I'd made up my mind just then. "Right. I am so not worthy of this." I struggled with the bracelet.

"Why do you think so?"

The bracelet wouldn't give. Stupid glue. "It's because of my best friend. She's changing. Because of me."

"That's partly true." Clio ran her fingers over the rest of the folders on her desk. "You read the success stories. These files here . . . well, let's say our tactics aren't always successful." Clio sighed. "This job, *our* job, isn't easy. And it requires courage, but mostly, hope. Annie always hoped. Have you given up on your best friend already, Callie?"

I shook my head. Of course I hadn't. I bent down and picked up the dropped folder and the clippings, putting them away carefully. Lastly, I put away the picture of the muses. Tia Annie seemed to be staring at me pointedly.

"I'll give it another chance," I said, and put the file folder back under the plate, Raquel's words, *You'll find your IT, Callie*, still ringing in my head.

"Good," Clio said. "Now that you're here, I'd like to show you something. But first," she said, stopping mid-sentence. She rubbed one of her earrings. The tiny golden trumpet shone under the office lights. "Headquarters, junior muses," she called into the air. I could feel my brace-let warming up. I looked at Clio anxiously. "Give them a minute," she said. Soon, I heard footsteps on the spiral staircase, and Thalia's tinkling laughter.

"What's the emergency?" Thalia asked. She was wear-ing her school uniform—a plaid skirt and blue blazer.

Clio held up one finger, and her eyebrows rose as she waited. Then there was the sound of more footsteps, and Clio's office door opened again. Mela and Nia stepped through. Nia was wearing an apron with a swirly picture of the Milky Way and the words IN THE KITCHEN. NEED MY SPACE. Underneath, she wore a green dress with a golden ribbon at her waist.

"It's Thanksgiving, for the love," she said. "I'm making a grilled cheese casserole, and it had better not burn."

Mela was in her pajamas, and she was rubbing her eyes and yawning.

Clio walked around her desk and opened the door to

the office. "Come along, you four," she said. "It's time the junior muses got their first assignment."

Thalia coughed the words "Muse Squad," and the rest of us pretended not to notice.

We followed her through the library, down a set of stairs, passed through a gallery full of glittering jewelry, and down a hallway lined with paintings. Finally, we stopped in front of an old, speckled mirror that was about the size of a refrigerator.

"This mirror was a gift from Athena to the first Muse of history." It was set into a marble frame with owls carved into each corner. "For the gods, time does not exist. Everything to them is just the now. The past is now. The present is now. All possible futures are now. The mirror allows me to see as they see, which is useful in understanding Fated Ones."

Clio stroked the surface a few times, as if she were petting a dog. Our reflections blurred, and a different picture appeared. It wasn't like looking at the television. It was more like peering through a window. I reached out, thinking I could touch what was on the other side, the way Alice had walked through the looking-glass in her book, but Clio held my wrist.

"Don't touch," she said, but didn't explain why.

The mirror showed us a city, half-submerged in water. I could see the tops of buildings, and how ocean foam lapped at windows.

"Is that the past? Or the future?" I asked.

"A possible future," she said. "Here's another." She touched the mirror again, and the image shifted into a room with white walls. A bank of computers lined one side. A woman in a lab coat peered at one of the screens. She had a streak of rainbow in her hair, which was parted into two braids. Even though she was a grown-up, there was something about her that reminded me of a kid.

"Who's that?" Nia asked.

"A Fated One. She could save the world someday," Clio said. "And she's all yours."

A mission. A real mission! I thought of Tia Annie's files, and all the good work she'd done. This was the first step for us. The first face in the file.

"But wait. The flooded city. You said that's a picture of the future, too," I said. In the mirror, the rainbow-haired woman turned to face us. Her brow was wrinkled in concentration, then her face lit up with an idea, and she ran to a tablet and started typing. There was something about her face that seemed so familiar.

"It is. It's a *possible* future. Many years from today," Clio said. "But this Fated One might help humanity prevent it."

"So the Fated One. She's a kid right now? Like us?" Mela asked. She had headphones around her neck again. I'd have to ask her sometime about the kind of music she liked.

Thalia bounced a bit, her loafers slapping the shiny floor. "We're sharing her? One Fated One and four muses?"

"She must be important," Nia said.

Clio hummed in agreement. "She's definitely important," she said. "Fate of the world and all that."

I got closer to the mirror. The woman was facing us again, and she was chewing her bottom lip. A funny feeling grew in my stomach. My hands tingled. I couldn't shake the idea that I knew her. Those brown eyes seemed very familiar, and the curve of her nose, too. She started talking to someone in another room, moving her hands as she talked, as if she were doing . . .

"A hula," I whispered.

"What now?" Clio asked. I looked up at her. From Clio's face I could tell that she knew that I knew. The woman in the mirror wasn't a stranger.

"That's Maya Rivero," I said.

"Well done," Clio said. She touched the mirror again and the picture faded, leaving only its old, tinfoil-like surface behind. "She's your Fated One."

I took a step back. "M-my Fated One?" I wasn't ready for that. Maya Rivero? Why did it have to be her? There wasn't a test she couldn't ace, a teacher she couldn't impress, or a weird outfit she could turn down. Why did she need us?

"So who is this Maya Rivero?" Thalia asked.

I faced the other muses. "She's a girl in my grade. A

genius. And a total dork." Maya, of all people! Maya and her tutus, and her SAP club, and her giant brain. I had no idea how a girl like that could ever need help from someone like me.

"She's important to the future," Clio said.

Nia stood up straight, squaring her shoulders. I wondered if she'd learned that authoritative pose from her dad. "When do we start?"

"But she's in Miami," Mela said. "I was sort of hoping that my first Fated One would be somewhere snowy."

"We're going to Miami?" Thalia squealed.

Clio shook her head. "For now, all I want you to do is some homework." Absently, her hand went to her back pocket, where she'd put the bronze key. "There's been a situation. The four of you have some legwork to do. Cassandra. Look her up."

The four of us groaned at once. Hating homework was universal.

"You, Callie. Keep an eye on Maya in the meantime. Be a friend," Clio said.

"I *am* her friend," I said, but it wasn't really true. I didn't talk with Maya much. Sometimes, I didn't even notice if she was absent from school. Clio gave me a pointed look, and I glanced away.

"Now if you don't mind," Clio said, and waved her hand at us in a shooing motion.

None of us moved.

"Go home," Clio said, then she swept past us, her hand already removing the key from her pocket.

"'Cassandra. Look her up,'" Thalia repeated, copying Clio's voice. "Ha! She might as well have said, 'Look up Becky.' Or 'Look up Larry.' It's just a name."

"It must mean something," Mela said.

"Right," Nia added. "Plus, we have a Fated One. This is awesome."

I didn't say anything. Didn't mention the key, or the fact that I'd come to headquarters unsure of this muse stuff. I'd be leaving with even *more* responsibility.

"We'd better go," I said, and the others agreed. We left the library, then went our separate ways to our entrance points. When I was sure the others couldn't see me, I ran through the museum, not bothering to look up at the statues and other priceless things on display. Why would Clio assign anyone to me? Especially someone who might save the world someday. I'd made a mess of things with Raquel, hadn't I? Plus, that *someone* happened to be the strangest and smartest girl at school. I wished she'd skipped a couple of grades when she had the chance. Maybe someone at the high school would have been tapped for this muse stuff instead of me.

I found myself back in the garden. The fountain tinkled in the distance. It was nice being there when it was all so empty. There wasn't a lot of breathing room in my small house. Even when I was alone in my room, Mami often busted in wanting to sweep the floor, or one of my brothers would leap from the closet, scaring me to pieces. This garden was different. It was peaceful. I followed the row of bushes, bopping the leaves as I went. I sat down in a shady spot and closed my eyes.

I leaned back, and my head struck something hard and metallic. Turning around, I noticed that behind me were two large plaques. One read:

IN MEMORY OF JIM.
DIED 1879, AGED 15 YEARS.
FAITHFUL DOG OF SIR HENRY COLE OF THIS MUSEUM.

The other read:

To TYCHO, A FAITHFUL DOG
WHO DIED
V-I-AN-MDCCCLXXXV

Dog graves, gross, I thought, then reread them. Tycho. Tycho? Tia Annie's book! So that's where she got the funny title. I felt a little flip in my stomach. Up until now, in spite of the magical entrance points, and the stopping of time, I still couldn't quite believe that Tia Annie, *my* tia Annie, had lived this same experience. But here it was, the evidence in the form of a dog's grave. The plaque felt warm to the touch.

"Oh, Tia Annie," I whispered as if anyone could hear me. "What am I even doing?"

There was silence, of course. I swallowed hard against the lump that had shown up in my throat just then. Got up, dusted my butt, and made my way back to the Great Bed, back to home and my never-as-peaceful-as-that-garden house.

When I got back, the first thing I did was creep into my mom's room. She was taking a nap, so I was careful not to wake her. In the dark, I felt the top of her nightstand, my fingers lightly touching her reading glasses, loose change, and then, ah! There it was! Mom's copy of Tia Annie's book, *Tycho*, which I now knew was named after a dead dog, of all things.

I picked it up, and slid out of the room with the book held tightly against my chest. I turned on a lamp in the living room, and began paging through the poems. Tia Annie had dedicated it to me, and I couldn't help but wonder if there was some message in the poems she had wanted me to understand, muse to future muse. I ran my finger along the table of contents. The poem titles were short, all one word: "Tales," "Happy," "Porcelain," "Sister," "Camden," "Christmas," "Miami," "Tycho," "Lost," and on and on. I selected my first poem and read.

> *TYCHO*
> *I pushed aside*
> *The small dog, its*
> *Bones white as*

Snow. Behind,
a Path. Beyond,
Secrets we
Were meant
To learn.

Did my aunt go digging in that dog's tomb? I wondered. I shivered. The plaque looked pretty well cemented in place. She must have meant it figuratively. But how? If Tycho was a metaphor for something, what was it? And who was "we" in the poem? Maybe the next one would reveal something more.

> *LOST*
> *My inquisitive friend*
> *Sought out the searchlights,*
> *Drawn to light like an insect. She*
> *Grew radiant with fury, she*
> *Bid me goodbye. Then she*
> *Was gone.*

My skin prickled. But what did that mean, "Sought out the searchlights"? A searchlight draws attention to something. Was Tia Annie's "inquisitive friend" chasing attention? Was she chasing fame? My mind flickered briefly to Raquel. Fame, as it turned out, had chased *her* thanks to *me*.

Frustrated, I read a few more poems. My language arts

teacher, Ms. Salvo, always said that we shouldn't confuse the speaker of a poem with the poet, that the poet isn't necessarily telling us about something real. "Invention," Ms. Salvo said, "is what a poet *does*. They are not to be trusted!" She would say the last bit with a wink, letting us know she was only kidding.

But even if I didn't assume Tia Annie was the speaker of the poems, I *still* didn't know what to make of any of it. None of it made any sense to me.

Muse of epic poetry, my butt.

Chapter 10
IT HAPPENS AGAIN

A surprise awaited me at school on Monday. Hanging over the front gates was a huge banner with Raquel's face on it and the words, "Miami Palms Middle School is Team Falcón!"

I guess word had gotten out about her audition.

I found her in homeroom with a new haircut, wearing bright red lipstick, and surrounded by all the popular kids in school, including Violet, Max, and Alain. Seeing her with them made me feel like I had been picked last for a team in PE.

"Raquel?" I asked, hovering at the edge of the group.

She perked up, found me, and shouted, "Make way for my bestie!" Students moved aside as if they'd been ordered to do so, and I guess they had.

"Your hair," I said. The sides were shaved, the short

part dyed pink. The top was still dark and curly, but the curls were glossy, perfect ringlets.

"I know," she whispered. "It's all so crazy. My publicist said—"

"Publicist?"

Raquel said, "I know," again, her eyes wide. She lowered her voice. "Nobody is supposed to know this, so shh. I thought I was there to audition, but it was, like, a formality. I'm on the show! My first-round performance airs in two weeks! And guess what? Jordan Miguel is a judge this year!"

"Raquel!" I squealed, and hugged her hard. I was happy for her, but part of me was worried. My best friend was going to be on television! She would have fans, probably. She'd have to go to California. My brain buzzed with a million thoughts, and underneath it all was a question— would she still want to be best friends with me?

"I wish Principal Jackson hadn't put up that banner. We're supposed to be discreet." She shrugged, then craned her neck to look behind me. "Hey, where's your project?"

I looked around. Everyone in homeroom had a science project with them. I watched as the triplets came in, balancing their coffee cups on their project boards. How did I miss all those huge boards? Worse—how did I forget to do my science fair project?

"Oh my God, Raqui. I forgot. I *forgot*. Ms. Rinse is going to be so mad!"

The situation was hopeless, and Raquel knew it. She gave me a gloomy look and pushed her own science fair project away from her with her foot. Too late. I'd already seen it in its perfect, glittery glory. I was dead, dead, dead.

Then I had an idea. I gripped the charm on my bracelet and whispered, "Nia? You there?" She was the Muse of science, right? If anyone could help me, it would be her.

Nothing happened.

It had been a stupid and desperate idea. I looked up and Violet was watching me, her lips twisted in a smirk.

"What are you doing?" Raquel asked me in a tone that suggested I'd nearly cratered her popularity with one gesture. What was that even about? Since when did Raquel care what the cool kids thought?

"Jeez. Nothing," I said, then added in a whisper of my own, "Violet Prado? Really? You're hanging out with her now?" but Raquel only shrugged. I decided to change the subject. "Hey, what's that?" I asked her, pointing to a jeweled box on her desk. It was round and covered with red stones packed closely together.

"Oh, it—it—was a gift I got in California. Um. It's nothing," she said, and started to put it away.

"It's pretty," I said. "Is it a secret or something?"

Raquel took a deep breath. "Sorry," she said. "It was a gift from Jordan Miguel. A 'welcome to the show' gift. I didn't want to tell you because—" She paused. "Because you might get jealous. Because Jordan Miguel, right? Your celebrity boyfriend?"

I punched her in the arm—not too hard, of course. "You're ridiculous. I'm happy for you, see?" I grinned like a maniac. "*Happy*. Now what's inside?" I asked, my hands reaching out to touch.

Without answering, Raquel swept the box away in one smooth motion and dropped it into her open backpack. I was about to punch her again, harder this time, when Ms. Rinse walked in. Our teacher was wearing her usual—a polka-dot dress. She greeted us all with high fives. But when she saw me without a board, she pulled her hand out of reach. "Callie Martinez-Silva," she said, "I'm shocked at your brazen empty-handedness."

"I had a concussion!"

"You've had this assignment since September," Ms. Rinse said. "Do you really have nothing at all?"

I shook my head. I'd started the project at the beginning of the year. It was on growing a backyard garden. I'd planted arugula and basil, tomatoes and chili peppers. They were getting sort of tall and lush, too. But with the concussion and the muse stuff, I'd forgotten all about abstracts and bibliographies and poster boards.

Scanning the room for Maya, I wondered what I was supposed to do now that I knew she was my Fated One. It's not like Clio gave us any directions. Maya walked in right as the bell rang, without a science project board. Did she forget her project, too? Maybe Maya *did* need help. She sat down at her desk and drummed her fingers nervously.

I was about to ask her about her missing project when Ms. Rinse said, "Anagrams, children!"

Every day, Ms. Rinse would put a science vocabulary word on the board. As she took attendance, we were supposed to come up with anagrams for the word. Maya always got the most. Today, the word was "photosynthesis."

As usual, I could only come up with three-letter words.

Maya's desk was next to mine. She rested her head on a closed fist as she worked, and I got a long look at her. Yes, I could see the way she would grow up into the woman we'd seen in the mirror. I glanced at her paper. She'd written down "hypnosis," "honey," and "isotopes" within the first minute, and she was already scratching out a new word. I didn't even know what an isotope was.

"What are you staring at?" Maya asked without looking at me.

"Oh," I said, startled. "Nothing. Sorry."

Maya glanced at me, chewing her bottom lip just like the grown-up version of her had done. She didn't say anything else.

"Okay, anagrams away," Ms. Rinse said. "It's Science Project Day!" she announced. She pressed a button on her desk, and rock music filled the room. She put her arms in the air and danced a little, then shut the music off. Ms. Rinse was a strange one, that's for sure. She cleared her throat. "The top science project will be selected for the county science fair. The winner goes on to the Young Scientist Competition in Washington, D.C. I am hopeful that the winner is here among you," she said, wiggling her eyebrows.

Maya's hand shot up. Ms. Rinse nodded. "Can I go get my project from the SAP meeting room?" she asked. Ms. Rinse winked at her, and Maya took off.

Ah, I thought. *Of course she didn't forget an assignment.*

I watched as, one by one, my classmates presented their projects. Ms. Rinse had given us a simple prompt—think of a problem that science paired with inspiration can solve. The best I'd come up with was a garden, and two other kids did, too. Letty, Lisa, and Leo each had brought in a different kind of battery made from household materials. Raquel's project was on solar energy, and Violet presented on mangrove trees and soil erosion. Max measured the effects of temperature on a hockey puck's speed, and Alain Riche did an experiment on the effectiveness of different sunscreens.

But every project paled next to what Maya Rivero came up with. She walked in from the SAP meeting room at last, pushing a cart with a glass tank full of water. Inside was an elaborate machine of some sort. Beside the tank was a pail. Maya herself was in her glory—she had put on a hat with an orca's face on it. She'd pulled an aqua-blue tulle tutu over her uniform skirt, and was wearing tights with what appeared to be clownfish all over them. Her T-shirt, also pulled over her uniform, read SAP in bubble letters.

"The earth is warming up and the seas are rising," she began softly.

"Speak up," Ms. Rinse said from the back of the class-room.

"THE EARTH IS WARMING UP AND THE SEAS ARE RISING," Maya shouted, pronouncing "seas" like "THees." Everyone laughed. She continued. "MIAMI IS A VULNERABLE CITY. OUR CHILDREN MIGHT NOT HAVE A MIAMI TO CALL HOME."

"Not quite so loud," Ms. Rinse said.

Maya took a deep, shaky breath. "I've designed a model pump. On a much larger scale, these could be installed in low-lying areas, underneath homes and roads, to pump out the seawater."

Inside the tank were two layers. The top layer was a piece of Astroturf, bright green and shiny, mimicking land. Underneath was water, and a bottom layer that was rocky and sandy. A plastic tube had been pushed through the rocks and sand, out over the top, and into the pail out-side the tank. Beneath the tank was a motor of some sort. Maya pushed a button on it. The machine inside the tank began to shake. Bubbles frothed in the water, as if it were boiling. The cart wobbled. "Hold on, hold on," Maya was saying to the pump. It shook even more violently, and a crack formed in the glass. Now Maya was shaking, too.

She couldn't seem to turn it off. Water splashed out of the sides of the tank, soaking Violet, who was in the front row.

Violet wiped water off her face and started saying something under her breath about nerds, something Maya heard, because she froze in place and her chin trembled.

As smart as she was, Maya was in trouble. Clio had only given me one job. *Be a friend,* she'd said, and it was now or never. I rushed out of my seat. "Calm down, Maya, you know what to do," I said, touching her shoulder. Then it happened. The tingly, hair-raising, crying feeling. It scared me, because I knew something was going to happen next, but I didn't know *exactly* what.

Maya looked at me. She said, "Oh. I do." Her hands steadied, and just like that she popped open a section of the motor, and thrust her fingers inside. The water stopped sloshing and the pump whirred smoothly to life. Water poured out of the tank and into the pail, without a single splash.

"The problem of sea level rise is a Goliath. And while this is one possible solution—a David, if you will—we'll need to develop many others. Not to mention cut back on carbon production immediately. If we're creative, and hopeful, we may just be able to hold back the sea," Maya said. She was composed, her voice at just the right volume.

Hold back the sea, Maya had said. I thought of Clio's mirror, of the submerged city I'd seen. I took in Maya's wild outfit, and started picturing her in a lab coat, her hair dyed in rainbow colors.

Finished with her presentation, Maya said, "My apologies for the little mishap earlier." I peered at Maya and noticed that her teeth were somehow . . . straighter. Was I imagining that? Then to Ms. Rinse, Maya said, "I don't know what happened."

"I know what happened," Violet said loudly, wringing her skirt. "You're an idiot."

"Come on, Violet," Raquel said from the back of the room.

Violet turned around and glared at Raquel.

I heard Raquel clear her throat. She didn't do confrontations well. "You don't have to be so mean all the time," she said softly.

The class went "Ohhh," and Violet's cheeks began to turn pink.

"That's enough," Ms. Rinse said, but Violet ignored her.

"If you think I'm so mean, why did you want to hang out this morning?" Violet said to Raquel. "What a poser you are. You can't even sing and your hair is stupid."

The room felt chilly all of a sudden, as if Ms. Rinse had turned down the AC a couple notches. I turned to stare at Violet. What was the matter with her, anyway? Hadn't she and Raquel been chatting this morning, all buddy-buddy?

Raquel crumpled for a moment. I'll admit I felt a little vindicated. What was Raquel thinking, hanging out with Violet?

"You're so rude, Violet. Leave Raquel alone," Maya said. Her lisp was utterly gone. Did I do that? *This is so bananas,* I thought. I rubbed my hands together, the feeling slowly coming back to my fingers.

Violet made a shocked little sound. Then she threw her pencil at Maya, who dodged it with a quick side step. Everyone gasped.

Maya, the nerdball genius, was suddenly a lot cooler than she'd been five minutes ago.

"What the—" I started to say. Raquel was on her feet, a balled-up piece of paper in her hand, aimed right at Violet's head. I wanted to cheer on my best friend, or hug her, or both.

Finally, Ms. Rinse was standing, stalking to the front of the room, her eyes narrow and full of purpose.

A pencil hit me on the chest and Violet grinned at me like a murderous clown.

"Girls, listen to me," Ms. Rinse warned, but it was too late. I'd dipped my hand into Maya's tank, cupped some water, and splashed it onto Violet's face.

Clearly in shock, Violet said nothing, only sat there, dripping.

Ms. Rinse also said nothing. Instead, she slammed her hand against the security call button beside the door. Someone from the main office piped in through the PA system. "Ms. Rinse, do you need help?" came the tinny voice.

"I do," Ms. Rinse said. "Please send school security. They need to escort three errant young ladies from my class."

"Three? What about Maya?" Violet argued, but Ms. Rinse gave her *the look*, and she didn't say another word.

The security guard, a woman we all knew simply as Ms. Rosa, was at the door at once.

"Callie. Raquel. Violet, off you go," Ms. Rinse said, exiling us from class for the day.

We don't need to go into everything Principal Jackson said to us. He was disappointed. He called our parents. Then he assigned us detention in the afternoon. I wasn't listening too closely. Instead, I was thinking about IT.

IT had happened again.

I hadn't meant to do IT, to inspire Maya in any way, but there was no doubting what I'd felt, and how Maya had been able to turn things around.

The problem was, I didn't know how to turn IT on. Would I just be randomly inspiring people for the rest of my life? And what if I was the one who needed inspiration? Was this . . . magic or power, or whatever it was, sucking me dry? Is that why Tia Annie had gotten sick?

Raquel was a mess all day worrying about detention. And I could tell that she was still upset about what Violet had said to her. While I didn't like the whole detention thing, I did like the fact that Raquel was being plain old Raquel again—worried about getting in trouble at school and talking my ears off. We walked down the hall together to Ms. Salvo's language arts class. Every so often, someone would stop us and say something to Raquel about the show. "Good luck," some kids said, or "You're so lucky!" But it didn't help Raquel's mood.

We quietly took our seats in language arts. Violet and Max sat two rows away, but we could hear them talking about what had happened in science. On top of that, Violet had somehow gotten her hands on the biggest Band-Aid ever made, and had taped it to her forehead. She turned toward me, pointing at it. "Twinsies," she said, laughing so hard she snorted.

I put my head down on my desk.

A moment later, I overheard Violet complaining to Max. "Detention, can you believe it? It's all that Maya's fault. Such a horrible dork."

Maya walked in then, her feet dragging. She was still wearing her tutu and orca hat, but it all seemed sort of sad now.

"She's not so bad," I heard Max respond, his eyes following Maya as she sat.

"Yeah, right," Violet said.

Ms. Fovos walked in, and I fumbled with my pencil. Fovos was a tall, thin woman with long, blond hair. She resembled a lizard, one of those long-faced anoles that were everywhere outside. Her pale skin even seemed to have a greenish tint to it under the fluorescent lights. She was the school's permanent substitute teacher.

I heard a student at the back say, "Oh no," at the sight

of her. Ms. Fovos whipped her head around, trying to figure out who said it, but we all kept our heads down. Not making eye contact with Fovos was always the best approach.

"Your language arts teacher, Ms. Salvo, seems to have come down with food poisoning," Ms. Fovos said. "Please avoid the salad bar at lunch." Then she began to hand out photocopies of an essay. "It's an informative essay. Let's do some popcorn reading," she said.

It took a while for everyone to quiet down. Ms. Salvo always read to us, and she would perch on her desk like a kid while she did it. Ms. Fovos was a walker—snaking her way around the desks as she spoke. Popcorn reading went like this: everyone took a turn reading a few sentences, and then you would say the name of someone who would read next.

I went first, reading the title of the essay out loud: "Cassandra, Princess of Troy."

I gasped. Clio's homework assignment! I'd forgotten to do it, which seemed to be a theme with me lately.

Ms. Fovos interrupted me. "I hate this kind of stuff," she said, waving the handout a bit. "Myths, and gods, and curses. It's all so dramaaaatic."

"Like a telenovela," Letty, one of the triplets, said, and then the class got derailed again as people started talking about the latest episode of *Soñar Despierto,* the new telenovela on TV.

"Martinez-Silva, read on," Ms. Fovos said at last, once she got the class quiet again.

The essay was about the Trojan War, and a princess named Cassandra who could tell the future, but the god Apollo cursed her, so that nobody ever believed anything she said. She tried to warn her family about the war, but it was useless. They cast her aside in disbelief. It made me so sad to read about this Cassandra, especially now that I knew it was probably a true story.

Then again, maybe it wasn't just Cassandra's sad fate making me feel this way. I wondered why Clio wanted us to know about her. I stopped reading. Usually, I picked Raquel during popcorn reading. This time I called out, "Maya," who was so shocked to hear her name called—nobody ever called Maya's name during popcorn reading—that she stumbled over the first few words.

I made my way to detention in a fog of overthinking. Raquel was beside me, chattering away nervously, but I wasn't listening. Suddenly, detention seemed like too minor a detail in my complicated life.

Detention was held in the music room and was overseen by, who else? Ms. Fovos. During the day, she was a substitute teacher, but in the afternoon, she lorded it over detention like an evil queen. Cell phones were confiscated without her batting an eye, and silence was mandatory. She even yelled at a student for sneezing once. Or so I'd heard. I didn't end up in detention often. Or ever, really. Neither did Raquel, who sat in the seat in front of me with tears in her eyes.

The classroom was freezing and we shivered while Fovos took attendance. When she called Violet's name, she smiled warmly. Then she summoned her over to her desk. Violet pulled up a stool, and the two of them chatted in whispers. Sometimes, they would both glance out, their eyes landing on me for some reason. Fovos licked her teeth when she looked at me. It was unnerving, to say the least.

I scribbled a note and passed it to Raquel when Fovos and Violet were chatting. It read: *F keeps staring at me. Am I imagining things?*

Raquel read the note, then hid it under her thigh. I watched as she watched Fovos.

After a few minutes, Raquel scratched the back of her head and flashed me a Y in sign language.

Yes, she'd noticed it. No, I wasn't going crazy.

Meanwhile, Violet and Fovos were still chatting, like old friends. *Evil likes evil,* I scribbled onto a note that I passed to Raquel.

Maybe they're related. Like Fovos is her aunt or cousin or something, Raquel scribbled back. That made sense. In fact, I saw a resemblance. They were laughing now, Fovos and Violet, as Fovos showed her something on her cell phone.

Just then Maya walked into detention. She was soaked to the bone, her tutu limp, her orca hat in her hand.

Soggily, she handed a slip of paper to Fovos, who read it and actually smiled.

"Over there," she said, pointing to a seat by the AC unit blasting chilled air.

"I'm wet and cold. Can I sit somewhere else instead?" Maya asked.

Fovos frowned, then shook her head. "Sit," she said. I swear, it sounded like "Ssssssit."

I watched as poor Maya shivered in her seat. She put her head down. I'm pretty sure she started to cry. But detention was over soon after. Raquel and I waited for Maya by the door.

"What happened?" Raquel asked her.

"I was taking my science project home and my tank fell over. Principal Jackson was standing nearby. You can guess the rest," she said. Then, Maya walked away from us, leaving wet footprints in her wake.

"Poor Maya," Raquel said. "And how bizarre was Fovos? She was definitely fixating on you."

"Beyond bizarre," I said.

Raquel brightened a little. "Hey, I'm sorry I was short with you earlier. Things are so crazy, they're getting to me. Do you want to come over and see my audition footage? I have so much to tell you, Callie," she said, gripping my hands.

"Yes, I'd love—" I started to say, but the bracelet Clio had given me began to heat up.

Thalia wasn't kidding. This wasn't warm. This was *hot*.

"Ouch," I said, and pulled my hands out of Raquel's.

"You okay?" Raquel asked.

"Yes," I said, spinning the bracelet to cool it off. "But I gotta run. I'll watch the audition tape some other time, okay?"

"Oh. All right," Raquel said. I left her, and ran down the hall, out the doors, and down the street as fast as I could.

I juggled the keys to the front door of my house, the bracelet burning all the time. I tried to take it off on the way, but my mother's superglue trick had worked. That sucker was on permanently. "Ow, ow, ow," I muttered as I opened the door, closed it behind me, and ran to my room.

"Where are you going?" Mario asked. He and Fernando were in the kitchen, devouring bowls of cereal. My brothers had breakfast at every meal, and for snacks in between.

"Nap!" I shouted as I ran past them.

I heard Fernando say, "You don't look tired, but whatever," as I closed my bedroom door and slid under the bed like a baseball player diving to base.

I closed my eyes and counted until I felt the chill of the museum.

I sighed. The bracelet had stopped burning, but I was freezing cold again.

Chapter 11
THE REST OF THEM

"Listen up, Miami girl, you're going to catch pneumonia coming to headquarters dressed like that. Also, why are you trying to call me in the middle of the day? Not cool. There are rules, you know."

I was wearing my short-sleeve uniform polo shirt and khaki shorts. Goose bumps prickled my skin. Nia was crouched on all fours, staring at me under the Great Bed. She thrust another cloak from the dress-up room at me. This one was wine colored.

"It worked? You heard me?" In my excitement, I tried to sit up and smashed my head.

"Hey, that bed's a priceless treasure. Watch it," Nia said, reaching out a hand. I took it, and she pulled me out.

"Right," I said, rubbing my head. I hoped I didn't bust a stitch. I was going to have permanent brain damage before

I got the hang of this muse thing.

"Yes, I heard you. So did my dad. He checked the whole house, thinking we were under surveillance. He's retired CIA. He's, um, antsy sometimes," Nia said, her dark eyes wide and full of meaning.

"Sorry," I said, putting on the robe and feeling instantly warmer.

"No worries," Nia said, but I'm not sure she meant it. "How about your mom? Is she suspicious yet? I know she's at the dentist's office all day and . . ."

"How do you know my mom is a dental hygienist?" I asked. It was like they'd been briefed on me or something.

"We were briefed," Nia said.

"Well, I haven't been . . . briefed on . . . hardly anything. And now I get this—this *call*," I said, holding up my wrist and jiggling the bracelet, "which burns, by the way, and I'm supposed to just come running."

"Which you did. Because you trust your instincts. Above all else, a muse trusts her instincts," Nia said. I noticed she was wearing a NASA T-shirt, this one reading, IT'S NOT ROCKET SCIENCE. OH WAIT. YES IT IS!

"What is that, rule number two?"

"Rule number one, actually."

"I give up," I said.

Nia gave me a reassuring squeeze, and I followed her down the stairs and around a bend, into a small, dark theater. It was just like a movie theater, with plush mustard-colored seats and a big screen.

We sat down and I took an aisle seat. "We're about to be briefed on something."

"How do you know?"

"You know the message you got? On your bracelet? It's like Morse code. There's a pattern to the heat that tells you what you're in for. When it's intense like that, you'll know it's important, like a serious briefing. When it's just training we're coming in for, it gets a little warm in short bursts, on and off. When it feels like you might literally catch fire, then come running, and pray that the V and A is still standing when you get here." Nia said this last bit in a whisper, but I wasn't sure if it was because she feared a call like that, or because she had actually experienced one.

Before I could ask, I heard voices in the hall.

Three women came in. One was pushing a fourth in a wheelchair. The other muses! I recognized some of them from the photograph Clio had shown me. The woman in the wheelchair extended both hands toward me. She was very old, her dark skin papery, her black eyes glittering. Her hair was gray and cropped short. I took her hands. "Greetings, Calliope," she said, in a lilting accent I didn't quite recognize. Normally, I correct people who call me Calliope, but one look at this woman told me I shouldn't.

"My name is Etoro," she said. "Muse of love."

Etoro held my hands and I felt it all at once—my

mother's love, my brothers', my father's, and my step-mother's. Shocked, I pulled my hands away. Gently, Etoro reached for them again, and there it was, Tia Annie's love. Raquel's love. I felt the love of my dog, Lola, and my cat, Misu. It was overwhelming. My eyes filled with tears.

"How blessed you are, girl," Etoro said, then released my hands. The sensation dimmed a little, but didn't go away entirely. "What you do for the world, you do for them. Keep them in your mind's eye, always," the old woman said. Then, she rolled her chair into the wheelchair space at the front of the theater.

Another of the women pushed forward. She was my height, and her hair was dark. When she spoke, it was in Spanish. "Paola, musa de lo sagrado. Bienvenida, divina," she said.

Even though I mostly understood Spanish, I had a hard time speaking it, a fact that disappointed my mother to no end. "Muse of the sacred?"

"Sí," Paola said.

"Colombia?" I asked. Sometimes, you can tell where a Spanish speaker is from just from their accent.

Paola smiled. "Yes," she said in English. She gave me a kiss on the cheek. She put her hand on my forehead and closed her eyes as if in prayer, then she found her seat.

The remaining women greeted me together. They were younger than the other two, and both wore their dark hair in high ponytails. The first introduced herself as Elnaz,

Muse of music, and the other as Tomiko, Muse of dance. They took turns asking me how I was doing, expressed awe about the Great Bed of Ware, and asked questions about Miami. Turns out they were from Istanbul and Tokyo, respectively, both college students and performing arts majors. "We spent last summer with Etoro in Nigeria," Tomiko said.

"Maybe she'll invite you someday," Elnaz said. I laughed. If my Cuban mother knew I was currently four thousand miles away, she'd invent a way to teleport to my location and ground me for life.

Then it was just me and Nia again. "The muses, they're from *everywhere*," I said to Nia quietly. I don't think I managed to keep the awe out of my voice.

"Inspiration knows no borders, and all people and places are equal and worthy of inspiration," Nia said. "Those are rules number four and five, by the way."

"Oh," I said.

Soon, Thalia and Mela showed up, and they took seats next to us. Thalia was chattering away at Mela, who had her headphones planted firmly over her ears. Thalia had a worn copy of *The Lion, the Witch, and the Wardrobe* on her lap. Thalia and Mela were in matching pajamas— blue, with yellow hearts all over.

"You two plan this?" I asked.

"No," Mela said, scowling, tugging her headphones off.

"Yes!" Thalia said, giggling.

I thought of the theater mask rings they both wore—happy and sad. They really did seem like a balanced pair. I watched as Thalia opened her book and thrust it in Mela's face. "Proof that it's real," I heard her say.

"For the last time, it's *fiction*," Mela said roughly.

Finally, Clio arrived. She was wearing a dark business suit. Her white hair was done up in an elegant bun and her face was drawn, dark circles ringing her eyes.

"Muses, welcome home," she said. She walked behind a large podium and fiddled with some controls. The lights dimmed. The screen began to glow. "Now that you are all here, I have a story to tell."

The first slide came on the screen. It was a painting of nine faceless women.

"Are we about to get a lecture?" I asked, incredulous. I left school for . . . more school?

Mela leaned over and whispered, "Weren't you listening? You're about to hear a story."

Chapter 12
CLIO'S TALE

"For the benefit of the newest among us, who has yet to make her decision about staying, I thought a brief history was in order," Clio began. I knew they were all staring at me. I probably should have waved or something. I was biting my lower lip so hard I thought I had made it bleed.

Clio gestured toward the image on the screen. "The original nine Muses were the daughters of Zeus and the Goddess of memory, Mnemosyne. They were tasked with inspiring poets, musicians, scientists, artists—and heroes. Their influence was profound. The nine were protectors of the human spirit and its creative light."

A new image appeared on screen. It was a black-and-white photo of the V and A.

"We have always had our headquarters in museums. We inspired the very name of these places. The earliest headquarters were in Greece. They were temples then, where artists came to worship us. Later, our home was in Alexandria, Egypt. We made the Ashmolean in Oxford home for a long time. The Louvre in Paris. The Quito Astronomical Observatory in Ecuador, and The Gyeongju National Museum in South Korea. Then there was the Indian Museum in Kolkata. We were there quite a while. And, for the last several years, here at the V and A."

Thalia's hand shot up. "Why not stick around one place?"

Clio clicked a button and the picture changed. Now it was a drawing of an ancient, smoldering building, fire licking the walls. "Sometimes, our location gets compromised," she said darkly, before adding, "Look at us. We speak many languages. We sing different songs. We worship in different ways. As a group, we don't belong to any one place. Besides, it's fun to get new entrance points in new places, don't you think?"

Mela beamed, and I knew she was thinking about that unicorn tapestry.

Clio stepped away from the podium. Behind her, the screen glowed with the image of the muses, frozen in cold marble. "There can only be nine of us. That was as our mother, Mnemosyne, wished. When a muse dies, or decides that she can no longer serve, a new muse is awakened."

"We lost several muses who had been with us a long,

long time," Paola clarified, turning to look at us, her face full of sadness.

What had happened? I wondered. Had there been some kind of attack on headquarters? The thought frightened me, and I wrapped my arms around myself.

Clio must have noticed, because she said, "As much as I wish it didn't, time marches on without a care. We are mortal, after all. The last muses of science, comedy, tragedy, and the epic poem all left our sisterhood over the course of the last two years. If you've done your math, you'll realize that the transfer of power doesn't always happen right away. The time has to be right," Clio explained.

"A new muse receives her powers in a moment of a peril. Not her own, but that of others. It is a test of her will, and her love, given freely even to strangers," Etoro added.

Clio turned her attention to Nia, Mela, Thalia, and me. "You four are very young. Eleven years old, all of you." I could hear some of the older muses taking a deep breath. I wondered what they remembered about being eleven.

"Nia?" Clio prompted. "Might you share your story with us?"

Nia cleared her throat. "A little kid fell into Lake Michigan back in February. Don't know where his parents were. But I took him out of the icy water, wrapped him in my coat, and called nine-one-one. The next day, Clio was our substitute teacher in my social studies class."

"And you did very well on that quiz I gave you," Clio

said, which made Nia smile. Clio nodded at Mela next.

Fidgeting in her seat a bit as she spoke, Mela described the night an alarm went off in her apartment in the middle of the night. "But the strange thing was I woke with a start *before* the alarm went off. It was a carbon monoxide detector. I woke my family, then my nani, and I went around the building waking people up and getting them out. Clio was among the police who had come to check on everyone. You looked very smart in that uniform, Clio," Mela added.

Thalia laughed. "I've got you beat. I was in maths class, and our teacher was giving out lollipops, and I was like, 'Bags the strawberry sort!' And anyhow, this one girl, Sarah, starts to choke on her lollipop, and I thought, 'Well, that's pants,' so that's when I went over there and gave her the Heimlich, and out popped the lolly. She puked all over me afterward, true story, but that was all right because she was okay, wasn't she?" Thalia didn't wait for an answer. "Then Clio shows up at our door that night with takeout from my favorite curry place, and freezes Mum and Dad right on the spot, didn't you, Clio?"

I stopped blinking for Thalia's entire speech.

"Your turn," Thalia said, shaking my shoulder and snapping me out of it.

"Pass," I said. They'd all done such incredible things. Brave things! What had I done? Stood there in terror while almost falling out of a moving elevated train, that's what.

Or maybe Clio wanted me to tell them about accidentally turning my best friend into a pop star. How very heroic of me.

"Callie?" Clio prompted.

"No thanks, I'm good," I said, as if I were turning down one of her brownies.

Etoro turned in her seat. "It's all fine," she said. "You are meant to be here."

I didn't say anything, but I'm sure my face said, "I'm not so sure."

Clio looked at me as she spoke, her voice strong and clear. "Callie inspired an entire train car of people to risk their lives for one another's safety."

Tomiko spoke first. "She made heroes on her first try?"

Elnaz let out a long whistle. "Wow, girl," she said, and high-fived me from a distance. I lifted my hand weakly and high-fived her back.

"I don't know how—I didn't—I didn't mean to," I said softly, unsure if anyone actually heard me.

"Yes, impressive," Clio said. "But there is still a lot of learning to do, especially for you four," she added, turning her gaze on Thalia, Mela, Nia, and me.

Clio worked the podium's electronics again as I sat there, confused as ever. Weren't they going to tell me *why* what happened on the Metrorail was impressive? I glanced at Nia and she was staring at me, wide-eyed. "You didn't tell me you did *that*," she said.

"For the last time, I don't know what I did," I whispered back.

Before Nia could say anything else, Clio pushed a button and a new image appeared on the screen. Three figures came into view, cloaked in dark hoods, only their bright teeth visible in the shadow.

"We empower the light within others. We conduct it. We guide it. But where there is light, there is also darkness."

Paola started to mutter something like a prayer in Spanish. Tomiko had drawn up her knees to her chest. Elnaz was staring straight ahead, her mouth a grim line, while next to her, Etoro had her eyes closed tight.

"There are always three, and they have had many names. The dark muses. Temptresses. Sirens. They are our counterparts—vengeance, jealousy, destruction. They can travel long distances in an instant. Through time, they, like us, arrive in different forms," Clio said, then clicked on another picture.

Now an image of a ship appeared. The sailors were tied to the masts, while three smiling women, winged and sharp-toothed, reached out from a rocky outcropping. "When the sirens tried to derail heroes of old, the muses plucked their feathers until they were bald chickens. Our ancestors defeated them in the past. We may be called to do so now. They have been quiet for a long time, working their dark influence in small ways, ways we can't track easily. But something has changed."

Now Clio loaded up what appeared to be security camera footage. It was a familiar but empty courtyard.

"That's my school!" I whispered to Nia.

A long shadow formed along the pavers, followed by a water tank, followed by none other than Maya Rivero, pushing said tank. She stopped for a moment, adjusted her tutu, and kept going. Principal Jackson appeared from the opposite direction.

I held my breath. I knew what was going to happen next—Maya was about to get the mother of all detentions.

The two of them chatted for a moment. Suddenly the sky darkened. Three black birds, glossy and large, swooped between them, knocking Maya down. As she fell, she bashed into the water tank, toppling it over and dousing Principal Jackson.

We watched as Principal Jackson began to yell at Maya. She pointed to the sky, but he looked at her as if she were crazy, as if she'd pushed the tank over on purpose.

Whatever she was saying, he didn't believe her.

Clio switched off the video at that point.

"As you can plainly see, this particular Fated One, a girl named Maya Rivero, was recently attacked," Clio said.

All around me, the muses were shaking their heads and whispering to one another. Thalia and Mela were discussing something vigorously, while Nia had jumped into another row to ask Tomiko a question. Then there was me, an island in the center of the theater, confused as ever.

I raised my hand and waited. If I had to sit through a

lecture, I might as well behave as if I were in one.

Finally, after a long moment, Clio's eyes fell on me. "Yes, Callie?"

"I have a question," I started, my voice low.

I swallowed. "Why, in the name of all things Greek, or holy, or whatever, does Maya Rivero getting whooped by some random birds matter?" I asked.

Clio nodded. "Not random birds. Sirens. Fated Ones are rarely targeted by beings from our world. Titans, centaurs, nymphs—they tend to mind their business these days. The fact that *sirens* are after Maya is of concern to us all. We will all be involved in protecting her in some form."

Nia hopped back into my row, sat up, and whispered, "This is big. This is *huge*." I shrugged her away. I bounced my leg up and down until Nia put her hand on my knee to make me stop.

"Excuse me." I raised my hand again.

Etoro spoke. "Sirens only interfere when the Fated One is particularly important."

Once more, I tried to get them to listen to me. "Guys. I mean, ladies. Muses. I have a question about Maya—" But the room erupted in conversations, and I felt like a little island in the middle of them again. I fought the urge to just get up and go back to the Great Bed.

Clio clapped her hands to get everyone's attention. "The sirens appear in different forms. They may be human, or not. They are disrupters who do not show their faces easily. Remember that we have defeated them in the past, and we can do so again. Because Maya is also eleven, and because she and Callie attend the same school, I have assigned Maya to Callie. Nia, Thalia, and Mela are on this assignment as well."

"Are you certain, Clio?" Paola asked.

"Honestly, they're, like, seventh graders," Tomiko added.

"Sixth, thanks," Nia said, and Tomiko shook her head.

"They are up to the task," Clio said.

The older muses stared at us then. I didn't think they were convinced. I mean, I wasn't even convinced.

Clio passed around a plate of brownies as the older muses made their way out of the theater. The four of us exchanged glances and stayed in our seats. We could talk when we were alone. "Thank you for your attention. You are dismissed," Clio said when the last brownie was taken.

"I'm supposed to protect Maya Rivero from demented birds? Can someone explain this?" I asked Nia, who started to say something when Clio popped back into the theater. "Junior muses, to my office," she said.

"We are the MUSE SQUAD," Thalia yelled back.

Nia frowned. "Junior muses is a terrible name, too," she said, stomping out of the theater. Thalia, Mela, and I followed.

"I hate birds," Mela muttered over and over again as we walked through the cold and dark museum, back to the library.

Chapter 13
ASSIGNMENT: MAYA RIVERO

I had about a million questions. "Let me get this straight. Those muses I just met? They each have a 'Fated One' assigned to them? Is that how it works?" I asked as we walked.

"There are hundreds of Fated Ones," Nia began. "They mainly don't need us day to day. Sometimes they get stuck on an idea, or need a jolt of courage."

"And you go about inspiring them or something?" I asked.

"Yes, but sometimes, it's more hands-on than that," Mela said. "For example, Etoro was in Cairo last week helping a Fated One who's starting a school for girls. Etoro used to be a school principal."

"I was on Instagram the other day, and it looked like Tomiko was back volunteering at that dance academy in Sozopol," Thalia said. "I wonder if muses fly first class?"

she asked out loud, but nobody answered her.

"Mela, Thalia, and I haven't done much of anything yet. I got here in February. Thalia and Mela got their powers this summer. We're learning, just like you," Nia said.

"You all know more than I do, that's for sure," I said. "I think I accidentally made my best friend famous," I said.

"Yikes," Nia said. "The worst I've done is inspire my science teacher back home to give us too much homework."

"That's awful," Thalia said. "The worst I've done is ruin a school play. It was *Romeo and Juliet*, but the whole school started laughing in all the wrong parts thanks to me." Thalia turned a deep shade of red.

"I keep making people cry at parties," Mela said. "Honestly, how is that even helpful?" Her lips turned down into a frown, and I felt my eyes pricking with tears.

"Quit it, Mela," Nia said, swiping at her eyes.

We reached the library, where Clio was waiting for us.

"Follow me," she said. We trailed behind Clio as she went through door after door, until we were no longer in any part of the museum that a visitor might see. When she reached the last door, she dipped into her pocket and pulled out the key I had seen the other day. She slid it into a large bronze lock, twisting and pulling on a massive door handle shaped like a bat until the door creaked open. We were in a vast storage room, with rows and rows of shelves full of items of every shape and size. Three sarcophagi sat in one corner. If there were any mummies inside I didn't want to know. On another shelf were hundreds of teacups. Another held silver spoons. Tiaras lined a different shelf, glittering in the light.

Clio led us past more and more shelves. "These are the museum's stores," she said. "Not everything makes it to an exhibit. Most items are here because they aren't all that significant. Others remain in the stores because they aren't safe."

She stopped in front of an open case with several small wooden boxes in it. Some were so old and beat-up that they looked like they belonged in the trash. Others were decorated with stones or gems.

"Treasure chests?" Thalia asked, reaching out to touch one.

Clio grabbed Thalia's wrist. "There are curses inside many of these."

The smile on Thalia's face died at once. We all took a step back.

"But here," Clio said, pointing to an empty spot on the shelf, "is our biggest problem. Up until last week, there was a small wooden box upon this spot called the Cassandra Curse. You've all done your homework?"

The others nodded, and I did, too. I hadn't technically done any homework, but I knew who Cassandra was.

"As you all now know, long, long ago, Cassandra, an ancient one *and* a Fated One, was cursed by Apollo to speak prophecies that no one would believe."

"Like the boy who cried wolf," Nia said.

"Correct," Clio said. "You can imagine how that went for her. She would warn people that an invasion was coming, and they would laugh her off, saying, 'Oh, Cassandra.' Then later, she'd have to watch her loved ones die, and her city burn. Again and again she warned people, but they never listened. It must have been torture," Clio said, her brow furrowed in concern. "Before her death," Clio went on, "Cassandra rid herself of the curse briefly, and she managed to lock it into a small chest like the ones you see here. It was only a short respite for poor Cassandra. She probably meant to hide the box, but somehow, it was taken from her. Now, whoever opens the box receives the curse."

"How did she lock the curse away?" I asked.

"Some say that she uttered a truth that she'd been afraid to tell even herself, and so she was cured and the curse was trapped again." Clio ran her hands along the empty spot on the shelf, leaving a clear line in the dust that had settled there. "The box went missing last week. We had just discovered the threat when Callie showed up here unannounced."

I took a tiny step backward. No wonder Clio had looked so frazzled that day.

"I believe a siren took it," she said, then drew a single red feather from a pocket in her suit.

At the sight of the feather, Mela let out a little squeal, but otherwise she held it together.

A thought tickled the back of my mind. I don't know

how else to explain it really. But there was something about these boxes . . .

"Follow me," Clio said, and we did, all the way to her office, where a fresh plate of brownies was waiting for us.

We took up seats in the four chairs in front of her desk. Clio cleared her throat before beginning. "Now, Nia, Thalia, and Mela—as you know, Maya is your first assignment. It's early in your training as junior muses and—"

"Muse Squad, ma'am," Thalia interrupted. We all glared at her. Clio's nostrils flared a little.

"As I was saying, though it is early in your training, the incident at Callie's school with the Fated One named Maya Rivero is of the utmost significance."

"How are we supposed to help her?" I blurted. "Maya is a nobody at our school. She's smart, yeah, but weird. *So weird*. She doesn't have friends. She doesn't hang out with anyone, like ever, and, and . . ." I stopped myself. I remembered how weird I was sometimes, and how Tia Annie in my dreams had told me to "let go." And I remembered my mother's words: *If you are loved, Callie, you'll be okay.*

Suddenly, I knew what we were supposed to do. I took a deep breath and said, "Maya is not loved. At least, not by many people. Not at school. And she needs to be okay, right, Clio? She's Fated, and if she isn't loved, well then, she'll go off track."

Clio smiled. For the first time ever, I saw her teeth. They were very nice teeth.

"Maya Rivero is very important to us all. The choices

she will make in her life are vast and far-reaching. Do you remember the mirror I showed you? The flooded cities, the destruction? There may be a chance to stop that future, and Maya could hold the key. But now that I know for sure that sirens are involved, your mission is far more urgent." Clio stared at each of us in turn. "And Callie is right. Maya Rivero is not loved. Yet. You will all help."

"But how? Maya is all the way in Florida," Mela said.

"Miami!" Thalia said, then made a "whoop, whoop" sound.

"It's not all beaches and coconut drinks," I muttered.

"How?" Nia asked, all business as usual.

"I cannot hold time back home for each of you for this particular assignment. It's too lengthy, and would disrupt the planet's timeline. Thus, your parents will be informed of a once-in-a-lifetime opportunity for the three of you to travel to Florida for an exceptional academic experience this semester. They will not be opposed," Clio said. I shuddered. Just how powerful was she? My mother would *never* let me leave home. I wasn't even allowed to go to slumber parties. "It's a Cuban thing," my mom always said, and my dad and stepmom backed her up. Thank goodness, this particular problem wasn't mine. Nia, Mela, and Thalia would be coming to *my* town.

"Callie," Clio said, turning to me, "your mother will be thrilled to accept three exchange students."

"Roomies!" Thalia shouted, and tried hugging us all at once.

I wiggled out of that most awkward hug. "My house is tiny!" I protested. Not that I didn't think it would be fun, but we had only one bathroom.

"Now to the mission at hand. Thalia, Maya will need your expertise in socializing. Smiling. Making friends. Tender-hearted Mela, you'll know what to do. Nia, you'll find in Maya a kindred spirit and a like-minded scientist. Keep her on track." Nia nodded solemnly. "Now, Callie, Maker of Heroes, you've already done what you need to do twice now, inspiring Maya to stand up for herself."

I shook my head. "No, just that one time before she got detention."

"Incorrect," Clio said. "Maya stood up for Raquel before, at her audition." That's right! Maya had gotten on her feet and shouted out that goofy SAP war cry, or whatever it was she called it.

"I did that?" I asked, knowing the answer.

Clio rose to her feet. "If Maya is going to grow up to be the person humanity needs her to be, she needs—"

"Friends," I said.

"Yes. And more than that. She needs protection. I'm afraid that whoever stole the Cassandra Curse means to use it on Maya Rivero," Clio added. "Sirens can take many forms, but they often work in threes. I believe the sirens are in Miami, sticking close by, watching for an opportunity to strike."

My hands balled up into fists at my sides at the thought of monsters in my hometown.

"Sirens love chaos. They are pulled to it the way bugs are drawn to light. So keep calm. Find the three, break the curse, and save the future. This job will take the four of you, working together. You four can do what no single muse can, understand?" Clio finished.

"The Muse Squad is on it," Thalia said.

The rest of us only took a deep breath before Clio tried to dismiss us.

"But—" I began. Clio stared hard at me. I steadied myself. "But I don't know how to do it. The muse magic. I don't know how." My cheeks felt hot.

"That's something we can work on," Clio said. "Come with me."

Chapter 14
MUSES IN TRAINING

Clio chatted as she walked, leading us through the museum until we stopped in the courtyard with the pool again. I spotted the Tycho grave out of the corner of my eye. It was cold and raining outside, but the dress-up cloak helped. "Wait here," Clio said, then disappeared into the museum again.

"Now what?" I asked, but the others didn't respond. The lights were off in the café across the pool. They switched on suddenly, the door opened, and there, under a pair of bright red umbrellas, were Paola, Muse of the sacred, and Elnaz, Muse of music.

"Greetings," Elnaz called out, smiling at us, perfectly dry under her umbrella. She looked like any other college kid, except that her left eye was brown, and her right eye was blue. "It's a lovely day for training, don't you think?"

She and Paola walked around the pool, reaching us quickly.

Water dripped off the tip of my nose. Lovely, my butt. At least it wasn't one of those torrential Miami rainstorms.

"Don't tease them, Elnaz," Paola chastised, and handed each of us a plastic poncho with the V and A logo emblazoned on the back. Cheesy, but it would do. I slid it on and the plastic immediately stuck to my thighs. Paola's long skirt was soaking up water. At her waist was a thin chain composed of silver hoops, from which hung tiny silver bells. She jingled as she watched us. The wrinkles around her eyes deepened whenever she smiled, and she smiled a lot.

"It's one thing to inspire a Fated One. We use different methods. We talk to them. We encourage them. We get to know them so that we understand what makes them afraid, or reluctant. Inspiration, girls, is easy," Elnaz said.

"But we can't inspire a siren to be good," Paola said. "Just like you can't inspire a minotaur not to lower his horns and attack. Believe me, I've tried."

I couldn't picture Paola—so old, tiny, and sweet—facing off against a mythic monster.

Elnaz cracked her knuckles. "Today, you'll learn to fight."

Paola cleared her throat. "And later, we inspire," she said softly, catching Elnaz's eyes. The younger muse bit her lip, and gave Paola some room.

"Mela, Nia, and Thalia have all had some training already, haven't you, girls? Consider this a refresher," Elnaz said.

The three girls nodded beside me. *Great*, I thought. I was further behind than I'd realized.

"Pair up as so," Paola said, and turned at once to face Elnaz, as if they were about to dance or box. "Mela," Paola said, "you know what to do."

I felt Mela grab my arm and watched as Nia and Thalia stood off to one side.

"You're stuck with me, I'm sorry," she said.

I opened my mouth to ask why she was apologizing when Mela's hands flew up before her face, fluttering her fingers, her eyes closed.

Tia Annie's face filled my mind. The day she'd died, she'd told me, *You'll make the whole world spin, Callie.* It didn't make any sense. Her voice was like a foot crunching gravel. Her nails, usually perfectly manicured, had weakened and split. She was pale. She was dying. I remembered holding on to Mami, who shook and held me tight. I remembered the heartbeat monitor slowing down, the beeping stopping, stopping, forever silent, stopping . . .

"Stop!" I cried out. My face was wet, not from rain but from tears, and I was on the ground, my dress-up cloak soaked through. Mela's arms went around me at once, and she was going, "Shh, shh, forgive me, my friend."

When I looked up, everyone was a bit misty-eyed, but no one had faced the brunt of Mela's powers like I just had.

Elnaz cleared her throat. Her voice was shaky. "Mela has such strong control of her power because she has mastered her kódikas."

I looked at the other girls. Nia's brow was furrowed, but Thalia and Mela both nodded in understanding.

"We say 'kódikas' in Greek, the word the first Muses used. 'Código,' en español. 'Code' in English. A secret code. A gesture. One that helps her tap into her powers, the way a key unlocks a door," Paola said slowly, mostly to me. "Así," she said, and began to hum.

Paola's voice was not strong. It was an old woman's voice, but she carried a lovely, lilting tune. The bells at her waist accompanied her song. Suddenly, everything seemed so . . . important. The hydrangea bushes around us, the way the leaves clung damply to the thin branches, and the people in the buildings beyond the museum, I worried about them so much. Should I go to them? My feet took a step toward the exit, just as I remembered the grass beneath my feet. We were trampling it. Was it okay? A beetle scurried over my shoe. I bent down to pet its mottled, shiny back.

"Sacred things," Paola said, her song ending. "You have felt what is sacred in all living things, and you have felt the desire to protect them." Thalia had her cheek pressed to a patch of dirt. Nia and Mela were hugging Elnaz, who scowled at them both. "My song is my kódikas," Paola said.

Elnaz shrugged off Mela and Nia, and clapped her hands. "Let's move on then," she said. "Thalia, why don't you try to focus your magic? Pick your target." Thalia closed her eyes and pointed at Mela, who began to say, "Don't you dare, Thalia Berry," when Thalia launched into a laugh, one so infectious and sudden that Mela was soon clutching her sides and wiping happy tears off her cheeks.

"My kódikas is laughter, and it's *hilarious*," Thalia said.

"And powerful, mi niña," Paola added.

A bird chirped in a nearby tree, and I jumped at the sound. How was any of this going to help us fight sirens?

"What about you, Elnaz?" Mela asked, interrupting my train of thought.

Elnaz smiled, and drew a small silver instrument from within her sleeve. It was a flute of some kind. "Tin whistles. Portable instruments. My favorite is the cello, but you don't want to carry that around." She held it to her lips and paused. "Ever get a song stuck in your head and think it will drive you crazy?" We nodded. "I can play one for you. One that will dig its way into your brains, consuming your every thought until you drop," she said, her mouth popping on that final *P*, her expression deadly serious.

Oh, I thought. *That's how she'd fight a siren. She'd break their brains with a killer earworm. Got it.*

No thanks. We all shook our heads vigorously. Elnaz slowly lowered her flute.

"Good," she said, and put the tin whistle away. "How about you, Nia? Have you figured out your kódikas yet?"

Nia looked down at her sneakers. "I'm working on an app."

"An app? Like on your teléfono?" Paola asked, her brow furrowed.

Nia nodded. "Something like that. Closed source. Just

for me. It measures the placement of the stars, whether anything is in retrograde, the likelihood that any move I make will be successful, that sort of thing. Descendant of Urania, right? Goddess of the stars?" Nia didn't seem too confident as she spoke.

"I don't know what I'm doing either," I said, feeling as if I should speak up and come to Nia's rescue somehow. "Except for this tingly feeling all over. I can't control it. But when I feel it, I know that muse stuff is about to happen."

"You control your kódikas, not the other way around," Elnaz said.

"But—"

"But nothing, Callie. Your will must be stronger than your magic," Elnaz said firmly. "As for you and that app, Nia—" she began to say, but halted at the sight of Tomiko and Etoro, waving us over from inside the gift shop.

Paola cleared her throat. "We must end things here, queridas. But remember that a muse must never use her magic against her sister. Never. Today was for training only."

"Rule number three," Nia said. "Got it."

"Good. It's time for your next lesson," Elnaz said, winking her blue eye at us. We peeled off our ponchos and handed them to Paola, then went to the gift shop.

Chapter 15
WHAT *NOT* TO DO

Once inside the store, I resisted the urge to jump into a mountain of stuffed animals—teddy bears with glitter eyes called out to me in their fluffy adorableness. Nia trailed her fingers along some colorful geodes on a shelf, while Thalia stopped at a bin full of rubber bouncing balls and had to be dragged off by Mela. Finally, we reached Tomiko and Etoro, who were in the back of the gift shop, in front of the most tantalizing display of candy I'd ever seen. There were gummy bears the size of my head, and a chocolate Great Bed of Ware, and bundles of lollipops. I wanted to eat it all.

Despite the candy, my stomach felt all jumpy. Paola and Tomiko had complained when Clio had announced that Maya was our assignment. Their lack of confidence in us made me even more nervous. If the other muses didn't believe in us, how could we?

"Welcome," Etoro said. A colorful blanket rested over her legs. Her right hand was very still upon it.

"Your lesson begins here," Tomiko said. She was wearing a crisp white sweater and khaki cargo pants. Her hair was dyed bright orange, and she reminded me of a living flame. Tomiko walked over to the shelf that held the giant gummy bear, her glossy, fiery ponytail bouncing against her back.

I caught a glimpse of the price tag. I didn't get enough birthday cash last year to cover the cost of it. When she picked it up, I thought Tomiko was going to buy it for us. The gummy ear alone would fill me up for hours. Then she said:

"If you were to choose, you could each use your magic to take anything in this store for yourselves," she said. Tomiko put back the gummy bear. "You, Thalia, could make a cashier laugh so long and so hard that he forgets to breathe. As for Mela, grief kills as well. A person consumed by sadness without any relief is capable of doing terrible things out of desperation. In an instant, you could bring everyone in this museum to their knees. Nia could drive a guard to distraction with a curious thought, making her think she should test her own powers of flight off the top of the building." Here Tomiko paused. I felt a shudder that started at my shoulders and made its way down to my toes. I risked a glance out a nearby window, imagined a body falling, falling . . .

I suddenly lost my appetite.

"And, Callie," Tomiko said at last, "you hold within you the power of self-confidence. Too much of it leads to arrogance, and therein is the first ingredient in making an egomaniac, a monster, and an unstoppable force for self-ishness."

"These would be wicked deeds," Etoro said, rolling toward us. "A muse lives her life in the service of others. Not just the Fated Ones. All of humanity is in need of inspiration. Service is derived from love. We do not inspire anything in a person that does not have love at the source."

"What about self-defense?" Nia asked.

"Well, loving yourself matters, too," Etoro said.

"We won't practice the things we talked about here, not on each other, not ever," Tomiko said. "Temptation will always be part of this job," she added softly. "And temptation is what the sirens do. It's what they embody. We are the opposite of that."

"We are love. We are sacrifice," Etoro said, her voice a deep purr. "There have been other muses," Etoro continued. "Ones who have given in to the longing that sometimes accompanies our powers. For them, there have been no second chances."

The four of us waited for Tomiko and Etoro to speak again, but they were quiet for a long time before Etoro put her hands on the wheels of her chair and moved out of the gift shop. "Come on then," she said, and we followed her out.

She wheeled up to a window that overlooked the city. "London. It's a big city, like my Abuja in Nigeria, like your Chicago, your New Delhi, your Miami, your Tokyo," she said, talking to us all in turn. "It is a rare thing, you know, that all nine muses are city women." Etoro took a deep breath that seemed to fill her up entirely.

I thrilled at the word—"women." Maybe before all this muse stuff happened, I would have hated it, would have protested, "I'm a kid!" But it really did feel like I'd grown up a lot in the last few days. Maybe I wasn't a woman yet, but one day I would be. I suddenly felt a lot more confident than I had before, threw my shoulders back, and stood a little straighter.

"The city is full of heroes and people in need of inspiration. They simply do not know it yet," Etoro said.

Tomiko leaned her head against the glass, which reflected her hair color so that it seemed all of London was aflame. "Only nine of us, and so many of them out there," she sighed. I'd forgotten how young Tomiko was, too. She was nineteen. In college, sure, but still a teenager.

"Outnumbered, but not outmatched," Tomiko said. She glanced at the candy behind us. "We've taught you how to fight. And you know what not to do. We don't use our magic this way unless we absolutely have to."

"Like fighting sirens," Thalia said, balling her hands into fists.

Tomiko grinned. "You got it, little sisters." She grew

serious. "You are all very young and you've been given a Fated One very early. You'll need to be brave, and you'll need to fill your hearts with love," she said.

"But you aren't fighting alone," Etoro said.

"We've got your backs," Tomiko added, and I felt a lot better. Maybe they trusted us after all.

When the lesson was done, we parted from one another at the nearest staircase. I looked at my soon-to-be-roommates. "Well, see you in Miami," I said.

Mela took a huge breath. "I don't know how Clio will manage it."

"She always does," Nia said.

"I, for one, can't wait. Muse Squad, out!" Thalia said, and took off running, gripping Mela's wrist as she went.

"Hey!" Mela protested, and we could hear the two of them bickering on the way to their entrance points.

"Those two are bananas together," Nia said.

I nodded. "Hey," I said, tugging on Nia's shirt. "I don't know what I'm doing."

Nia stared at her sneakers for a moment. "Me neither," she said. Her phone was in her hand, and I could see the app she'd designed for her kódikas. It looked really cool. "But my dad always says you can't know what you're good at until you try. I'm going to try, Callie. For Maya," she said.

"Right." We hugged, and then Nia walked off toward

the fireplace that would transport her home to Chicago.

I made my way back to the Great Bed of Ware, and slid underneath the bed like a cat. I didn't close my eyes at first, didn't want to go back. Because when I did, everything would be different. I looked at my bracelet. *There's still time to say no,* I thought.

Maya Rivero needed friends to show her the hero's path. And somehow, I was supposed to help her do it. My breath hitched for a second. It was a feeling like tripping over something and falling so fast you weren't sure what had just happened.

I thought of Nia, Mela, and Thalia. We did make something of a team. A squad, Thalia would say. Maybe we really could help Maya Rivero become the hero she was meant to be.

I closed my eyes and the world grew warm and familiar again.

Chapter 16
MUSE MAGIC COMES IN HANDY AT HOME

The next evening, as I was watching *America's Next Star* with my mom and brothers, Mom's phone rang.

"Mm-hmm. Yes. I think so. How wonderful," and on and on she went, scratching down notes on a piece of paper. My brothers tuned her out and, instead, held their cell phones, texting one another.

"You're right next to each other," I said.

"Yeah. So?" Fernando responded without looking up.

"We don't want you to eavesdrop on our conversation, obviously," Mario explained.

It's not like I cared what they were saying. I was focused on the television. Raquel's first-round performance was about to air, and my stomach was in knots. When I'd begged her to tell me more about it, she told me she couldn't. "I can't say much, Callie, except that

Jordan Miguel is *so cute* in person."

I'm not going to lie. I was jealous. Happy for her, too. But definitely jealous.

Mom was still on the phone, taking notes. My little dog, Lola, jumped up onto the couch and curled up in my lap. Jordan Miguel came on the screen. He was wearing a red leather jacket over a white T-shirt. A tattoo of an eagle peeked out from under his shirt collar. His brown eyes twinkled. My cell phone buzzed. It was a text from Fernando.

> Close your mouth, boba.
> What are you doing, catching flies?

Mario texted next.

> You look like Lola's twin.

I glanced down at my dog, whose mouth was open, her tongue lolling out. She looked ridiculous.

I threw a pillow at both of them. It was Raquel's turn. She was onstage wearing tight jeans and a cute blue top. Long silver earrings dangled from her earlobes, and her hair was in a high ponytail.

"Where are you from?" one of the judges asked. It was Will Branson, a music producer who wore his hair in a faux-hawk.

"Miami, born in Venezuela," Raquel said. Her voice shook a little. I focused on her, thinking of that day she'd sung for the school play auditions, thinking I could help before I remembered that this was pre-taped.

Her name and age blinked at the bottom of the screen—Raquel Falcón, 12.

"What are you going to sing for us today?" Jordan Miguel asked. I thought I saw Raquel's knees shake a little.

"A Spanish bolero. It's my mom's favorite. 'Bésame Mucho,'" she said. The judges nodded, and the music began. The trumpets swelled, the camera took in the audience, and then Raquel sang the first note.

Fernando and Mario put down their phones. I heard my mom say, "Wait a moment" to the person she was talking to, then she joined us.

"Bésame, bésame muuuuucho." Raquel sang a song about kissing, a thing I knew for a fact Raquel had not done yet. The hairs on my arms stood up. This wasn't muse magic. No, this was just the feeling you get when you hear something beautiful. And Raquel did sing beautifully. She was born for this.

The judges clapped. Jordan Miguel even gave her a standing ovation. Five stars from him! Five from Will Branson! And five from the other two judges, too—Marty Quinn and Josie Zelda, '90s pop stars.

Raquel jumped up and down onstage, and we all stood up and screamed. Lola barked once, offended that she'd been pushed off the couch. Mario and Fernando even hugged me. "Your famous friend better hook it up!" Fernando said.

"Hook what up?" I asked.

"I don't know. Free tickets to concerts and stuff," he said.

"She learned everything she knows from us, after all," Mario added. Then they left the family room together, talking about a video game they were going to play with friends online.

"Wow," my mom said, having finally hung up the phone. She gave me another hug. "Raquelita is amazing. Just amazing."

"Yep," I said. Something small and ugly stirred in my heart. She was amazing, but I had helped. I had helped a lot. I watched as Raquel was interviewed by the show's host, watched as she blew kisses into the camera. She looked so thin, and sophisticated, and pretty. I glanced at my phone. I should probably text her and congratulate her. My fingers hovered over the screen. I put the phone down.

A muse trusts her instincts. Nia had said that was rule number one. I couldn't figure out what my instincts were telling me, or if these feelings weren't instincts at all. Would my instincts be this petty? This unfriendly to my best friend? Was this a "deep feeling" like the ones Clio had talked about?

My mom dropped a kiss on my head. "It's hard

sometimes when the people around us seem to have all the luck, isn't it?" she said. I know muse magic isn't inherited, but surely my mom has *some* sort of gift, otherwise how did she know what I was feeling?

Maybe it was just mom magic.

"Yeah," I said. "I'm happy for Raquel. I am. It's just complicated."

"Your feelings are valid, Callie. Go ahead and feel them. And once you allow that to happen, your heart will still be in the right place, guiding you." She clicked off the television. "Anyway, I have a distraction for you."

"Oh yeah?"

My mom scooched closer to me. She fiddled with her nails, something she always did when she was anxious. "I just got off the phone with Principal Jackson. Don't look at me like that, it's good news. There are three exchange students coming to your grade. And Principal Jackson wanted to know if we might host them here. The PTA nominated our family! Our little family. Can you believe it? Three girls. Your age. What do you think?"

I'd been wondering when to expect them. I'd assumed Clio would take a week or two to arrange things. She was faster than I'd thought.

"Oh," I said, trying to play off my excitement. "Where will they stay?"

My mom took a moment, then cleared her throat. "I thought that we could put two bunk beds in your room.

Principal Jackson said there was some money involved for host parents, and well, we could use it. But I won't agree unless it's okay with you. Just for the semester. They'd get here this weekend." Her nails clicked together rapidly. I could tell she wanted to do this. Whether that was Clio's magic, or my mom's big heart, I couldn't know for sure, but I had a hunch it was the latter.

"Of course. I've always wanted sisters," I said, which was true. When I was younger, I would wish for a sister every time I passed a fountain. I would say it out loud and my parents would laugh and say, "Maybe someday." But then my dad met Laura. I thought uneasily of the baby on the way. How often would I even see him or her? The kid would grow up without me in their life, and be nothing like me. My new sibling was going to be a New York kid who played with snow, a kid who wasn't around for my birthday, and who wouldn't have my mom's nose, like me and my brothers did.

Mom interrupted my thoughts. "Are you sure? Because 'no' is a complete—"

"'No' is a complete sentence. I know. But I would love to share my room with them. Tell Principal Jackson yes," I said.

My mother nodded. Then, she went to my brothers' room. She would have to ask them, too. This was a family decision.

I hovered outside their door.

"NO WAY," Fernando said. "No way. Callie is enough middle school girl for one house. If you need the money, I'll get a job bagging groceries, Mom."

"What he said," Mario replied. I could still hear the video game beeping and pinging, and the voices of their friends online shouting commands.

Now was my chance. Clio had said I needed to tap into my "deep feelings." Did I even have deep feelings about my brothers? I thought about how one time, Mario had taken me to the mall and some boys from my grade were there, and they had teased me about my weight. "Fatty Callie," they had said. Mario had only glared at them. But when we got in the car, he'd turned to me and said, "Cal, you are so stinking gorgeous. And I'm not just saying that. Those boys are idiots. But you are smart, and sweet, and the most beautiful kid. Like, a stunner. Plus, you know I always tell the truth," he'd said, and I'd hugged him so hard.

I could hear Mom explaining things—where the girls were from, the extra money. Lola wandered up to me and licked my left ankle.

Another memory came to me—the time when Fernando had saved Lola. She'd choked on a piece of a chew toy, and he'd shoved his finger into her throat and pulled it out. He'd handed her to me with tears in his eyes, then told me, "Take care of your dumb dog."

My brothers were sometimes my heroes. The thought seemed to thrum deep within my chest. I think I even said it out loud. "My brothers, my heroes." Then I felt it. My eyes stung, the hair on my head rose up a little.

"Hey," I heard Mario say, his voice sounding a little softer. "Now that I think about it, this could be good for Callie. I'll bet they're nice kids. Smart kids to get a scholarship like this. Super smart. They could help us with our homework."

"Do our homework for us, even. Yeah," Fernando said. "Go ahead, Mom. We're cool with it."

My mother left their room and was startled when she saw me standing there. "Why are you crying?" she asked me, and wiped my cheeks dry. I couldn't explain what I'd felt, how I'd tapped into some really deep feelings for a moment there. So I told my mom a different truth.

"They said yes. Sisters!" I said, and my mom gave me a big hug.

"Sí, mi amor. Sisters. For a semester at least. I'll call Principal Jackson."

Chapter 17
BIENVENIDO A MIAMI

It was the middle of the night when I heard it.

"Psst. *Psst.* Callie. Are you asleep?"

I sat upright in bed, breathing hard. It was quiet. Maybe I had dreamed hearing a voice.

"Callie. Answer me! I can't make an international call on my mobile, can I? I have loads of packing questions!"

I wrapped my hand around my bracelet. How did this thing work anyway? I raised my arm and talked over it. "Thalia? Is that you? It's the middle of the night."

"Not here it isn't. I have a question. How hot is it in Miami, really? How many bathing suits shall I pack? Flip-flops—yay or nay?" She spoke loudly, and in the background, I could hear the sounds of kids playing some sort of game.

"Are you at school?" I asked.

Thalia sighed. "Yes. It's games period over here. People are playing footy. It's a bore."

"I have no idea what any of that means." I was whispering, though I don't know that I needed to. The walls of my home were made of poured concrete—built strong enough to withstand hurricanes. That said, my mother had ears like a bat's.

"Oy, watch it," Thalia shouted at someone. "Callie, any tips?"

I rubbed my eyes and looked at the clock. It was three in the morning. "Thalia. It's hot. Flip-flops are great. I never go to the beach, plus we have a job to do. Maya Rivero, remember?"

"Gotcha," Thalia said. Then everything went silent again. I hoped I hadn't made her feel bad. She was only excited. Just as my guilt was starting to get the better of me, another voice filled my room.

"Callie? Are you there?"

It was Mela. "Hi," I said, mid-yawn.

"I have a question, if you don't mind. You don't have a pet bird, do you?"

"No. I have a dog. She's a mutt. Very stupid, but very sweet. And a cat named Misu."

"A cat? Wonderful!" Mela said. "See you soon, then."

I fell back on my pillows. Sisters, huh? This wasn't going to be easy. At least Nia had the sense to—

"Hey, girl. You there?" Nia's voice came through the bracelet.

"I'm here. Why are we awake?" I asked her.

"I'm sorry!" Nia said. "Listen, it's just that my dad is so suspicious, I can't do anything weird during the day."

"CIA, right, I remember," I said.

"Yeah. Listen. There isn't anything about your family I need to know, is there? Like something I need to prep my dad for? Because he is going to investigate all of you. *Hard*."

I laughed. Maybe the CIA had a record of the time my brothers left all the faucets running at the middle school on purpose. Mami and Papi had punished them for weeks. "No, Nia, I think we're good. Nice and safe."

I actually heard her say, "Phew."

"Okay. Sorry to wake you. Sleep tight," Nia said.

"'Night," I told her.

Sisters, I thought again. This was definitely going to be interesting.

The bunk beds were delivered just in time and set against the walls in my room. We had to take my old dollhouse out and put it in the garage. It wasn't like I played with it anymore, but sometimes I liked to sit in front of it, arranging the tiny rug in the tiny living room, fluffing the tiny pillows, setting the mother and father on the couch together. Now, in its place were two towering bunk beds. Mom bought three colorful comforters and three new teddy bears, each wearing a small T-shirt with the words "Fun in the Sun" on them.

"I bought them at the dollar store. Think they'll notice?" she asked nervously.

"They're great," I said.

"Good. There's one for you, too," she said, and handed me a bear of my own. It smelled like the dollar store—disinfectant and junk food. She surveyed my room, bent down to pick up a jumble of hair from the floor, and nodded in approval. "Looks like we're ready. Let's go get the girls."

We parked at the airport and made our way to the north terminal first to pick up Nia. She played it cool, acting as if she'd never seen me before, commenting on the long TSA lines at O'Hare International in Chicago, and asking about the drive to Cape Canaveral, where NASA was.

"It's about five hours away," my mom said. "Callie and I have never been."

When my mom wasn't looking, Nia gave me a wink and a thumbs-up.

We didn't have to wait long for Mela and Thalia to appear at the international terminal. They spotted me at once, and they ran to me and gave me a giant hug. They both started talking a mile a minute before realizing that we weren't supposed to know one another this well. I was carried away, too. Nia cleared her throat, and Thalia, Mela, and I froze.

"Wow," my mom said. "Callie isn't usually this . . .

enthusiastic." She gave me a weird look, and I contained myself.

"I'm just excited," I said. "My name is Callie." I extended my hand like a car salesman waiting for a handshake. Then the others introduced themselves just as awkwardly. They followed us out, the glass airport doors opening and letting in a gust of hot air.

"Whoa, that's warm," Thalia said.

"Just like home in the springtime," Mela added with a smile, as my mom led us through the parking lot.

We slipped into the back row of the minivan, snug like sardines in a can. My mom turned on the radio and started to sing along, so we were safe to talk.

"Such a long flight," Mela said. "I had a layover in London, where I met Thalia. We flew over to Miami together. But this one wouldn't stop talking," she added, pointing to Thalia, who stuck her tongue out. "Plus, my headphones went missing."

Thalia laughed nervously. "Oh, you mean these?" she said, and pulled Mela's headphones out of her bag.

Nia, however, was busy digging through her backpack. "So, the mission at hand," Nia began to say.

"Find the three. Break the curse. Save the future," I said, repeating what Clio had told us the last time we were at headquarters.

"Yep," Nia said. "Clio sent us a message via chat." She pulled out two pairs of earbuds and a splitter for the jack.

"Share," she said, plugged in the earbuds, and opened up a video on her phone.

I pushed the bud into my ear just in time to hear Clio say, " . . . should be receiving her county science fair invitation this week. You all must be at this fair. She must win. Watch out for anyone trying to keep her away from the event. Remember your training."

The screen went blank. "That's it?" I asked. "That's all the help we get?"

We were quiet. Mela spoke up next. "The sirens could be anybody. Men, women, animals. They're shapeshifters. One of them could be your mom!"

"What?" my mom asked from the front of the car.

"Nada, Mom. Just messing around back here," I said, trying to keep my tone light. To the others I said, "My mom is *not* a siren. But I get your point. Where do we begin?"

"Chaos. Sirens quite like it, according to Clio. I'm rather good at chaos myself. We could create a siren trap," Thalia said, rubbing her hands together.

"Please don't destroy my house, or my school, or my city, for that matter," I said, making Thalia chuckle.

"No promises, mate," Thalia said.

"The box," Nia interrupted, putting us back on track. "The Cassandra Curse. Especially anywhere near Maya Rivero. She shouldn't accept any gifts, right? Maybe we can tip her off somehow and keep an eye out for something that might be the curse."

Mela and Thalia murmured their agreement. I gasped softly. Whenever one of us had a realization in language arts class, Ms. Salvo liked to announce that "the penny had dropped." I never really understood what it meant, but I liked the idea of it, of a penny falling, and falling, and landing at last with a *plink*.

Plink. The Cassandra Curse rested inside a box. A jeweled box, Clio had said.

Plink. Very much like the one Raquel said that Jordan Miguel gave her.

Plink. A gift she was keeping secret for some reason.

"Callie? Callie?" Mela was nudging me. "Is this your house? Because it's adorable," she said as the van came to a stop. My house had a Spanish-tile roof, and a flamboyán tree in the center of the yard. My mom had planted roses in front of the porch, one tree for each of her kids. Our front door was bright red. It was small, but I guess it *was* kind of cute.

"Yeah. C-come on. I'll show you around," I said, but my heart wasn't in it. What if someone was using Raquel to safeguard the curse?

Thalia, Mela, and Nia dragged their suitcases up the porch steps and into the house. I stood outside for a moment, watching as they looked around at our furniture, the blue paint on the walls, my enormous First Communion portrait, complete with me in a white dress and white veil, a picture that Mom had framed in gold, next to a pair of similar portraits of my brothers in their white suits. "Classic Cuban Catholic," Mario had called them. "Tacky," Fernando had added. "Beautiful," my mom would say. "Mortifying," would be my take.

Nia stood before the portrait. "I'm a Methodist. Never took pictures like those before."

"It's a Cuban-Catholic thing," I said, feeling my cheeks blush. Then I thought of something. "Hey, Nia. How does this even work? I mean, if there are Greek gods, then what does it mean for the rest of it?" My mom insisted on going to Mass sometimes, and for me, it was always a peaceful time. I'd hold Mami's hand through the service, and sing the songs, and recite the prayers. I liked it.

"I wondered that," Nia said, "but Paola explained that the universe is big enough and mysterious enough for all our beliefs to matter, and for all our versions of God to exist. That our magic was sacred in whatever way made sense for each of us. Basically, if it's true in your heart, it's true. I'm okay with that."

I looked up at the three portraits, and for the first time in a long time, I didn't feel so embarrassed when I saw them. "I'm okay with that, too. Thanks, Nia," I said.

I grabbed Thalia's book bag, but it felt like it weighed a million pounds.

"What's in here?" I asked.

"All the Narnia books," Thalia said. "You wouldn't happen to have a magical wardrobe in your house?"

"Nope. Just a magical bed," I said, which made everyone giggle.

"For the last time, those books are fiction!" Mela said, but Thalia only rolled her eyes. Then my cat, Misu, strutted up to Mela, who cried out, "Kitty!" and scooped her up.

Nia sneezed. "Oh no. You have a cat?"

"Sorry," I said, while Nia started digging around in her bag for allergy medicine.

An ambulance roared past, its siren on full blast. The others jumped, startled. I didn't even hear it.

"Ambulances are just part of the neighborhood's sounds," I said. They looked at me skeptically. I took a deep breath.

Sisters, I thought, and followed them in.

Chapter 18
THE NEW KIDS IN SCHOOL

Thalia was the first to say something on Monday as we stood outside my school. "Miami Palms Middle won't know what hit them," she said. Nia and Mela weren't as enthusiastic.

"Here goes nothing," Nia said under her breath as we went through the front doors.

"Gods help us," Mela muttered, adjusting her backpack.

Nia, Mela, and Thalia were given my schedule, so we would be together all day. More importantly, I shared all my classes with Maya Rivero, too.

"There she is," I whispered soon after getting to school. Maya sat alone on the floor, her legs crisscrossed, a Rubik's Cube in her hands. She clicked the sections of the cube back and forth, trying to line up the colors. Some of the stickers that made up the colors had peeled off, but Maya seemed to know which colors they had been.

All around Maya, other kids were busy talking, or looking at their cell phones together, or shoving one another playfully. Maya, sitting in the center of it, reminded me of the eye of a hurricane.

"She's lonely," Mela said.

"She's concentrating," Nia added.

"Doesn't look like fun to me," Thalia said.

I was about to suggest I introduce them to Maya when I felt a tap on my shoulder. I turned around, and there was Raquel. Behind her were Violet, Max, and Alain.

"Hey," Raquel said. "New friends?" Her hair was different again. The pink was now blue, and her curls were gone, replaced by stick-straight glossy tresses. When she'd moved on to the next round on *America's Next Star*, she hadn't bothered to text me when it happened. I hadn't bothered to congratulate her.

"Um, yeah," I said. "You?" I gestured at Violet and company.

Raquel laughed in a way I didn't recognize. It was high-pitched, different from the way she normally threw her head back and guffawed. "Don't be dumb," she said. "You know these guys."

By this time, Thalia, Mela, and Nia had turned around. Thalia was the first to speak. "So are we going to have a dance-off or something? Is that what we do in America?"

Violet opened her mouth to speak, one hand already

on her hip, when I cut in. "These are my new friends. Exchange students staying with me. Thalia, Nia, Mela, meet Violet, Max, Alain, and Raquel." I paused. "Raquel is my best friend," I added.

What I'd hoped was for Raquel to say, "Yeah," or to put her arm around me, or something. But she only stood there and stared at the muses, then back at me, as if they were proof of something.

Alain broke away from our awkward introductions and sauntered over to Maya. Nearby, one of the triplets (Lisa? I couldn't always tell the two girls apart) was hanging up a sign that read "Don't Be a Sap! Join SAP!" Alain glanced at the sign, said, "Why are there so many nerds in this school?" and then plucked the Rubik's Cube from Maya's hands. "Hey!" Maya shouted.

He tossed the puzzle back and forth, flipping it in the air, then bouncing it off his knee like a soccer ball.

"Give it back," Maya said. "I've almost solved it!"

"Oh," he said, then gave the cube a couple of twists, undoing Maya's work.

"Jerk!" Thalia shouted at him.

"Shut up, Queen Elizabeth," Violet said.

"How dare yo—" Thalia began to say, when all of a sudden, Alain burst into tears.

Mela had placed one hand on his wrist and stared at him with her big brown eyes. Her other hand fluttered softly by her side, her kódikas at work. Whatever he was remembering, it clearly had broken his heart. He dropped the Rubik's Cube and ran out into the courtyard. Violet chased after him.

"Sorry about him," Max said to Maya, picking up the Rubik's Cube and handing it to her. "I love these things," he told her, then followed his friends out.

"You're scary, you know that?" Nia whispered to Mela, who took a deep breath and seemed to shake off the moment with a shimmy of her shoulders.

Nia went over to Maya and started pointing out other ways to solve the puzzle. Mela and Thalia sat beside her and watched as Maya deftly twisted the cube, getting the colors to line up at last.

That left me and Raquel alone, so to speak.

"You're doing really well on the show," I said.

Raquel wrapped a blue lock of hair around her finger. She'd never seemed to care what her hair looked like before. She did it again, then held up the hair to the light, as if admiring it. The gesture looked wrong on her.

"You look really pretty on TV," I added. "And in real life, too. Of course. Not just on TV."

"Thanks," she said. She turned to look behind her, craning her head to see where Violet and the others had gone.

"Raquel, I thought we were best friends," I said at last. My voice quivered. I could have kicked myself for being so direct.

Raquel took a deep breath. "Look at your phone, Callie. Go ahead. Look at it." I pulled my phone out of my bag. "See the missed messages? I called and texted you lots. It's an L.A. number, so you didn't recognize it. But it's been me. *I've tried*."

I looked at my phone. There they were. Her messages. How could I tell her I didn't have cell service in England, of all things? Or that I was so busy with my new roommates that I hadn't checked my phone that much?

"You have an L.A. phone number now?" I asked, my voice weak.

Raquel waved the comment away. "It's like you've disappeared. Violet says you're just jealous because . . . because . . ." She couldn't seem to find the words.

My chest tightened. Jealous! *Jealous?* "I am *not* jealous," I said. "I don't even *want* to be a singer. Or famous." If only she knew, I thought. I didn't want any attention at all. And here I was, in charge of saving the world from sirens, and protecting a Fated One. I didn't want this.

"It's not just that. You're jealous of other things, Violet says."

I blinked furiously at her to keep from crying. "Other things? Because Jordan Miguel gave you a gift? Or because I'm fat and you're not. Or maybe because your parents are together and mine aren't. Is that why I'm supposedly jealous?"

All of it had spilled out of me so quickly that I wondered

if she wasn't right. Maybe I was jealous after all. I sniffed and pressed the heels of my hands against my eyes.

Now Raquel grabbed my hands. "No, Callie! I—I don't know why things are different with us. But they are. I wanted you there with me at every step. But every time I call you, you're missing. And now these new girls? I feel like I don't know you."

I could have said the same thing about her. In fact, I almost did. But at that moment, Raquel's backpack slipped off her shoulder, and out tumbled the box.

I gasped. What if it popped open? Would we all be cursed? But the box stayed closed, and I noticed a little gold latch and keyhole.

"Is that Jordan Miguel's gift?" I asked.

Raquel nodded. "Yes. He told me I can't open it until I win. He really believes in me."

"Oh," I said. That stung a little. Then a notion struck me. "Raquel, did he give it to you *personally*?"

"Ha, ha, technicalities," Raquel said, her lips pursing tightly. She didn't say the word "jealous" again, though I knew she was thinking it. "No, his assistant did. A nice lady named Kim something or other. She wears the prettiest feather earrings I've ever seen. Peacock feathers. Everyone in L.A. wears them."

Siren feathers, I thought. "Raquel. Don't open the box without me. Promise? And keep an eye on it at all times." It was all I could think of to say, the only safeguard I could imagine. I didn't know how to stop a curse, but I would try.

Raquel pursed her lips. "You're being weird again. Listen, go back to your new besties before they make a poor friend choice over there." We both glanced over as the girls were laughing with Maya. Thalia had them doubled over with laughter.

"That's mean, Raquel," I said, but she shrugged, turned, and went off in search of Violet.

The bell rang, and people started to disperse. "Where to?" Nia asked.

"Science class," I said.

Nia pumped her fist into the air. Today, her shirt read: IF LOST, RETURN TO NASA.

"How many NASA T-shirts do you have?" I asked as we made our way down the packed hall.

"All of them," Nia said, wiggling her eyebrows.

There were three new desks at the front of the science classroom. Ms. Rinse was obviously expecting Nia, Thalia, and Mela, but she ignored them when we walked in. That's because Ms. Fovos and Ms. Salvo were there, too, and the three teachers were talking excitedly by the chalkboard. Ms. Fovos tugged at her turtleneck while she talked, and Ms. Salvo clicked her long nails against a clipboard. Ms. Fovos called Violet over, and the teachers whispered something to her, and she nodded. They seemed . . . obviously nervous about something.

I looked over at Mela, mouthing the name *Violet Prado* at her. Mela narrowed her eyes, elbowed Thalia, who then nudged Nia with her foot.

We were on alert.

The tardy bell rang, and Ms. Salvo and Ms. Fovos hurried out, late to their own classes.

"No anagrams today. It's a day for announcements," Ms. Rinse said. We sat quietly for once. The vibe in the room was strange, and we had all picked up on it. "First, we have three new exchange students. Mela Gupta, Nia Watson, and Thalia Berry. Ladies, welcome to Miami Palms Middle." Ms. Rinse clapped, then clapped harder when the rest of the class didn't follow suit. She clapped until we were all clapping, and it was beyond awkward, I can tell you that. Thalia's ears turned pink, Mela put her head down on her desk, and Nia stared up at the ceiling through all of it.

"Second announcement. The winner of the science fair is—drumroll, please?" Alain drummed on his desk, but when Ms. Rinse said, "Maya Rivero! Congratulations," Alain stopped and said, "Boo!"

Maya didn't seem to hear him. She was beaming. The muses turned to look at her, then to me. Thalia gave me a thumbs-up. I turned around to give Alain an evil look and noticed that Raquel, who normally sat in front of him, wasn't in class. I searched the other rows for her, but she was 100 percent absent.

But I'd seen her before the bell rang.

What if she'd opened the box?

What if my best friend was now cursed?

"Maya," Ms. Rinse continued, interrupting my dark train of thought. "The county science fair is on December 20th. And I have tickets for all of you to attend. We'll make it a field trip for the class, and root for Maya," Ms. Rinse said.

Everyone clapped again, sincerely this time. There was nothing better than a field trip.

"Third announcement," Ms. Rinse began, then paused and looked at the clock. "Okay, everyone. Quietly, without running, we will make our way to the cafetorium for a special assembly."

We got up loudly, everyone chattering about what it could be. "Quietly," Ms. Rinse shouted, and I heard her sigh, "Why won't anyone ever listen to me?" before heading out into the hall.

I caught up to Maya and tapped her shoulder. "Hey, congrats!"

"Thanks," Maya said. "I'm excited. Ms. Rinse said she would help me with my project, so there aren't any accidents like I had in class."

"I can help, too," Nia said, catching up to us.

"I can, as well," Mela added.

"Don't look at me, I'm rubbish at science," Thalia said. "But I'll provide snacks!"

Maya scratched her head. "Um. Okay. If you guys want,"

she said. Then she hurried away toward the cafetorium with the others, half running, as if she couldn't wait to get away from us.

I hung back with the muses. "Listen. Slow down a bit," I told them. "You're going to scare her away. Besides, we've got to focus here. You know the Cassandra Curse? I think Raquel has the box. And she was supposed to be in class just now, but she wasn't."

All three muses stopped cold.

"Your best friend? The one who was incredibly mean to you?" Thalia asked.

"You noticed," I said. The others nodded. I pressed on. "Jordan Miguel gave it to her and asked her to keep it closed. And yes, she's become a total mean girl. Suspicious, right? Like the presence of the curse is . . . affecting her in some way?" I didn't say that maybe I was being a little bit of a mean girl, too.

Mela cleared her throat. "I think we have another problem," she said, and pointed toward Violet, who was carrying two big buckets and creeping toward a door that led to the backstage area of the cafetorium. A pair of red feathers floated out of one of the buckets.

"Siren feathers," Nia said.

"This assembly," Thalia muttered, "is about to get real really fast."

Chapter 19
BEST (WORST). ASSEMBLY. EVER.

The hallways were packed as students snaked their way to the cafetorium. Mela, Nia, Thalia, and I linked hands, and I led them through the throng. There was shoving. There were weird body odors. Mela lost a shoe and we had to backtrack to get it.

"Good going, Cinderella," Thalia said above the chaos. Mela ignored her.

All around us, students were asking the obvious question: What was going on? Once in the cafetorium, we were met with a row of huge, muscled security guards in tight black T-shirts and black jeans. Each of them wore headsets. None of them smiled.

"Is this . . . typical?" Mela asked.

"No," I said, "this is bizarre."

The inflatable turkey in the corner had been replaced with an inflatable snowman and an inflatable dreidel.

Though it was only the first week of December, some kids were already starting to wear Santa hats to school. The security guards' stern looks clashed with the festive decorations, big time.

Nia was staring at the stage. "Where did that girl go? The one with the buckets?" she asked. I'd been wondering, too.

"Don't know," I said. Then I gestured for a huddle, and we all put our heads together. "Let's be ready for whatever happens. Remember our assignment," I said, realizing that Maya Rivero was sitting directly in front of me. Silently I pointed at the back of her head. The others nodded.

Just then, Ms. Fovos, looking more lizardy than ever in a green blouse and brown slacks, called Maya's name from the end of the row. "Maya. Come with me," she said, waving Maya forward. Her long red fingernails flashed in the light.

"I don't like the look of that teacher," Mela said.

We watched as Maya got to her feet and proceeded down the row, saying "Excuse me, excuse me, excuse me," stepping on everyone's feet as she went. I remembered detention, how Violet and Ms. Fovos had seemed to be conspiring about something, how mean Ms. Fovos had been to Maya, making her sit near the cold AC unit even though she was soaking wet.

"Let's go," I said. There was no way I was going to leave Maya alone with Ms. Fovos.

The four of us rose, only to be shouted at by Ms. Rinse.

"Sit down, you four. At once!" At first, we didn't do it. Instead, we watched as Maya followed Ms. Fovos to a small door on the side of the stage. I assumed Violet was in there, too. Waiting.

"What do we do? What do we do?" Thalia whispered furiously.

"Sit!" Ms. Rinse yelled again, and suddenly, the lights in the cafetorium cut out.

Some of the students yelped. A spotlight turned on, baking the center of the stage in a warm yellow light.

"Boys and girls," came the voice of Principal Jackson. He was standing on the edge of the stage, but in the darkened room, I couldn't make him out. "It is my pleasure to introduce the one and only JORDAN MIGUEL!"

The room erupted into a thousand squeals, so high-pitched that I covered my ears. Everyone was on their feet now, and I could no longer see the door through which Maya had disappeared.

Jordan Miguel walked over to the microphone stand at the center of the stage. He was wearing a white V-neck T-shirt, a silver chain with a guitar pendant around his neck, and blue jeans torn at the knees. "Miami Palms Middle!" he said into the microphone, and everyone went wild.

I, for one, was standing on the seat of my chair, one hand on Mela's shoulder and one on Nia's for balance. My throat was already raw from screaming.

I know, I know.

We had a mission.

For all I knew, Maya Rivero was already cursed. Maybe Raquel was, too.

But Jordan Miguel was here, in our school, and at the moment, I wasn't thinking straight.

Then he put his fingers to his lips and went "Shhh," managing to shush the entire school at once. "I have a little list here," he said, pulling out a piece of paper from his back pocket. Everyone screamed. Why we were all screaming was beyond me, but it was as if every simple gesture he made was enough to send some of us into a frenzy.

Okay. Me. It sent *me* into a frenzy. Mela had already tried to pull me back down, and Nia had taken out her cell phone to take snaps of me losing my head over Jordan Miguel.

"This little list has some naaaaaaames on it," Jordan Miguel said.

More screaming.

"Now, I know you've all been voting for Raquel Falcón on *America's Next Star*."

Screaming.

"And y'all know she's gonna win, right?"

Totally bonkers screaming.

"Sirens love chaos, remember?" Thalia said, and my stomach dropped a little. "And this is utter pandemonium—which, by the way, I did not cause."

We had to be sharp, I reminded myself. The cafetorium

was so packed with people, though, and there was Ms. Fovos at the end of our row, keeping an eye on everyone.

Jordan Miguel continued shouting excitedly into the microphone. "But this is a talented school right here! Raquel isn't the only superstar." He waved the list in the air. "We've got Keneisha Truman, who earned the highest Florida State Exam score in the county this year. Give it up for Keneisha!" The spotlight shone on Keneisha, an eighth grader, who emerged from backstage. Jordan Miguel gave her a huge hug before Keneisha took her seat again.

Jordan checked his list. "Where is my boy Rajiv Singh? RAJEEEEEEV!" Jordan called out, his arms in the air in a victory pose. Rajiv, a quiet seventh grader who wore his hair over his left eye, took small steps out from backstage. It seemed to take him forever to get to Jordan, who gave him a double high five. "This guy," he said, as if he'd known Rajiv his whole life. "This guy has been named the youngest violinist in the Miami Junior Orchestra!" Jordan mimed playing the violin, and Rajiv gave him a lopsided smile before taking his seat again.

Jordan shushed us once more. "Now this next name," he said, and squinted at the list, making a big show of it, as if he hadn't read all the other names perfectly. "This one right here? She's not only representing your school in the county science fair, but if she wins, she'll be invited to WASHINGTON, D.C., for the Young Scientist Competition. So, we've got to support her! Give it up for MAYA RIVERO!"

The velvet curtain to the left of Jordan Miguel rustled. We watched as Maya became tangled in it and couldn't get out. Jordan stood there, mic in hand, and didn't move to help. Finally, Maya got herself free and stumbled toward center stage.

"So that's why she went backstage," Nia shouted up at me. I couldn't relax entirely. Though Maya didn't seem to be in any immediate danger, the fact was we still didn't know what Violet was doing.

"There you go!" Jordan said, as she walked over to him. Just like he'd done with Keneisha, he gave Maya a giant hug. She stiffened up like a telephone pole, staring at the rest of us as if saying, "Help?" Then it was over, and Maya was back in her seat in front of me.

Keneisha was now happy-crying, her friends rubbing her shoulders as if, by touching her, they were touching Jordan Miguel. Rajiv was slumped in his seat, hair over his eyes, arms crossed. And Maya? Well, she had pulled out a notebook covered in doodles of whales and busied herself by giving one of them stripes with a blue pen. The tips of her ears, however, were very red.

"So much to celebrate," Jordan said, when the cheering died down.

I wondered if he was going to sing or not. I thought he'd give Keneisha, Rajiv, and Maya some sort of gift. A certificate maybe? But all they got was a hug or a high five.

The lights dimmed some more and the spotlight on him grew brighter. "And what better way to celebrate than with a song?" he said dramatically into the microphone. Then all the lights went out with a snap. I teetered a bit on my chair.

When the lights came on again, Jordan Miguel was gone. In his place was Raquel, in a sequined top and a full red skirt with pockets. She wore black heels. I didn't even know Raquel could walk in heels. I knew I couldn't. She was holding a bedazzled microphone.

"Hey, guys," Raquel said. "I'd like to thank you for supporting me. I want to congratulate my classmates Keneisha, Rajiv, and Maya. And all of you for being so awesome," she said, and everyone cheered.

For the millionth time, I thought: *Who is this person in the shape of Raquel?* She was so smooth and poised, and my heart sped up while I watched her, the way it did whenever I saw a celebrity on Miami Beach walking down the sidewalk.

The opening chords to a song began softly. Raquel talked over them. "I'm going to dedicate this song to my real friends. You know who you are," she said, and swept her arm before her as if to indicate: *All of you are my* real *friends.* Everyone screamed some more. But that couldn't be true. They weren't all her friends. Before all of this, Raquel had had one best friend. Me. Now, it felt as if she really did mean everyone in the room. Everyone *but* me.

She sang beautifully, her mouth forming perfect Os, her fingers dancing along with the music.

Above her, I noticed a single feather floating down. I scanned the room for Violet, but she was nowhere to be seen. Another feather rode the AC currents for a while before hitting the ground.

Then another.

Sirens.

Mela said, "Callie," my name sounding like a warning. I stepped down from the seat. For a second, I thought Raquel noticed and frowned.

A red feather landed on Raquel's left foot.

"I see them," I said.

More feathers. Some glitter, too.

"What in the world . . . ?" Nia said.

We watched intently. Everyone in the cafetorium was swaying. Some had turned on the lights to their cell phones and waved those overhead. But the four of us? We were as still as a held breath. I could feel it in my chest, on my scalp, a buildup of muse magic. I was ready for . . . something. Beside me, the others were tense, too. Mela was holding my hand. Thalia's foot kept tapping the floor. Nia was looking at the app on her phone, which showed her the formation of the stars overhead. *They're always there, even in the daylight*, she'd told me the night before. *They can tell us about the future sometimes.*

"It doesn't make sense. I'm not reading any disturbances here," she muttered, maximizing and minimizing the screen.

Finally, Raquel's song was over. "That was 'Friends of a Feather,' and it's my new single," she shouted over the cheering. Jordan Miguel approached her just as the lights turned on again.

"Feathers, of course," Thalia said. "It's the blasted song title. The feathers were a *gimmick*. Just a stupid gimmick." She leaned back in her chair and draped her arm over her eyes in relief. Violet came out from backstage, feathers stuck in her hair. Ms. Salvo and Ms. Fovos each gave her a high five. That's what they'd been whispering to her about before the assembly. Violet had just been helping with the special effects.

We all sighed. I could feel the energy draining from me, leaving me exhausted, as if I needed a nap. No sirens here.

"We have a surprise for everyone, don't we, Raquel?" Jordan said. Raquel nodded, smiling brightly at all of us. "What's that in your pocket?" he asked her.

Raquel reached into her skirt pocket and drew out the box.

The box.

The four of us shot to our feet.

"There's something special in there, Raquel. Something you need to see. In fact, if you'll all reach under your seats . . . ," Jordan said.

"Oh no. Oh no, oh no, oh no," I heard myself saying. All around me, my classmates were bending down, reaching under their dusty seats, and finding boxes identical to the one Raquel had been carrying around for days.

"What if they're all curses?" I said.

Thalia was the first to act. "Not on my watch," I heard her say, laughing, and suddenly, Principal Jackson, who had been standing at the edge of the stage the whole time, began doing a funny dance, jutting out his chin and wiggling his butt. Unfortunately, his "moves" made his pants slip down and puddle to his ankles, revealing boxer briefs covered in Christmas trees.

The entire cafetorium erupted in hysterics.

Then Mela's hands started fluttering, and thankfully, my scalp started to buzz right on time. We both hit everyone at once with muse magic, inspiring the whole school to suddenly sing Raquel's "Friends of a Feather" song at top volume, and moving themselves to tears as they did so. People were holding on to one another, crying and singing at the same time.

Cool-headed as ever, Nia plucked a box out of Maya's hand, then proceeded to collect them from everyone she could reach. They gave up the boxes without a problem, too busy crying and singing to care. Even Raquel and Jordan Miguel had sat down and were wiping each other's tears and singing into the microphone without any accompaniment. Principal Jackson, his underwear still on display, was pretending to hold a microphone of his own, and wailing into it in a voice deep and rich.

My scalp felt like it was on fire. I could feel them all, each and every one of my schoolmates, tapping into the place in them that made them want to express themselves. I swayed a bit, felt Nia's hands on my shoulders.

"You can't hold them forever," she said. She checked on Mela next, whose eyes were starting to get droopy. Thalia, for her part, was still giggling at Principal Jackson. I watched as she patted her own back, literally reaching around and patting herself with pride.

I grew more tired by the second. The singing was already growing quiet. Raquel and Jordan Miguel were blinking, as if they'd just woken up. At least Maya no longer had a box. Nia had dumped as many as she could into the big trash can in the hall.

This was no solution, I knew. If the boxes held curses, or even if only one did, there was no way of knowing which one. And we would never know, unless we tested them. Someone had to be first.

I reached down and found the box under my seat. I shook it.

"Don't," Mela said.

"I think . . . I think it's all right," I said. How bad could a curse be, I wondered. So what if nobody ever believed me again? It's not like anyone would ever believe this muse stuff anyway.

I took a breath, and cracked open the box.

Inside was a small, folded paper. I opened it, and read:

"The finals," I said to myself. "These are tickets." I wilted into my chair.

Jordan and Raquel were on their feet. He scratched his head. "See how they loved your song?" he said, a little weakly. Then, his voice growing stronger: "You loved the song, right?"

More cheering. The triplets from Tampa were hugging and jumping up and down. One of the girls (Letty, maybe?) seemed to faint midhug, and Leo smacked her cheeks until she stood up again. Max and Alain were high-fiving one another. I could hear everyone's voice was a little raw. They'd all be voiceless tomorrow, too.

I watched as Jordan gave Raquel a little golden key, and she opened the box she'd been carrying for weeks. She read the note inside.

"The finals are going to be here? In Miami?" she asked softly, her voice breaking. Jordan nodded, and she jumped into his arms. The cafetorium went utterly wild. Violet emerged from backstage and emptied the rest of the feathers all over Raquel. Then the two of them hugged and bounced up and down.

"AND YOU'RE ALL INVITED!" Jordan Miguel

yelled, pointing to the boxes. "Now, if you want Raquel to be a finalist competing here in her hometown"—more screaming—"then you know you need to watch this week's *America's Next Star* and vote!"

There was a bit of confusion when some students realized their boxes had gone missing, until Principal Jackson, his pants back on, discovered them in the garbage can and began to pass them out again.

A single box came down the row and landed in Maya's lap. She didn't open it.

"It's okay, Maya," Nia said, "free ticket. Pretty cool, right?" I could tell Nia was feeling bad for taking Maya's box away in the first place.

"I can't go anyway," Maya said, her voice sounding so sad. "It's the same day as the county science fair."

"Oh," Nia said. "Well. I'll join you."

"Me, too," Mela said.

"Count me in," Thalia said.

"And me," I added.

Maya smiled at us weakly. "You really don't have to. I'll be okay. *America's Next Star* is a big deal. Way bigger than a dumb county science fair." She said it but didn't mean it. Not at all.

We watched as Maya left the cafetorium.

Soon, the room was empty, and it was just the four of us. Nobody seemed to notice we weren't in our second-period class. I didn't really care that we were missing it, either.

"Well," Thalia said. "I'm done in. Utterly. Strike two for the Muse Squad."

"We are very bad at this," Mela said.

Nia and I nodded.

You might say the four of us were uninspired to do, well, anything.

Just when I thought I might actually suggest we make our way to social studies, which was where we belonged, I felt a warm tug on my wrist. The tug grew hotter. It was my bracelet.

"Heavens, must it be now?" Mela said, wrapping her left hand over the ring on the right.

"Ow, OW," Thalia said.

"Run," Nia said, and that we did, out the back door of the cafetorium and the five blocks to my house, and my bed.

It was the first time I had ever skipped school. My heart was pounding as we ran into my room. The floor was cool against my back. The others pushed against me until I was squeezed tight, like being crammed into the backseat of a car with my brothers. I felt I could almost fall asleep. Everything went dark, and then, a rosy light, and the smell of old things and polished wood filled my senses.

"Home sweet home," Thalia said with a sigh.

Chapter 20
SIRENS UNDERGROUND

It was only 2 p.m. in London, which meant the V and A was slammed with people. From where I lay under the Great Bed of Ware, sandwiched between Nia and Mela, I could see the tourist-feet all around us, their owners speaking in more languages than I could keep track of.

Mela raised her ring to her lips. "Clio? We are surrounded by people. Please advise," she said calmly.

No answer.

"What are we supposed to do? Lie here until nightfall?" Nia asked. As if in response, Thalia's stomach growled loudly.

"I'm starved," she moaned.

"Shush," the rest of us said at the same time, also too loudly it turned out, because suddenly, a flashlight appeared beside Thalia, the skirt of the Great Bed lifted, and there was one of the museum's security guards, scowling at us.

"What are you lot up to?" he said, and we scurried out the other side, like bugs scattering in a sudden light.

"Run!" Thalia said, and we followed past mothers pushing babies in strollers, and past a class of art students sketching a dress. Nia leaped over a bench, and Mela took a little tumble, righting herself at once, her long braid sailing behind her. We were faster than the guard, who we could hear chattering away into a walkie-talkie.

Thalia led us straight to the library. We pounded up the spiral iron stairs, making a horrific racket as we went, and we didn't stop until we were at Clio's door, hammering at it to let us in.

The door, however, remained stubbornly closed. And before we could decide on our next move, we found ourselves blocked by the security guard and one of his friends.

"Game over," the breathless guard said, smirking and obviously proud of his catch.

"Out with you," his companion said. She took me by the wrist, squeezing way harder than necessary, and led me down the stairs first. Behind me, Thalia began to shout, "Oh no, we won't go!" again and again at the top of her voice. She was, as usual, making a scene.

Out of the corner of my eye, I watched a young man taking a video of us with his cell phone. He was laughing as he held it up, and chanting along with Thalia's "Oh no, we won't go" song. Nia noticed too, and the next thing I knew, he was swearing at his phone, saying, "Deleted? I deleted it?"

"Thanks," I said to Nia just as she closed her app, the one she'd rigged to work as a kódikas. She'd confused him somehow, caused him to misuse the tech that made the phone work. Good thing, too. The last thing we needed was to be subjects of a viral video. How would I explain it to my mom? Or to Clio, for that matter?

We were led in the world's most embarrassing parade (Thalia stopped chanting once Mela elbowed her, hard) through the lobby and out of the building, the guards pushing us one by one through the revolving door.

"Cheers, loves," Thalia said to the guards.

"Now what?" Mela asked, scowling at Thalia.

"Clio?" I said into my bracelet. "We have a problem."

"I know, that's why I summoned you all in the first place," came Clio's voice, clear and crisp around us. We huddled together away from the building's entrance.

"What do we do?" I asked.

"Come out to Bethnal Green. The V and A has a sister museum there. The Museum of Childhood. There was an incident here this morning. You are needed immediately."

"Okay. Right. We'll be there in a sec. Um, over and out. Ten four," I rambled into my bracelet.

Nia faced Thalia. "Get us to where we need to go, London girl."

Thalia clapped her hands and rubbed them together. "Lucky for you lot I still have this," she said, and waved a little yellow card that she'd produced from her pocket. "Transportation card. Good for bus, rail, underground," she said, sounding like a voiceover on a commercial. Then she added, "I don't intend to walk all the way to East London."

We marched half a block before it hit me—I was freezing. My uniform skort and thin polo shirt weren't cutting it. My teeth chattered, too.

"I can't do this," I said weakly. The others were rubbing their arms, too. Something cold touched my nose. A flurry. "Is it . . . is it . . . snowing?" I shouted. I'd never seen snow before.

"We'll catch our deaths," Mela said.

"No, we won't!" Thalia said, and led us straight into a tourist shop. "Sale section," she muttered, stopping before a wall of the tackiest scarves and hoodies and gloves imaginable.

Each and every one had a picture of a winking Prince Harry.

"I'd rather freeze," Nia said, and started heading for the door.

Thalia dug her hand deep into a pocket. "It's a clearance sale for a reason," she said as she pulled out a soft bill. "Twenty quid gets us each a souvenir and a bit of warmth." Then she plucked four hoodies off the rack.

"Besides, Harry is quite fit for a ginger, don't you think?" she asked, tugging at one of her own red locks.

She paid for the hoodies and I swear the cashier was trying to hold back her laugh.

Nia, Mela, and I turned ours inside out before putting them on.

Thalia did not.

The snow picked up. I tried hard not to let it distract me. Thalia led us back onto the sidewalk and south of the museum, and we followed her like ducklings.

It took me a moment for it to sink in—I was in London. Flipping London. Me, a Florida girl who had never even seen snow. I mean, I'd been there before, but never outside of the museum. It had been like stopping in an airport—just because you flew through Miami International Airport didn't mean you'd actually been to Miami. I took a deep breath and smelled diesel and roasted chestnuts.

The red double-decker buses, the black gates with gold-painted details, the bright white rowhomes with their black-and-white-tiled front porches—all of it seemed like a movie come to life.

The streets were crowded with pedestrians. A harried mom ran over my foot with a stroller. A street performer, painted entirely in silver, seemed to levitate with only a cane for support. Another performer beat on a plastic bucket to a rhythm in his head. Three little kids zoomed past on scooters, and every so often, a giant red bus would blow by, the people inside looking like apparitions—here one moment, gone the next.

Thalia turned a hard left and stopped before the entrance of what looked like a small shopping center. A gate outside, with wrought-iron letters, read "South Kensington and Metropolitan and District Railways." She gave us a wink and entered. Left and right were tunnels leading down, and underneath my feet, the ground was rumbling.

Thalia stood before a colorful map with lines leading in every direction.

"They look like neurons," Nia said. "I love them."

"Subway?" I asked. I thought of the Metrorail and shuddered. At least these trains weren't up in the air.

Thalia shook her head. "Not a subway. Welcome to the Tube." She ran her fingers along a blue "neuron" and then a red one. "Piccadilly to the Central line," she muttered to herself, then peeled away from the map. We followed her down the stairs and through a turnstile, with Thalia sliding her card through the machine once for each of us.

Underground now, the Tube was hot and oppressive. We pulled off our Prince Harry hoodies and waited for our train in silence. A couple folks looked at us oddly, and I realized that we were still in uniform, the patches on our polo shirts reading MIAMI PALMS MIDDLE in big yellow letters. We looked like kids who had gotten lost during a transatlantic field trip.

When the train arrived, we got on and sat together.

The only other person on the train was a woman in a pink suit and running shoes. She gave us a little smile, then dug through her briefcase for a pen and notebook. Her hair was disheveled, and her mascara had run a bit. We must have been staring, because she giggled and said, "I keep missing my stop. Don't know what's come over me."

The train rumbled along through the tunnel peacefully, stopping every so often. A singsong voice would announce, "Mind the gap between the train and the platform's edge," at each stop, and soon, Nia and I were repeating it in British accents, prompting Thalia to mutter something about "Americans."

"Careful, or we'll dump all your tea into the nearest body of water," Nia said, and Mela actually giggled.

It was all very pleasant until the feathers.

They were tiny orange feathers and were, suddenly, everywhere.

"Not again," Thalia said. "It was a wild-goose chase the last time we saw feathers."

Mela started coughing at once. "I think I snorted one. It's up my nose!" she yelled.

"Where are they coming from?" Nia asked, rooting around in her pocket for a tissue to give to Mela.

"There," Thalia said, pointing at three robins that were darting back and forth in the train.

The woman who was sitting across from us tsked, pointed her finger, and said, "They aren't bothering anyone, poor things." The notebook was now open on her lap, and it looked as if she'd tried to write the same sentence three times, scratching out each attempt.

The birds kept darting back and forth, back and forth, and each time, they'd get closer to us. We sat even closer together.

Were they just some unfortunate robins, trapped inside the train car, or were they . . . something else? After a while, they quit flittering about and perched on the seat beside the woman, as if they were her tiny pets. They looked like small, puffed-up toys, their sharp little beaks opening and closing as if they were out of breath. Their eyes were little black beads, and the orange feathers on their chests were the color of the sunset. One of them slipped into the woman's briefcase for a moment, then hopped out again.

Maybe they were just regular robins.

Whatever they were, we didn't take our eyes off them.

That's how we noticed the teeth.

Thalia screamed and Mela buried her face into her knees.

One of the birds made a low, rumbly sound. It was as un-birdlike a sound as I'd ever heard. Another snapped its beak open and shut, the noise it made like a ruler clapping on a desk.

"Did those birds just . . . growl at us?" Nia asked in a whisper. At this point, I was too terrified to say anything at all.

"And why do they have *human teeth*?" Thalia said, shutting her eyes tightly.

The automated voice on the train speakers called out, "The next station is Bethnal Green."

Then, as if on cue, the birds began to sing. They warbled softly, trilling long, pretty notes. Mela lifted her head, tears having run down her face in rivulets. Thalia and Nia cocked their heads to one side, listening. I listened too, and my heart seemed to beat faster.

Almost as if I were very far away, I heard a voice repeating "Bethnal Green, next station, Bethnal Green, next station," but even as the train slowed, the birds got louder, drowning other sounds until the birdsong was all I could hear.

Scratch that. All I could hear was the siren song.

And that's when I snapped out of it.

"Girls," I said, clapping my hands in front of their faces. When that didn't work, I put my hands over Nia's ears. She blinked, then understanding dawned on her face. She did the same to Thalia, who then pulled Mela's headphones from around her neck and put them over Mela's ears.

The train rolled to a stop. The doors slid open. Our hands still over our ears, the four of us rose and made to leave.

But the sirens sang a little louder, lifted into the air, and hovered before the woman with the notebook.

Whatever they told her, she took the direction well, because she was on her feet and blocking the door, her pen in her hand the way a person might hold a knife.

"Ma'am, you need to move. Like, now," Nia said.

Then the birds dive-bombed us.

"Get off!" Mela shouted. The woman laughed, but her eyes were glazed over, and I had a suspicion she wouldn't remember any of this later. The door began to close.

The sign outside the train read "Bethnal Green." This was our stop. The other muses needed us. Or maybe we needed them a little more at the moment.

The woman adjusted the grip on her pen. Then I remembered her notebook. Slowly, I put my hand around her fist, both our hands controlling the pen now. I concentrated on my skin, the way you can sometimes feel your own pulse if you're still enough. Then I felt it. The buzzing sensation. My kódikas. And I'd made it happen on purpose!

"I don't know what you're writing," I said to her, looking into her glassy eyes, "but I bet it's going to be awesome." My eyes pricked, my scalp tingled, and the woman's eyes dropped to her notebook. "Such a great idea. I know you can do it," I urged her. "Why don't you sit down now, right this minute, and get to it?" My fingers went numb, but I could feel her grip loosen.

The birds sang more loudly, but the woman shook her head, sat down, and picked up her notebook, writing in penmanship that was really nice and flowy. She was so lost in thought that when a big gloppy drop of bird poop landed on her sleeve she just glanced at it and kept writing.

Nia had shoved her foot between the doors, and we

worked together to pull them open again. I watched as the robins descended on the woman's briefcase. They flew up, the bag's strap between their teeth. The birds disappeared into the dark tunnel ahead of the train, the briefcase trailing behind them like the tail of a kite.

"I hope an oncoming train splatters you!" Mela shouted into the darkness, then she wiped her eyes.

"What was in the bag?" I wondered.

"Pink-suit lady just got mugged by birds and she didn't even say 'hey,'" commented Nia.

"That was fun," Thalia said, without even a hint of a smile. "Let's go." We followed her out of the tunnel and into the light of Bethnal Green.

Chapter 21
TOY TRAGEDY

The V and A Museum of Childhood was in shambles. The skylights in the domed roof above had shattered, and as we walked in, our feet crunched over the glass. There was no other sound except for the insistent wailing of a woman down in the café. Huddled around her were the other muses—Paola, Etoro, Tomiko, Elnaz, and there, her hands on the woman's shoulders, was Clio.

She spotted us at once, stared at our Prince Harry hoodies for a moment, and beckoned us over with a flick of her head.

"This is bad," Mela was saying, and Thalia nodded her head over and over again.

The woman continued to cry, and now I could make out what she was saying. "I was here before sunrise, to get ahead of things, when they came. B-birds. But, but, like, *human*-birds. With wings and t-t-teeth," she was saying. "And there was a woman with them. She wore pink head to toe, even her trainers, and she had a blank look in her eyes."

Thalia gasped.

"Pink," Mela said.

"And running shoes," Nia added.

"It's got to be the same lady from the train," I said. We stopped and took in the wreckage of the museum.

Two floors' worth of glass cases were turned over, shattered, toys everywhere. There was a giant dollhouse on its side, all the tiny furniture and tiny people on the ground like victims of a terrible earthquake. I spotted beheaded stuffed animals, puppets tangled up in their strings, and a pair of really creepy cello-playing monkeys turned upside down and dangling from the outstretched hand of a statue.

It was . . . a very big mess.

Clio brought us into the circle around the woman, and when we approached, the woman sobbed even harder. "Oh, the children," she said, and pointed at us. "This is *their* museum. And look at it now."

The woman broke down completely, sobbing and hiccupping.

Paola stroked the woman's hair and began to hum a song I remembered from childhood—"De colores, de colores se visten los campos en la primavera"—and on and on, a song about colors in the springtime, and about love and hope. Soon, the woman stopped crying.

"Sharon," Clio said, addressing the woman, "we are an

investigatory team from the V and A."

Sharon's eyes grew wide. "Oh. That's good," she said, sniffing loudly.

"Did the burglars see you, Sharon?" Clio asked.

"Burglars?" Sharon said.

"Burglars in costumes, yes," Clio said, and Sharon seemed relieved to think that no, she hadn't lost her mind, that nothing otherworldly had happened.

Sharon shook her head. "No, I don't think so. I was hiding behind the espresso machine over there," she said, pointing toward the café.

"Good. You were safe. What did they take?" Clio asked. Sharon lifted a shaky hand and pointed at a case on the third floor. The sign above read "Toys of the Eighties."

"They spent a lot of time there. Valuable pieces inside. Not sure what's gone missing. Stuff sells for a lot on eBay," Sharon said, rambling on a bit, but at least she wasn't panicking anymore.

Clio looked pointedly at Etoro and Paola, who had quit humming by then. Etoro pulled her wheelchair a little closer. "Fancy a cup of tea?" she asked Sharon, who nodded vigorously.

Paola clapped her hands. "Delicioso," she said, and led the way to the kitchen, Etoro and Sharon behind her.

"The rest of you, follow me," Clio said, and the Muse Squad, plus Tomiko and Elnaz, chased after her.

We walked gingerly over the broken glass, sidestepping all kinds of old and interesting toys. Only last year, I'd cleaned out most of my toys, making a huge donate pile of old baby dolls in the middle of the living room. My mom had looked at the pile, blinked a few times to keep tears away, and then helped me put them all into bags.

The truth was, I missed some of those toys.

The Toys of the Eighties case was smashed open. I spotted an old video game console. My brothers would each give an eye for that. A Cabbage Patch doll with its scrunched-up little face and yarn hair was on the floor. Thalia picked it up and gave it a hug before putting it down again. There were some action figures here and there— plastic muscle-men in colorful leotards. Cracked in half was the *Millennium Falcon* from *Star Wars*, the sight of which brought Nia to her knees.

"Noooooo!" she said, and cradled the two halves. "MONSTERS!"

"Monsters indeed," Clio said. "We know what they broke. But what did they take?"

Elnaz circled the broken toys. "They've already stolen a curse from the stores back at the headquarters. What could they have wanted from all this?" She gestured to the playthings.

Clio shook her head. She searched what was left of the case up and down, as if she could sense what was missing. She plucked a feather out from underneath a Superman lunchbox, and we all stared at it.

"The sirens attacked us," I said. "On the Underground. The woman in the pink suit was with them," I added.

Clio looked at us in alarm. "What form did the sirens take?"

"Robins," Mela said. "With human teeth."

"Incredibly creepy," Thalia put in.

"They were manipulating the pink-suit lady," Nia said, still on the floor with the *Falcon* in her lap. "Why did they need her at all? Couldn't they just take what they wanted on their own? Why do all of this?" Nia gestured at the broken toy on her lap.

Elnaz pointed at the security cameras. "The police will keep busy looking for the lady in the pink suit."

"And when they catch her, she'll be all confused and unaware. The sirens will have gotten their way, and also made a great mess of things, which they love. Am I right?" Thalia asked.

"Well done. That's their way," Clio said. "You escaped them. How?"

"Callie did it," Thalia said. "She was brilliant. Inspired the woman to sit down and pick up a pen, and she just blinked and did as she was told. We got away, and the sirens flew off into the Underground, down the Central line headed east. They took the woman's bag with them."

"Whatever they stole, it fits inside a briefcase," I said, eyeing the scattered items.

"Good eye," Clio said. "We muses inspire the best in others. The sirens inspire the worst. They sing a tempting song, and the lyrics are always the same. They say give up. They say you aren't smart enough. They say get angry.

They say trust no one. It's a powerful song. But we must sing a stronger one, a more compelling one. It's the only way to defeat them."

"And as a last resort," Elnaz said, "pull an Odysseus."

"Pull a what?" I asked.

"An Odysseus. Greek hero. Bit of a jerk. But the sirens called out to his sailors and they nearly crashed their ships. He tied them to the mast and plugged their ears. Then he did the same to himself," Elnaz said, mimicking the motion of shoving stuff into her ear canal. "It worked. They sailed on by."

Nia, Thalia, and Mela gave me a pointed look.

"Callie did that. She pulled an Odysseus on the train. Saved us all," Thalia said.

Clio looked at me, laid a hand on my shoulder, and smiled. She actually smiled. "Calliope, the first of the original nine muses. Coming into her own. But not quite yet." Then, Clio did the most unthinkable thing I could ever imagine her doing.

She winked at me. Like a normal human being.

I think I blushed all the way down to my toes. To break up the awkward moment, I said, "So, if we have to, we literally tie Maya Rivero down?" I asked.

"*And* plug her ears!" Thalia said. She gave me two thumbs-up, then stuck her thumbs in her ears.

"But first I need to figure out what drew them here." Clio nodded at the others, and they took off down the stairs in search of clues. "Junior muses, come with me,"

Clio said to us. Thalia opened her mouth, then closed it, the words "Muse Squad" hanging in the air, unspoken.

Clio gave us a ride in a black cab back to the V and A. It was a long drive with the traffic. The cabbie went on and on about how much he hated bicyclists on the road, but we mostly ignored him. Every once in a while, Thalia would point out a landmark.

"That's St. Paul's Cathedral," or "There's the River Thames." We all looked at the river as we rode in bumper-to-bumper traffic. Suddenly, I saw a woman pop her head out of the water. She had a massive amount of green hair, and she seemed to be looking straight at us with eyes that glittered like aluminum foil. Clio raised her hand in a wave, and the woman waved back. Then she ducked under again, followed by a thick, glossy tail.

My head was spinning. "Did I just see a mermaid?" I asked faintly.

"A naiad," Clio clarified. Mela was rubbing her eyes and staring hard at the water, while Nia had her face plastered against the cab window.

"Bloody hell, I missed it!" Thalia whined.

"You're telling me that there are naiads in the Thames?" I whispered. "Can everybody see them?" The cabbie drove on, and it was as if he didn't hear us.

"He can't hear us," Clio said, guessing my thoughts. "We can see mythical creatures because we are, in a sense, mythical creatures ourselves."

That weirded me out a lot. I always thought that "myth-ical" meant pretend. Imaginary. I dug my nails into my thigh. Yes, I was very real. I might have a mythical secret identity, but I was still Callie Martinez-Silva. I spent the rest of the ride either watching the water, or trying to remember if I'd ever seen anything that strange, or that cool, in all my life.

We reached the V and A at last. Clio gave money to the cabbie, and we all got out. On the way in, the security guards who had chased us gave us mean looks, but Clio waved them away and they began a lively discussion on the ancient Mesopotamians.

"Isn't history fascinating?" Clio mused as we passed the uniformed pair.

We walked up to the third floor, and straight to my entrance point.

"Find the three. Break the curse," Clio said when we got there.

"Save the future," the rest of us added in unison as we slid underneath the Great Bed of Ware.

"Easy-peasy," Clio said.

"Mermaids in the Thames," Thalia said, and whistled a long, low note. "And all this time, I thought the only things in there were eels and old boots."

She was still chattering away when I closed my eyes and the world went dark.

Chapter 22
PARROTS AND STRATEGIES

"We need a plan," Nia said as we walked home after school the next day. "We got lucky on the Tube. That whole mess could have been worse."

I agreed. "Waiting around for something to happen is not a good look," I said.

Thalia plucked a pink hibiscus flower from a tall bush. She nestled it behind her left ear as she talked. "I'm rather keen on my idea to start some kind of commotion and see if we can't draw the sirens out."

"And what? Get kicked out of school? Not helpful," Mela said.

"A *quiet* commotion, obviously," Thalia said.

Nia sighed. "We don't even know where to look for sirens. We just saw them across the Atlantic, for goodness' sake. They certainly travel fast."

"So do we," I reminded her. "Magic and all that."

"Clio said they were sticking close to Maya. And us, I guess," Mela said. She whipped her head from side to side, as if sirens were going to just pop up beside us. As it was, every chirp we heard made us jumpy. Earlier, a flock of tiny green parrots had streaked loudly over our heads, and both Mela and Thalia had screamed.

"All right," I said. "If there's a good time for it, we'll let you do your chaos thing, okay, Thalia?"

Thalia gave me a thumbs-up.

"We need earplugs. To block out siren song. All of us," Mela said.

So we walked to the dollar store down the street from my house.

"Hola, niñas," the shopkeeper called out loudly.

"Hola," we all said back in a variety of accents. We passed rows of potato chips, shelves full of carwash supplies, a stack of kiddie pools, and finally found some earplugs in the medicine aisle.

I plucked four packages off the rack, making sure I had enough pocket money. "Got them," I said, turning around to see Nia, Mela, and Thalia standing there, arms full of things like face masks, lip gloss, candy bars, and a stuffed dinosaur.

"What? I quite like dinosaurs," Mela said.

"It's your money," I said with a sigh.

We were making our way to the cash register when we

heard a shriek. Running, we saw the woman at the cash register waving a broom at three blue macaws. They were massive birds, their claws as big as her face.

"Quick!" I shouted, ripping open the earplugs, which we jammed into our ears. My whole body buzzed with magic.

"Stop, you," I heard Thalia shout. She chucked a candy bar at the parrots. The birds lifted up, seemed to pause in the air for a moment, then zoomed toward us.

They stopped in mid-air, eye-level to us, their big wings flapping hard to keep them aloft. A gush of air hit my face with each flap, knocking loose one of my earplugs. One of the birds opened its mouth, and I heard it speak in a parrot-voice, "CAW! You won't win. CAW!" In this form, the sirens could *talk*.

"Polly want a cracker?" I heard Nia ask behind me, and a package of saltines sailed over my shoulder, hitting one of the birds in the chest.

Out of the corner of one eye, I could see Mela's hands fluttering, and I could have sworn that one of the parrots started to get a bit teary.

The woman at the register hoisted a fire extinguisher over her head, and marched in our direction. She sent a blast of white foam at the macaws, who flew off, squawking loudly. We chased them out of the store, but they were gone, merely blue specks in the sky.

"Oye, you need to pay for those things!" the shopkeeper yelled at us.

Amazingly, Mela was still holding on to her stuffed dinosaur, and Thalia was clutching face masks in two hands. Plus, we all had earplugs in our ears.

"Of course," I said, apologizing in Spanish even as the woman kept grumbling at me about the birds, and people keeping wild animals as pets, and shoplifters. I noticed she wore a set of earbuds, the salsa music coming from them loud enough for me to hear. No wonder the sirens couldn't get her to do anything.

"That was intimidation, pure and simple," Nia said later.

"Maya wasn't even with us," Thalia said.

Nia was right. "They had a message to give," I said. The others nodded.

"But they won't win," Mela added as we reached my house. I walked in last, scanning the sky before closing the door.

Back home, we made our plan. Our first step was to list our siren suspects. At the top of the list was:

Ms. Fovos. We all know substitute teachers get the short stick when it comes to student behavior, and it had made her mean. And she was especially mean to Maya Rivero, and oddly, very nice to . . .

Violet Prado, suspect numero dos. Violet, who couldn't stand to see anyone being more successful than she was. Violet, who tripped Raquel on stage, who had been drenched by Maya's science project, and maybe had a reason to sabotage her later in front of Principal Jackson. And if we were including Violet, then we also had to consider . . .

Max Pascal and Alain Riche. Those two were the evil sidekicks to all Violet's best bullying moments, so that alone earned them the spot. Who was there when Violet put glue all over Kelly Bustamante's desk, gluing her to her seat in the third grade? Alain was. Laughing his head off. Who helped Violet spread the rumor that the first of February was "Wear Your Clothes Backwards Day"? Max. And who took photos of all the backwards-clothes-wearing dummies who fell for it, including me? Ditto Max.

And that was it. It wasn't much to go on, but it was a start.

We were sitting in my room, perched on our bunk beds, in our pajamas for the night. I'd been thinking. "Mela, I think you made that one siren a little sad."

"I tried. It was hard. Like trying to drive a nail into the wall with your bare hand," she said. "I could feel it pushing me away." She picked at her yellow pajama bottoms. They had tiny green dinosaurs on them.

"Okay," I said. "But they were parrots. Do they even have tear ducts?"

"Nope," Nia said. "I won a trivia contest knowing that." Her pajama top read BLACK GIRL MAGIC IS STARDUST, and had shimmery silver stars all over it. I kept finding glitter all over my room.

"But one of them did get all teary. I saw it," I said. "Maybe when they're in human form, we can affect them. Use our kódikas on them."

"Worth a try," Thalia said. She picked up the list we'd written. "Divide and conquer, I say."

We heard my mom call out, "Buenas noches," her cue to turn out the lights, lie down, and go to sleep.

"'Night girls," Thalia said, and the rest of us said our goodnights too.

I didn't sleep much, but when I did, I dreamed of a thousand birds on a telephone wire outside my house, the line sloping down so low it touched the ground. Every single bird had teeth, and they were all saying the same thing: "You can't win, Callie. Maya Rivero belongs to us."

Chapter 23
MAYA GETS A WIN

Ms. Rinse was out for a teacher's conference the next morning, and Ms. Fovos was our substitute. The first thing she did was yell at Thalia for wearing her Prince Harry hoodie over her uniform, and Thalia peeled it off slowly, grumbling the whole time. She looked over to me and mouthed the word *E-vil*.

Ms. Fovos announced our assignment. "We, and by this I mean you, are going to work in groups to put together a model heart pump using these items." On a table in the front of the class were water bottles, scissors, balloons, and plastic straws. Then Fovos quickly assembled the groups. "You, you, you, and you," she said, pointing at students to form their teams.

When she pointed at me, Nia, and Maya, I could have cheered. But then she added Violet, and all thoughts of cheering were gone. "Oh, crumbs," I heard Maya mutter behind me.

"Nobody ask for a bathroom pass," Fovos shouted as everyone started to get into groups. "You aren't getting one."

Letty, one of the triplets, spilled coffee, and Lisa slipped in it, soaking her uniform. Ms. Fovos angrily wrote out a bathroom pass for Lisa, then confiscated Letty's coffee mug for good measure.

Once the commotion was over, we settled our desks into a square, facing one another, while Maya fetched our materials.

"There are three too many nerds in this group," Violet said, then she huffed loudly so that the whole room could hear her.

The rest of us ignored it, getting to work reading the instructions and laying out the parts of the model heart pump. "The balloons are the ventricles, and the straws are the arteries," Maya said. "We need to start by connecting the two."

Violet huffed again.

"Lay off," Nia said.

"Why should I? And who appointed Maya the leader of this group?" Violet demanded. She grabbed one of the balloons and started shoving it into a bottle.

"Hey!" I said. "You heard Maya. We need to attach that to a straw first."

"Whatever," Violet said, dropping the bottle and balloon, and going up to Ms. Fovos to ask for a bathroom pass.

Of course Ms. Fovos gave her one.

Maya was quiet, fiddling with one of the straws. Nia leaned forward, whispering, "You can't let her treat you like that."

"How am I supposed to stop her?" Maya asked. It was a good question. Violet bossed *everyone* around. And she nearly always got her way.

Nia wasn't having it, though. She fiddled with her phone. "Maya, I can tell you have about ten brilliant ideas a minute. Maybe more. What's in Violet's head beyond trying to make people feel bad?"

"Twelve. Twelve brilliant ideas a minute," Maya said, laughing. Her eyes looked brighter, as if, in that instant, she really had thought up some amazing things. I glanced at Nia's phone. She had a privacy screen on it, so I couldn't tell if her kódikas app was open. I bet it was.

"Exactly," I said. I slung an arm around Maya, felt my fingertips slowly going numb, and that familiar buzz on my scalp. "You're tougher than you give yourself credit for. Don't you want to change the world?"

Maya nodded rapidly. "I do. Very much." She sniffed, wiping her nose with the back of her hand.

"Then you've got to stand up for yourself," I said. Maya looked at me, her eyes wide. Just then, Violet sauntered back into class.

She started talking as soon as she sat down. "Okay, nerds. First we—"

"When you get straight As in science for, oh, your whole life, then you can lead this group. Straws in balloons, everybody," Maya said.

Nia and I jumped to it. Violet sat very still. "Fine," she said at last, picking up a straw and a balloon. "This is stupid anyway."

I had a hard time keeping a smile off my face. Maya kicked me softly under the table. I didn't look up at her, but I knew she was beaming.

Phys ed class gave us a chance to investigate further. Our PE uniforms were simple—gray Miami Palms T-shirts and blue basketball shorts. It was a hot day, and Coach Navarro was sweating buckets. He had pulled a folding chair into the shade of a mahogany tree and announced, "Free play today. Take water breaks," then looked at his phone for the rest of class.

"Behold the dedicated educator," Mela said.

"Yes, shall we give him a prize?" Thalia asked.

"Come on," I said. "We've got a plan to put in place, and Coach just made it easy."

Nia went to go chat with Alain, who was throwing a squash ball against a wall. It rebounded hard and smacked him in the forehead. I watched as Nia swallowed a laugh and asked him to play a game.

Meanwhile, Thalia threw a basketball at Max, shouting, "Game on!" She was cracking jokes as they played, and he was laughing hard. "Ever been to London?" I heard her ask.

Mela was tagging along behind Violet, who kept telling her to buzz off. But Mela was nothing if not persistent. They walked along the chain-link fence for a while. I saw Violet swipe at her eyes with her sleeve, just at the moment when Mela asked, "Where did you get those feathers for the assembly?"

Meanwhile, I worked on Maya. She'd recently ironed patches of molecules onto her PE shorts, and today, she had a purple sock on her left foot, and an orange one on her right. "Tell me about your science fair project," I urged.

Maya had arranged a series of leaves in order of decomposition on the sidewalk before us. "I'm working on a smaller model at the moment. The problem with sea level rise in Miami is this," she said, and picked up a white rock from the ground. It was full of holes—like bleached coral, or Swiss cheese. "Limestone," she said. "It's beneath our feet. And it's porous."

I shrugged my shoulders, not getting it.

"Come here," she said, and led me to a puddle of water in the playground underneath the swings. Water always collected there, soaking little kids' shoes and socks. Someone had put yellow CAUTION tape all over the seats. Maya knelt and dipped half the limestone in the water.

I watched as water bubbled up through the holes in the rock.

"See that?" she asked. "When the seas rise, it won't come up on shore like a wave. It will get us from underneath. Hence the pumps to get the water out. I'm making a new model for the county science fair. It's the street where I live, with houses and everything, and underneath, running through the limestone, I'm stringing flexible tubes attached to a pump that will keep everything nice and dry. If I had more time, I could come up with a small desalinator to recycle the salt water and make it drinkable." I imagined ripples around Maya, each circle growing larger, impacting the world and making a difference.

"That's amazing. Will it work?" I asked.

Maya shrugged. "I don't know. We have to tackle this one small problem at a time, because the problems of climate change are numerous and variable. Patience and persistence are key. The greatest scientific mysteries are solved this way." Maya got a far-off look in her eyes for a moment. "I have other ideas," she said, snapping out of it. "Just sketches. Underground canals, stuff like that. Or we could come at it from the Poles. Lower the temperatures up there with geoengineering. Agrovoltaics are a possibility. Floating cities." I didn't understand any of it, but what I did see was that Maya got a sad look in her eyes for a moment. "The truth is, Callie, I'm not sure any of it will work. The grown-ups should have been thinking up solutions a long time ago. Maybe it's too late," she said quietly.

Maya's shoulders sagged. It was almost as if I could see the ripples fading around her as she lost hope.

"When have we ever been able to count on grown-ups to do the right thing?" I joked.

Maya looked at me in horror, her eyes wide.

"I mean," I tried to clarify, "I mean kids like us, we can make a difference, right?" I could feel it starting—the buzzing and tingling sensation on my skin. I willed it to get stronger. "The world needs people like you, Maya."

Maya smiled and shook her head. "You're a weird one," she said.

"Believe it or not, I've heard that before," I told her.

"Well, we have a SAP meeting after school, if you want to come." She said it like a question and didn't look me in the eyes.

"Yeah, of course," I said.

Maya smiled and dusted off her hands. "Great. See you at three thirty then," she said.

"Yep." I watched her as she returned to the leaves, turning them, examining them, then doodling something in her notebook. Her red sneakers had a hole in the left toe.

She really is going to save the world, I thought.

At lunch the Muse Squad took up the table closest to the exit. It was always empty because everyone wanted to be near the food line and the water fountains. Nia had made each of us a special grilled cheese sandwich for lunch. Mine had bacon. Mela's had spinach. Thalia's had extra cheese, and Nia had made herself one with tomatoes and broccoli. My brothers had watched with mouths open. "None for us?" they'd asked, and Nia had rolled her eyes at them.

The projection screen at the front of the cafetorium had been lowered, and the projector hummed in anticipation. We devoured those sandwiches.

"These are amazing," I said, my mouth full of cheese.

"Grilled cheese queen," Mela said, giving Nia a high five.

"You know it," Nia said, shimmying in her seat as she popped the last bite of sandwich into her mouth.

"So what'd you find out about Violet?" I asked Mela, who was wiping her mouth with a napkin.

"Nothing much. She got the feathers at the craft store. And while we were in London, being chased by evil robins, she was at the orthodontist getting spacers put in for braces. She opened her mouth and showed me, poor thing," Mela said. "She has a proper alibi."

"No sympathy for potential sirens," Nia whispered. "How about you?" she asked Thalia.

Thalia blushed a little. "Max doesn't plan on going to the concert. He says he'll be at the science fair instead. Also, he's very fit, isn't he?" she said, blushing a bit more deeply.

"NO CRUSHES ON POTENTIAL SIRENS," Nia said a little too loudly.

"Nia, what about Alain?" I asked.

"Girls," Nia said, and looked around, her face deadly serious. "That boy is as dumb as a sack of hammers."

"That's so mean!" I said. But we laughed, then Thalia snort-laughed, and we all laughed even harder.

Ms. Fovos came by and shushed us. She placed her knuckles on the table and leaned over. Her breath smelled like old coffee. "What are you up to, girls?" she asked, her eyes narrowing. I wanted to ask her the same thing. We stared at each other for a beat longer than what seemed normal. Then Ms. Fovos pointed to the screen.

A local television show, *Good Morning, Miami*, came on. There was Raquel in a yellow skirt and a denim off-the-shoulder top. She had on yellow sandals, too. Her hair was in a high ponytail, with a crisp denim bow clipping it together. Everyone went quiet and watched as the host interviewed Raquel then flashed pictures of her as a little girl. There she was in diapers in her backyard in Venezuela. There she was on her ninth birthday, standing behind her cake, and there I was, too, right beside her. I wanted to cry, but it had nothing to do with muse magic.

I looked around and found Raquel sitting with Violet and Max. They were both hugging her at the same time, their eyes on the screen. She must have taped the show earlier in the morning, because she had a lot of makeup on, and the denim bow was still in her hair, too. Alain was leading the cafetorium in a cheer of "Ra-quel, Ra-quel, Ra-quel."

"Hey," Mela said, and tried to put her hand on my wrist. I yanked it away.

"It's fine. I have to go to the bathroom. I'll . . . see you all at the SAP meeting," I told them, picking up my tray and leaving the cafetorium. I could see Ms. Fovos's eyes on me, but she didn't stop me from going.

I went down a corridor and then down another until I found myself in front of the library. I stepped inside and took a deep breath. Libraries had the best smell. They smelled like—

"Breakdown of chemical compounds in paper. That's what you're smelling," said Ms. Rinse, who was watching me from a table in the back of the otherwise empty library. "And it's really delicious." She picked up her book, something about the ocean from the looks of the cover, and put her nose in the binding.

"Sorry to interrupt," I started to say, but Ms. Rinse put her hand up. "No worries at all, Callie. Sit with me?"

"You're back from your conference," I said.

"Indeed. It was fascinating." She patted the seat next to her.

I joined her at the table, absently picking up a book on the way. It was a book of myths. On the cover, three witches held up a thread. One held scissors. They were all blind, except for the youngest witch, who had only one eye. It gave me the creeps, and I dropped it with a thud.

"I love that one," Ms. Rinse said.

I nodded. I didn't really want to talk about books. I missed Raquel. I missed the easy way we talked to one another. I missed giving her pep talks. I missed having her come over to my house for dinner and laughing together over videos online. The other muses were great. Just great. And Maya was interesting and all, and Fated or whatever, but none of them were Raquel, my best friend.

"The exchange students seem lovely," Ms. Rinse said. "How's it going at home? Big change, huh?" I didn't know what to say. It was fine, I guess. I mean, Thalia did leave her stuff everywhere, and Nia spent too much time in the bathroom, and Mela was so homesick that she cried every night, which put everyone in a weepy sort of mood.

"Fine. Super, um, fine," I said.

"Hm," Ms. Rinse said. She fiddled with a bookmark, tapping it on the table softly. "I had lots of sisters. It can be . . . difficult. Easy to lose yourself, your sense of who *you* are," she said.

A teacher had never shared anything so personal with me. I wondered if it meant that I was growing up, if sixth grade was the time when that kind of thing happened, when the teachers saw you as more than just a little kid.

"Any-hoo," Ms. Rinse said, suddenly cheerful, as if some spell had broken. "Are you coming to SAP? Maya mentioned you might."

"Yes," I said, happy that the subject had changed. "I

invited Mela, Thalia, and Nia to the SAP meeting."

Ms. Rinse beamed. "The more the merrier," she said. "We're planning a trip to Sea-a-Rama this weekend. Should be fun."

I hadn't been to Sea-a-Rama since I was a little kid. "I remember that place! Dolphin shows and stuff. They had these machines that turned hot wax into toys. I have a walrus somewhere at home," I said.

"Yep, those are still there." Ms. Rinse glanced at her watch. It had a blue strap and a smiling dolphin on the face. "Fifth period's about to start," she said. Halfway to the door, Ms. Rinse stopped to add, "Bring the superstar with you, too."

"Superstar?"

"You know who I'm talking about," Ms. Rinse said. She paused to look at a stack of books on a cart just right of the exit door.

The superstar. There was no way Raquel would come to a SAP meeting with me. Not cool enough for sure, and besides, she wasn't really talking to me these days. How long before everyone in school figured out that we weren't friends anymore? How long before they stopped asking me "How's Raquel doing?" as if I had the answers. I wondered, too, if anybody asked her about me, and if they did, what she said. "Oh, Callie? Her? She's probably stuffing her face at the moment."

The thought of it made me feel so low that I put my head down for a second, letting the feeling pass. A minute later, I said, "Hey, Ms. Rinse. I'm sorry for not doing my science project."

Silence. I looked up. Ms. Rinse had left the library without me noticing, and I had apologized to thin air.

The rest of the day rumbled on uneventfully, unless you counted the mouse that scurried over some kid's foot in sixth period, starting a chain reaction of squeals and stomping that Ms. Salvo had a hard time containing, so she gave up and showed us a video about prepositions. Then the final bell of the day rang at last. I gathered my things and made my way to the Activities Room, where SAP held its meetings.

The Activities Room had two worn and very beige couches in it, the fabric all nubby and gross. There was one table surrounded by six rusty aluminum folding chairs, two bulletin boards with notices from every club in the school, and giant rolls of colorful paper for making signs. By the time I arrived, Mela, Thalia, and Nia were already there, arguing with Max Pascal.

Max was holding Maya's Rubik's Cube in his hand, high over his head. He was the tallest boy in school, so there was no way that even Nia could reach it. "Give it back to Maya," she was saying, hopping up and down, trying to get her hands on the puzzle.

"She gave it to me," Max insisted. "What's wrong with you girls, anyway?"

I was about to go help when I heard Maya behind me

saying, "Leave Max alone. He's right. I gave it to him."

"Oh. Sorry," Nia said to Max.

"Whatever. Weirdos," said Max.

"Are we weirdos?" Mela whispered to me.

I thought for a moment, and because I was tired, or because I couldn't think of anything inspirational or muse-like to say, I said, "Yeah."

Mela gasped a little, but Thalia said, "Then we're in good company," and pointed her thumb at the students steadily pouring into the SAP meeting.

Ness Colucci came in with Janie Bustelo, two seventh graders best known for their K-pop obsession and their petition to force the school to offer Korean language lessons (it hadn't worked so far). They were followed by Dylan Garcia and Alex Contreras, both of whom were so obsessed with Underwatch, a team-based, shoot-'em-up video game, that they seemed to speak in a different language altogether, and insisted we call them by the characters they played— Tinker and Drang. Then three more girls sauntered in, all in volleyball uniforms, with their names on the back—Allie, Mia, and Diana. I thought they were staying for the meeting, but they each took an aluminum chair and dragged them away without saying a word, their long brown hair swishing against their backs. Finally, Letty, Lisa, and Leo Linares arrived, holding their ubiquitous coffee mugs.

"What are you doing here?" I asked Max as we found our seats.

"I won the school science fair last year, didn't I?" It's true. He had. I'd just forgotten. Then Maya came and sat between us. Max tossed the Rubik's Cube to her, and she gave it a few twists.

"Haven't solved it yet, Max?" she asked.

"I keep messing up the corners. I'm gonna try this next," Max said. He reached over and started peeling the colors off the little squares.

"Cheater," Maya said, laughing, and Max laughed back.

What in the world was going on? Since when had these two become friends? I very nearly asked them, when Ms. Rinse rose to speak.

"Wow," Ms. Rinse said, her own coffee mug in hand. "We've never had so many students come to a meeting. Welcome! Our first order of business is to talk about the science fair." Today she was wearing black-and-yellow polka dots, and I couldn't help but think of bumblebees. She went on, "As you all know, Maya has been selected to represent our school at the fair. If she wins, she goes on to compete at the national level. We have tickets for all club members to attend, and I hope you'll all be there to cheer her on."

Ness Colucci put her hand up. "I can't go, Ms. Rinse. I'm going to the *America's Next Star* finals instead." Janie Bustelo nodded vigorously beside her.

"But—" Ms. Rinse began.

"Hard same," Tinker and Drang said together.

Ms. Rinse took a big breath. She looked pointedly at Max Pascal. "I suppose you're going to abandon SAP, as well."

Max pursed his lips, crossed his arms, and leaned back into his chair, his long legs sprawling out before him. "Nah," he said. "I've got Maya's back."

I looked at him in surprise. Since when did Max treat Maya like they were friends? Suspicious, is what it was.

Ms. Rinse beamed. "Excellent news. Who else is coming to the county science fair?"

I put my hand up, as did the other muses, Letty, Lisa, and Leo, and Max again, for good measure. By this point, Tinker and Drang were taking turns pretending to explode in one corner of the room.

Clapping her hands, Ms. Rinse went on. "Okay, the field trip this weekend. Sea-a-Rama. Who's going?"

This time, everyone raised their hands.

"Great. You'll need to be dropped off by your parents or guardians, and picked up by them, too. Nine a.m. sharp. The park closes at five p.m. so make sure you have a ride home. Bring sunscreen and a notebook. We'll meet in the parking lot."

With one last reminder about being at Sea-a-Rama on time, Ms. Rinse closed the meeting, and everyone trickled out of the room.

I caught up to Maya, halfway out the door already. "Hey, Sea-a-Rama on Saturday!" I said.

Maya shrugged. "Can't go." She stared down at her

shoes. "I—I wouldn't be able to get a ride."

"My mom will pick you up. We have a van," I said. Maya still shook her head, her eyes not meeting mine. "Come on. It'll be fun. Fish and whales and stuff. That's totally your jam!"

"I don't think—"

"Mayaaaaaa," I said. I pulled out my cell phone and called up the Sea-a-Rama page. There, on the front, was an orca—Maya's favorite animal. "Look at it. Majestic fishiness awaits."

"Mammal. It's a mammal," Maya said quietly. Then, still looking as if someone had whispered "*You are DOOMED*" into her ear, she asked, "Why are you suddenly so nice to me all the time?" Before I could come up with anything to say, Max cut between us, turned, and asked Maya, "Coming on Saturday?"

I watched as her cheeks flared. She stuttered a response. "Of course, M-Max. Yeah!" Then she performed the world's most awkward fist pump.

"Cool," he said, leaving the room with a bounce.

Thalia, Mela, and Nia wandered over to us, having extricated themselves from a conversation with Tinker and Drang.

"Crush blush!" Thalia said, pointing at Maya's cheeks. Her eyes went wide and her hands flew to her face.

"Ignore her," Nia said. "You're coming to Sea-a-Rama, right?" she asked Maya, who nodded, fingers still splayed over her face.

"Type in your number and address," I said, handing Maya my phone. She did, and when she handed it back, I realized that she lived just two blocks over from me. How did I not know that already?

"We're practically neighbors," I said. "I'll walk over and get you, okay?"

Maya nodded, then left the room.

"That blush on her face explains things," Mela said. "Like why Max had Maya's Rubik's Cube."

"That Max kid is on our list of suspects," Nia reminded us.

"Maybe he has a crush on her, too," Thalia offered.

"I don't know," I said. "I don't think so."

"Why? Because she isn't 'cool' enough for him?" Thalia said. She was giving me a strange look, like she was judging me for thinking that way. But the thing was, I totally thought it. Since when did Max, definitely one of the cool kids, ever care about Maya, a Grade A nerd?

"It's suspicious, that's all," I said, uncomfortable. "I mean, don't you all think so?"

Thalia sighed. "I guess so."

"We'll keep an eye out," Nia said.

"Do you think they have birds at Sea-a-Rama?" Mela asked nervously.

"It's an aquarium," I said. "I think we're good."

Tempting fate has always been one of my strengths.

Chapter 24
AN INCIDENT AT SEA-A-RAMA

Early Saturday morning, Mom and I walked over to Maya's house.

"I had no idea she lived so close by," I said, kicking at leaves on the sidewalk.

"You'd think we'd have seen her in the neighborhood," Mom mused. She was wearing shorts and a T-shirt, and from a distance, we probably looked like sisters. I said so, and she told me to stop kissing up.

We stopped in front of Maya's house. They'd put up Christmas lights, along with a plastic Santa, whose cheeks were covered with purple marker streaks. I glanced down at my phone again, double-checking the address. The lawn was overgrown, and there were a couple of strewn bicycles. "I didn't know Maya had siblings," I said, pushing the doorbell.

A man with striking blue eyes opened the door, gave us a big smile, and called out, "Maya, your friends are here," before leaving us on the porch. From the depths of the house, I could hear the sounds of at least two kids arguing over the television, while a couple more kids, teenagers by the looks of them, zoomed down a hall, their feet pounding on the hardwood floor. Maya appeared at last. She was wearing black shorts over yellow tights, and a T-shirt with an orca on it that read SAVE THE SEA PANDAS!

"Funny," I said, pointing at the shirt.

Maya crossed her arms. "Thanks. Let's go," she said, and started pushing toward the door.

"Un momento," my mom said. "Can I talk to your mom or dad first?"

"Oh, um. Sure." Maya turned around and called out, "Alicia? Mike?"

My mother looked at me with wide eyes. If I ever called my mother Gertrudis, or Trudy, she would kill me. My brothers had once called my dad "Rafael" instead of Papi and they'd gotten grounded for a week.

The woman named Alicia came to the door to greet us. She had a squirmy toddler on her hip, his little face covered in chocolate. My mom went baby-crazy at the sight of him. "Hola, nené," she murmured, and started making weird sounds with her mouth. I cleared my throat and nudged her with my foot.

"Ah, yes. I'm Callie's mom, Trudy," she said.

"Alicia," the woman said, shifting the toddler a bit to shake my mom's hand. "Maya's been staying with us for, oh, how long has it been?" she asked, searching Maya's face.

"Six months," Maya whispered.

"That's right. She's a lovely girl. Helpful." A voice called out "Aliciaaaa!" from somewhere inside the house. "Maya, you have some money on you?" she asked, and Maya nodded. "Okay, kiddo. Have fun."

My mother's eyes jumped from Maya to Alicia and back. "You mean she doesn't live here full-time?"

Alicia shook her head. "Yes. Full-time. This is a group home for older foster kids," she said, bouncing the toddler, who was now pulling her hair. "This little one is here for an emergency stay," she said, "but mostly we take in kids over ten." Alicia smiled. "Lots of love in this house," she said, and gave Maya a kiss on the cheek. "But not a lot of time. Gotta run. You have fun. Call if you need me." Then Alicia and the toddler disappeared into the house.

As soon as the door closed, my mom threw an arm around Maya's shoulder. "Sea-a-Rama, here we come!" she said. I could tell she was trying to make things cheerful, but we walked in silence almost the whole way to my house.

We came home to a shouting match.

Fernando had eaten the last of Thalia's special cereal, which her mum and dad had sent from London, and she had her hands on her hips, giving him what for.

"Have you utterly lost the plot? Or are you always a git about other people's things?" Thalia was shouting.

Fernando looked at us and tossed up his hands. There were remnants of Thalia's Cheeky-Os on his chin. "I don't understand a word this girl says," he shouted.

My mom started yelling at him about hospitality, and Mela pulled Thalia away. "It's not like you can't just get more the next time we go to—" but she stopped herself in time to see Maya cocking her head over the conversation like an attentive puppy.

"Hey, Maya," Nia said, and Maya gave a tiny wave. "Love the shirt." Nia's own shirt today had a dinosaur running from a meteor on it, and it read: DINOSAURS ARE PROOF WE NEED A SPACE PROGRAM.

"Love yours," Maya said.

My mom finished telling off my brother for being rude, packed some snacks in a bag for us, and finally we went in the van, Sea-a-Rama bound at last.

When we arrived, there were about thirty protestors gathered outside the Sea-a-Rama gates. Their signs read "Free Otto" and "Empty the Tanks!" and other things. They booed and jeered at everyone who walked past them.

"I don't think this is a good idea," my mom said, but we could see Ms. Rinse coming over to the car.

Breathless, she waited while Mom rolled down the

window. "Glad you could come. The protestors are out-side, not in the park. They're here every weekend and gone by noon," Ms. Rinse said.

My mom was making a face, the same one she always made when she watched the evening news—as if she had taken a bite out of something really gross.

"It'll be okay," I said. "Yeah," Nia, Mela, and Thalia added. Maya was very quiet. She was staring at the protes-tors, her hands clutching her cross-body purse.

"Come on, Maya," I said softly, and she shook out of it a bit.

My mom finally relented, but I know she stayed in that van and watched us until we were all safely within the park gates. I waved her off from a distance, and she put the car in drive at last.

The other members of SAP were there too, huddled around a kiosk selling bubble wands and stuffed orca toys. Max was talking to Violet, but when he saw us, he broke away from her and came to stand next to Maya.

Thalia hovered behind me, and I heard her whisper in my ear, "Violet is here? Suspicious, right?" and I nodded a little.

"What's she doing here?" I asked Max, my eyes on Vio-let. "She's not even in SAP."

"Neither were you until, like, yesterday," he shot back, and it was true. I glanced over his shoulder and caught Violet glaring at us.

"She wanted to come, that's all," he said.

"What about Raquel?" I asked softly. I hated that I had to ask. Normally, I'd know exactly what Raquel was up to on the weekends.

Max raised an eyebrow. "She's in Los Angeles again," he said.

"Okay," Ms. Rinse said, "the park is yours." She handed out park maps. "We will all meet in the food court at noon for lunch and share what we've learned."

The first thing I noticed about the park was how much painted white concrete there was everywhere. Planters and benches and tables, all made of the stuff. White concrete–encased glass tanks filled with eels and puffer fish. There were so many layers of paint on everything that it chipped off like confetti, littering the ground.

We could hear the barking of sea lions in the distance, but we headed left, guided by Nia, who held the park map up before her like she was an explorer.

"The main event has got to be the killer whale show, right?" she said. I heard her ask, "What do you call a pod of musical whales?" When nobody answered her, she turned around and said, "An ORCA-stra! Get it?"

"My job. Jokes are *my* job, Nia," Thalia said. Nia laughed, ignoring her as she led the way, and chattering on about how orcas were actually a kind of dolphin but nobody ever called them that. Thalia and Mela walked up front, followed by Maya. And Max. Max and Maya. Talking quietly together.

I watched them anxiously. First Violet showed up on the field trip when she wasn't even in the club, and now Max was all cozy with Maya. Maybe it was just a coincidence.

I brought up the rear. Alone. We passed by one of those wax toy machines. This one made a wax penguin. I wanted to stop, quarters jangling in my pocket. But the others didn't wait for me.

They seemed so happy. Nia was in science la-la-land, going on about the intelligence of dolphins, Thalia and Mela had happily donned tank tops and flip-flops, every inch the tourist, and now it looked like Maya had a . . . boyfriend?

I had never felt so left out. I checked my messages for anything from Raquel, but there was nothing. The longer Raquel and I didn't talk or text, the more I felt as if maybe I'd never have a real friend again, as if having her for a best friend had just been dumb luck.

I toyed with my bracelet as we walked, tempted to whisper into it, if only to alleviate my lonesomeness. Would Tomiko respond? Maybe she was in one of her college classes and would get mad. Elnaz, perhaps? Someone had left a juice pouch on the ground, and I crushed it with my heel, walked on, paused, and returned to pick it up and throw it away.

When I rose, trash in hand, I caught Violet standing there, a smirk on her face. "It's empty. Can't suck any more juice out of it if you tried," she said.

"It's not mine. I was throwing it away," I said. The others were getting farther away from me, chatting among themselves. I looked in their direction.

"Sure, sure. Abandoned by your friends?" Violet asked.

"Same as you," I said. And it was true. Usually, where Violet was, Max was, too. That seemed to have changed in the last few days, though.

Violet flinched as if I'd hit her. But the moment passed, and she sniffed and looked at her watch. "Whale show in ten. Let's go. I hear you can get soaked if you sit in the first row," she said.

Which is how I ended up walking through Sea-a-Rama with Violet Prado.

"Max and Maya, huh?" I asked. Maybe Violet had the scoop.

Violet shrugged. "I don't get it. He says she's interesting. He's just hoping she'll help him with his science project next year, that's what I think," she said, but the way she said it suggested she didn't quite believe it.

I watched as Max bumped Maya with his hip, sending her staggering a little. She laughed and bumped him back.

"That's flirting," I said. I hadn't really had any crushes yet, not beyond Jordan Miguel, anyway. But I was pretty sure Max and Maya were doing that flirting thing, because it made my stomach all fluttery to watch. Violet had had a boyfriend in the fifth grade, a kid named Guillermo Diaz, and I remember how we had all watched them at the end-of-the-year dance. Only three pairs of fifth graders had participated in the slow dance, and you could reach out and touch the relief in the room when the DJ went back to playing reggaeton and hip-hop.

"Max? Flirting with Maya?" Violet scoffed. She was quiet after that, and I could tell watching Max and Maya together was bothering her. "He's my best friend," she said at last.

"I know what you mean," I said, thinking of Raquel. I expected her to tell me to shut up, but she didn't. Violet only nodded in solidarity.

"Raquel misses hanging out with you, in case you were wondering," Violet said.

"She has a funny way of showing it," I told her.

Violet only shrugged. "Believe me or don't. I don't care."

After that, I made a mental note to scratch Violet off our suspect list. A siren wouldn't be this human.

"So what's up with the new girls? They are *so* weird," Violet said after a while, interrupting my train of thought.

"I like them just fine. Thalia is funny and Nia is so smart. Mela tells the best stories. Tomiko and Elnaz are so cool, I wish I—"

"Who? How many people you got living with you, Callie?" Violet asked.

I gasped. I was *so* not good at this secret identity thing. "Nobody. I mean, besides my mom and brothers. And the muse—I mean, the girls. They're just, wow, hey look!

We're here," I said, pointing at the entrance to the killer whale stadium.

It was, like the rest of Sea-a-Rama, a concrete structure, blindingly white in the sun. A blue-sequined sign read "OTTO THE ORCA" in ten-foot letters over an oval pool. Pelicans sat peacefully on the sign, their saggy gullets twitching in the breeze. The place smelled powerfully of fish. The back wall of the tank wasn't glass, but rather, it was a gate that led out to the bay. A black dorsal fin pierced the water and drew circles on the surface.

The stadium was made up of aluminum benches. We all took our seats in the "Splash Zone," aka the front row. A smattering of tourists sat throughout the rest of the stadium.

Violet and I sat at the end of one of the rows, and she kept arching her neck to watch Max and Maya. "I don't get it," she said at last. "She's such a freak."

"She's not," I said. "She's going to do great things one day, just you wait."

"Oh yeah?" Violet said. "You mean to tell me *that* is not freaky behavior?"

I was almost afraid to look.

Maya had left her seat and was now nose-to-nose with Otto the orca through the thick glass of the tank. She had both palms on the tank and was talking quietly to herself. I rose and joined the muses.

"Budge over," I said, and they did. Nia had whipped out

her phone and opened up her kódikas app.

"This isn't right. This is definitely not right. That tank is way too small for that animal," she said, an edge growing in her voice.

"Look at his dorsal fin. Is it supposed to be all floppy like that?" Mela said. She was right, Otto's fin wasn't standing up the way it should. It was dog-eared, the tip touching his back instead of pointing to the sky.

"There is nothing funny about this at all," Thalia was saying.

"The protestors," Max said suddenly, and we all jumped. I didn't know he'd been listening to us. "That's what they're protesting. Otto's treatment. And they're right." He got to his feet.

"We need to do something," Nia said.

Thalia and Mela nodded in unison.

My scalp was buzzing, as if a thousand caterpillars were crawling on it.

"Girls," I said, but the other muses weren't listening.

That's when I heard them—the pelicans on the sign, three of them, screeching, sounding a lot like angry ducks, their bills opening and closing, clacking together loudly.

Nia was on her feet now, too, and she skipped down the steps to join Maya at the tank wall. They were talking furiously, pointing all around the tank. The trainer, who had been gathering tiny, limp fish into a bucket for the orca, was now laughing hysterically to herself for no clear reason at all. My eyes slid over to Thalia, who was staring at the trainer, her lips twitching into a smile.

"Thalia?" I asked, and touched her shoulder, but she brushed my hand off, hard, her eyes never leaving the trainer, who was now so distracted with her own laughter that she didn't notice Nia and Maya over by the tank.

Mela was on her feet, bouncing up and down, mumbling, "His little fin. It's so sad. He's trapped there," as her eyes filled with tears. Another trainer, who had been hanging up a wet suit, started sobbing into his hands. I grabbed on to Mela's arm, showed her the earplugs in the palm of my hand, and then plugged my ears. I pointed at the pelicans. Mela's eyes opened wide. She dug out her own earplugs, and then searched through Thalia's purse to find hers. When she found them at last, they were covered in chewing gum. She popped them into Thalia's ears anyway, startling her and breaking her concentration on the trainer, who quit laughing at once.

The three of us ran to the others. "Nia, your earplugs," I said, but when she turned to look at me, I took a giant step backward.

Nia's eyes, usually deep brown, were blazing, the irises golden, her pupils huge. "Save Otto!" she shouted into my face. Maya was still nose-to-nose with the tank, and the tips of her fingers were purple where she'd splayed them on the glass.

Shaken, I turned my attention to Maya. "Come on,

Maya. Come on. Let's go," I kept saying, but she would not move.

I concentrated my feelings, felt the numbness in my hands, and said again, "Maya, come with me," as forcefully as I could, but this time, instead of feeling the muse magic coursing through me, I felt . . . weak. My eyes focused on the back gate and not on Maya.

If it had a lock, then it could be opened.

And if it could be opened, then Otto would be free. Free of this too-small tank. Free to go anywhere he pleased. He wouldn't have to live in a too-small house. He would be fast and gorgeous and not fat at all. His parents would still be together and his best friend would be his best friend again and . . . and . . .

I stopped and looked down. I was no longer in the spot where I had been, but rather, I was standing with Maya and the other muses on the ramp that led to the back of the tank. How had our feet taken us here so quickly?

In the distance, a couple of trainers in wet suits were headed our way. In the stands, Violet and Max were on their feet, mouthing the words *Go, go, go.* Maybe they were shouting. I couldn't hear them.

The pelicans were above us now, diving into the water every so often. Otto was on the move too, circling the tank faster and faster, creating a whirlpool. The pelicans screeched, and it sounded like they were saying, "Dive in. The water's warm."

I felt dizzy, different from the last time the sirens had attacked.

Nia's voice cut through the fog. "Save Otto," she was shouting into my ear and into Maya's, shouting it to people in the audience, to her own reflection in the water.

Suddenly, I remembered what Tomiko had said back during our training session, how Nia had the power to inspire an idea, how she could encourage someone to jump off a building if she wanted to. I remembered looking out the window, imagining a body falling, falling . . .

"Nia! Stop it!" I said at last, and yanked her arm so hard that I almost fell into the tank.

Maya was now dipping her toe into the tank, the top of her sneaker getting wet. Mela seemed to wake up the same moment I did, and she grabbed Maya in a bear hug and pulled her back, both of them tumbling off the ramp and onto the ground below.

"Rule number three, a muse never uses her magic against her sisters!" Thalia was now saying, "Never, Nia!"

The pelicans barked at us. I thought I saw the glimmer of teeth.

Both things were happening at once—siren magic *and* muse magic. Nia's muse magic, in fact. She'd taken one look at that whale and inspired all of us to set it free. In the name of science, of course.

Otto was now just a few feet away. He seemed to be peering at us with one giant eye. Opening his mouth, he revealed a row of sharp white teeth and the largest, pinkest tongue I've ever seen. With one abrupt thrust of his jaw he sent gallons of water in our direction.

We might as well have jumped in the tank, we were that wet. Above us, the pelicans had gotten drenched too, and they shrieked off across the bay.

Nia coughed. She looked all around her, as if she was surprised to find herself on the ramp. "Did that whale just *spit* on me?" she asked. Her eyes were deep brown again.

I hugged her hard. Thalia did, too. "You're back," I said.

"Never do that again," Thalia said. Nia looked shaky, and in fact, her hands were trembling.

"To think, you didn't even need your app this time," Mela said.

Nia tried to smile, but grimaced instead.

But she was okay. The orca was still in his too-small tank, the tourists were staring at us with open mouths, and we were very glad it was over.

That is, until the trainers reached us, escorted us down the ramp, and handed us all over to Sea-a-Rama's security guards.

Chapter 25
THE MUSE COUNCIL

Maya, Mela, Thalia, Nia, and I were taken to an office behind the Sea-a-Rama gift shop. They made us sit on a wooden bench with a single pair of metal handcuffs attached to it, but they didn't bother trying to put them on one of us.

"This is where they put shoplifters," Maya said darkly.

"We tried to steal a whale, so it makes sense," Mela said.

"It's a dolphin, not a whale," Maya added.

"I can't believe they put us in Whale Jail," Thalia said.

Nia was leaning forward, her hands over her face. "I'm sorry," she mumbled into her palms. "I don't know what got into me."

"I do. Siren song," Thalia said, and I coughed loudly.

Maya wasn't fooled though. "Sirens?" she asked.

"Inside joke," I said, and Maya's face fell a little.

I wondered how often she felt that way—excluded. It didn't feel good. I thought about all the times I had excluded her in the past, like when we were picking teams in PE, or choosing a table in the cafetorium at lunchtime. A pang of guilt made my stomach flip.

"Not just that," Nia said. "It was me, too. I was so angry about Otto. It's not right how they keep him there. I lost focus," she said, her eyes falling on Maya.

Suddenly, Ms. Rinse opened the door, followed by a man in a suit. My whole body went cold. "Girls," she said. "You cannot understand the depth of my disappointment. There will be consequences for all of you, not the least of which," she paused dramatically here and looked at each of us in turn, "not the least of which is that I'm disqualifying Maya from the county science fair."

"No!" we all shouted at once, except for Maya, who only slumped in her seat.

"Aaaaaaaand," Ms. Rinse said, her hands on her hips now, "you all have detention with Ms. Fovos for two weeks. You're lucky that Mr. Dale here isn't pressing charges."

"Now, now." Mr. Dale spoke up at last, but didn't add anything else, as if "now, now" was all he could muster in the moment. He had on a name tag that read MANAGER.

"Please, Ms. Rinse. Detention is fine, but don't disqualify Maya. She's a scientist. The world needs her," I said, focusing hard on the teacher, waiting for that tingling sensation that told me I was drawing on muse magic, hoping to inspire Ms. Rinse to relent.

She stared at me for a moment, faltering. "Well," she began to say, then shook her head. "My mind is made up."

I concentrated on my hands, and yes, there it was, that strange buzzing sensation. Except it hadn't really worked. It was as if my kódikas had been put on a dimmer switch. I glanced out the window and scanned the sky for birds, but it was blue and empty. I felt a little nauseous. Maybe I was catching something.

Meanwhile, Mr. Dale had started pacing the room strangely, twirling the pen faster and faster, as if he were deep in thought.

Ms. Rinse called out to him. "Mr. Dale? Mr. Dale? Are you all right?"

But Mr. Dale waved her off. "I'm thinking," he said, then started to chew on the pen as he paced.

"What about Otto?" Nia asked. She was sitting up very straight, her hands in her lap, rubbing them together hard. Beads of sweat formed on her upper lip. She chewed on the inside of her cheek. Nia was using her muse magic again, tapping her kódikas without an app to summon it.

Mr. Dale stopped. "That's what I'm considering, young lady. Your passion today has . . . inspired me. We need to find a solution for Otto. Find a way to return him to his pod in the Pacific."

Nia was doing it. She was tapping into Mr. Dale's scientific mind. She was saving Otto!

But why couldn't I inspire Ms. Rinse? Had something gone wrong with my muse magic?

Mr. Dale shook our hands, one by one, and paused before Maya. "I once attended the county science fair. It was the highlight of my childhood. Ms. Rinse, don't deny this young woman the chance of it," he said without actually looking at her.

Ms. Rinse sputtered. "B-but there should be a punishment."

"To fit the crime, yes," Mr. Dale said. "Your punishment is the time you've already served here, in, um—" He paused.

"Whale Jail!" Thalia supplied, and Mr. Dale laughed.

"Yes. That's right. Whale Jail. You've been punished and now you're free to go," he said, a happy twinkle in his eyes. "Now, about Otto . . ." He muttered to himself as he left the room.

Ms. Rinse narrowed her eyes at us. "You got lucky, all of you," she said, and we followed her out of the back room. "Another misstep, Maya Rivero, and you're not going to the county science fair. I expect to see you at lunch. Try not to get arrested," she added, and left us on our own.

At once, we all faced Nia, who was smiling. "You did it," I said, giving her a hug.

"Did what?" Maya asked. Her arms were crossed and she looked angry. "Something is going on and you guys aren't telling me. What happened at the tank was—it was bizarre. I don't know why we aren't sitting in *actual jail* right now."

"April fools!" Thalia said.

"It's December," Maya said.

"Nothing's going on, Maya," I said. "But close call, huh?"

We heard a sharp knock at the window behind us. Letty, Lisa, and Leo were tapping on the glass with a coffee cup. "We're here to break you out!" Letty said, her voice muffled.

"We saw what you did back there! Incredible!" Lisa shouted.

"I love whales!" Leo added.

Lisa raised her cup and aimed at the window.

"No!" we all shouted at once and the siblings stopped in their tracks.

"No?" they asked in unison.

"NO," we shouted again.

They shrugged and walked away, toward the coffee shop next door.

"It's the caffeine, right?" Thalia said. "It's made them nutty."

We laughed, but Maya didn't. Her arms were still tightly crossed. "So you aren't telling me anything then?" Her voice was shaky.

"Maya, seriously, nothing is—" I started to say.

Maya sucked her teeth. Her eyes were watery. "Whatever," she interrupted. "I'm going to the bathroom." Then she wound her way out of the gift shop toward the rest-rooms.

We waited for her to leave before speaking. "Totally redeemed yourself," Thalia finally said to Nia, lightly punching her arm.

"Not by a mile."

We froze. None of us had said that.

The voice was disembodied, familiar, and coming from our jewelry.

Clio.

"Get to headquarters immediately. Your temporary entrance point is the slide in the Pirate's Playground."

Mela uttered a curse word under her breath and, with that, we headed out, ready to walk the plank.

The Pirate's Playground was next to the dolphin show, and we could hear their clicks and squeals, and the applause from the audience, as we climbed into the play equipment. The slide was a dark tube.

"I wonder where we'll pop out on the other side?" Thalia asked, before plunging in. We all watched the other end of the slide, waited a moment, and sighed when she didn't emerge.

"I suppose it works as advertised," Mela said, then slid into the tube herself.

Silently, Nia sat and pushed off. "This is so messed up."

Then it was just me. The last muse. I took a deep breath of the salty air. A sea lion growled. I looked out and saw

Maya wandering about with a map of Sea-a-Rama in her hands. It didn't seem fair that we had to keep her in the dark. Her head started to move in my direction, and I yelped, then flung myself into the slide before she could see me.

It felt like I was sliding in the darkness for a long time, the heat in Miami giving way to cool, damp air. When I tumbled out, I found myself inside a different kind of tunnel—with smooth stone walls and a light ahead. I followed the light until the tunnel opened up into a square room without windows. The walls were painted in hieroglyphics and a tall sarcophagus sat in one corner.

The elder muses—Paola, Etoro, and Clio—were seated in plastic chairs at the front of the room. Tomiko and Elnaz sat off to the side. And in the center of the room, on three stools, were Nia, Mela, and Thalia. Nobody spoke, so I took the remaining stool, which wobbled on its three legs.

There we were, all nine of us, silent in a dark tomb.

"It's not a real tomb," Clio said, as if reading my mind again. "It's the new exhibition—Designing Egypt. Not open to the public yet. Very convenient for these proceedings."

"Proceedings?" I asked, but got no answer.

Paola spoke next, her accent warm and familiar. But the words coming out of her mouth were less so. "To be a muse is a privilege. We are powerful beings, and the temptation to abuse such power is very great. Too great for some."

"Worse yet," Etoro said, "is when we turn that power

against one another. Our magic derives from love and understanding, which necessitate patience."

"Art cannot be rushed," Clio said. "Ideas cannot be rushed. Solutions to problems cannot be rushed. Our magic is meant to nudge, not push."

"I didn't—" Nia began to say.

"You shoved. You impelled the others in order to get your way," Clio said heatedly.

"To save Otto," Nia argued, her voice shaking.

Tomiko cleared her throat, obviously nervous about this role as elder muse. "Had you opened the gate, Otto would be as good as dead. He would have no family there. He would have performed his tricks in the bay alone, used to the schedule of his days, hungry for food he doesn't know how to hunt for. Reacclimating him to the open ocean would take time, and teams of scientists."

"But Mr. Dale said that he would find a way for Otto to be free," Thalia put in.

"Nevertheless," Elnaz now spoke, "it could have been disastrous had you succeeded."

"Not to mention Maya," Clio said. "You four almost managed to lose a Fated One today."

"But the sirens," Mela said. "There were pelicans."

"We know, how horrible," Etoro said, genuinely, kindly. "And yet you were too distracted to deal with them."

We were in so much trouble. My eyes hurt because I wanted to cry, and I couldn't look up at the muses. Instead,

I stared at the base of the sarcophagus, wishing I could hide inside for an eternity.

"Muses have been stripped of their magic in the past," Clio said.

I heard Mela make a little shocked noise. Thalia began to swing her legs back and forth. Nia covered her face with her hands and leaned forward, like she was going to puke. I just stared at the sarcophagus some more. *Move over, mummy,* I thought. *Make room for us.*

"Either they've abused their powers or gone to the searchlights. The reasons have varied."

I jumped in my seat. "What did you say?" I asked Clio.

"I said the reasons have varied."

"Before that," I demanded. She'd said something about . . . about searchlights. Where had I heard that before?

Nostrils flaring, Clio sighed and rose from her seat. "Your communications items," she said.

"Is that what they're called?" Thalia said, pulling off her ring. Nia removed her necklace, and Mela took her ring off, too. I struggled with my bracelet, the latch glued on and very much stuck. Clio collected everyone's things and stood before me, waiting.

"I can't," I said. "My mom superglued it."

Etoro hid a snicker with her hands, and Paola looked away.

"What is with your family?" Clio said. "Annie glued that latch together, too."

I shrugged. "I don't know. We're paranoid about losing things? We like glue?" I joked only because I was so nervous and sad. Were we being kicked out forever? Sent to the searchlights, whatever that meant?

"You're all suspended temporarily until we decide what to do with you. Tomiko, Elnaz, Maya Rivero is now assigned to you. Mela, Thalia, and Nia, you will return home immediately. Your parents are expecting you. When and if it's time to come to headquarters, I will let you know. That's a big *if*, by the way. You may exit via your regular entrance points."

Mela was crying in earnest now. "What about our classes in Miami? Can't we say goodbye to Callie's mom?"

"It's sorted," Clio said with finality.

Thalia was crying now too, no jokes in sight.

Nia kept whispering, "I'm sorry, it's all my fault."

We rose, eager to leave the tomb, when Clio said, "Calliope. You stay. Everyone else is dismissed."

The muses filed out until it was just me and Clio. Our voices echoed when we spoke.

"What happened?" Clio asked.

"It's like they said. Nia got upset about the whale's tank. There were sirens. Muse magic and siren song got all mashed up. It was too powerful for us. We lost control."

"Too powerful. Got it," Clio said, and started to wander around the perimeter of the room, her fingers trailing over the hieroglyphics. Her hand dropped toward a small hole in one of the walls. She put her thumb inside, then pulled, and the wall moved forward, revealing a hidden door. "Emergency exit. Come."

We exited the Designing Egypt exhibit altogether, and wound our way up to a room that was filled with clocks of every size.

"It's my favorite room in the museum," Clio said. There were cuckoo clocks, and clocks covered in diamonds and rubies. Another clock was a golden ship with actual working cannons, and another was a silver swan that unfurled its metallic feathers on the hour. Clio led me to a tall clock in the corner. It was a globe, held aloft by nine bronze figures.

"Muses, all nine," she pointed out. "Whenever a muse uses her magic for the first time, the globe on top spins. It stops in the place where the muse can be found."

I looked closely at the globe, and there was an arrow, set into the globe with a blue stone, stopped right on the tip of Florida.

"So that's how you knew to come get me. Because of what happened that night on the Metrorail."

"Indeed. It spun so fast for you, in fact, that it did not stop revolving for a full eight hours."

"Is that weird or something?" I asked.

"Unheard of, Callie," Clio said quietly.

I had a sinking feeling. "So the clock is broken? Am I not supposed to do this muse thing?" The others were temporarily suspended. Was I about to be permanently kicked out?

Clio gently touched the shiny surface of the globe. "The clock isn't broken. It merely recognized the power in you. Callie, you're the strongest among us. We are vessels of inspiration, but you, those you inspire, they change, don't they?" Clio leaned gingerly against a case holding dozens of pocket watches. "They change . . . physically."

I thought of Raquel getting taller, of Maya's lisp, now gone. I nodded.

Clio exhaled. "Remember Odysseus? How he was tied to a mast so that the sirens couldn't force him to crash his ship?"

I nodded.

"Later in the story, right before he comes back to his family again, the goddess Athena changes his appearance. First, she makes him a beggar so that he can sneak into his castle. Then she returns his youth to him, curling his hair and making him taller." Clio drummed her fingers on the globe. "There's more goddess in you than in the rest of us."

I touched the globe. It hummed underneath my fingertips. "I don't see how that could be true, Clio. Look at me. I'm just a kid," I whispered.

Clio reached out and brushed a lock of hair out of my eyes. Then she spun the globe softly and stopped when her finger landed over Greece. "Mount Olympus is here," she said, touching it lightly. "But you can't just hike up to the top and find the gods. Especially nowadays. Even so, we know that your aunt made a visit just before we learned she was sick. She told me afterward, but she refused to reveal what she'd learned there. You being here, being you, might have something to do with that visit."

"Oh," I said. What had Tia Annie known? What had she *done*?

"I'm afraid I've given you too much responsibility, too soon." Clio gave the globe another little spin, and it rattled around its axis, landing again with the arrow pointed at Miami. "There have been other muses who couldn't manage it. Lost Muses, we call them."

"They go to the searchlights," I said, and held my breath.

Clio seemed to be holding her breath, too. "Sometimes they do. But they shouldn't."

"I don't know what that means," I whispered.

"When a muse is no longer using her powers to inspire others, when she uses them for herself—that's the worst thing we can do with our gifts. Ambition. Selfishness. Anger. Nia came close to it, today. And you all aided her."

I felt myself growing angry. "Nia was right. Otto the whale needed help. And in the end, he's going to get it because of us," I told Clio.

"The four of you acted out of your own desire," Clio said.

"So what we want doesn't matter? What we want

doesn't count?" I asked. "I'm pretty sure, by the way, that Otto wanted out of that stupid, tiny tank," I went on.

A teenager wandered into the clock gallery, and I stopped talking. He was gazing into his phone. Clio took one look at him and he froze in place, his mouth parted, his finger touching the screen mid-scroll. She walked over and plucked the phone from his hand.

"Take it," she said, handing it to me. "I've seen your phone. It's, what do the kids say, 'busted'? This one is new, see?"

"It's not mine," I said, confused. The teenager stared into his empty hand so oddly.

"Don't you want it?" she asked.

"No. I mean, yes. But not his. I'll get a new phone, eventually. Maybe Christmas. Why are you doing this?"

Clio returned the phone to the teenager's hand, delicately placing his finger in the right spot on the screen again. She released him, and he walked through the gallery, barely giving us a glance.

"Then you clearly know the difference between using your magic to act on a desire and waiting for the moment when you won't need magic to achieve it," Clio said.

"It's not the same thing. What we did at Sea-a-Rama was good for everyone," I said, quietly this time, unsure even as I spoke.

"We aren't superheroes. We aren't genies. We can't solve every problem. But when we focus we can be effective.

The success of the Fated Ones can move mountains, but it requires patience from us. Patience that is derived out of love and understanding."

I hadn't realized that I had stopped breathing as Clio spoke, and when she was done, I gasped for air. "That's what Etoro said."

"And Etoro is right. As always."

"Clio, please don't assign Maya to someone else. I can do it."

Clio shook her head. "Love and understanding, Callie. Without it, your magic won't be strong enough." I stared at my shoes, and felt Clio's hand on my wrist as she unlatched my bracelet with a yank. I gasped again.

"Off to the bed," she told me. "I'll be in touch."

"Okay," I said, though I was pretty far from okay. In tears, I made my way to the Great Bed, slipped underneath, and looked around before closing my eyes.

I couldn't concentrate. I stared at the cases filled with old things, at the leaded windows, at London outside, and said goodbye to all of it.

I let my eyes close at last, then tumbled out the other end of the slide at the Pirate's Playground.

Slamming straight into Maya Rivero.

Chapter 26
GETTING TO KNOW MAYA

"How did you *do* that?" Maya asked, peering past me and up into the slide's tube.

"Do what?" I climbed out of the slide, dusted the tops of my jeans, and tried to walk past her.

"I saw you go down the slide, and then you got sort of . . . stuck. I went to help and you weren't in there. I blinked, and then you were back. Is it a trapdoor or something?" Maya asked, starting to climb up the slide.

Think, Callie, think.

"No, of course not. I saw you. Waved and everything. You looked right through me. So rude," I said, and curled my lip at her, pretending to be put off.

"I didn't. You weren't—"

I waved her off. "No worries, Maya. Probably a trick of the light. It's so sunny. Soda?" I asked, and shook my purse in front of her, the coins inside jangling.

Maya nodded, confusion still playing like shadows on her face. "Sure," she said, and the two of us walked over to a soda machine a few feet away. I bought us each a drink, and we sat down on a picnic table under a flamboyán tree that kept dropping its tiny red blossoms on us as we talked.

She hadn't asked about the others yet. I wondered . . .

"Hey, Maya. Nia was really upset about Otto," I said.

Confusion on her face again. "Who's Nia?" she asked.

I took a deep breath. It was like the Muse Squad had never been in Miami. I thought of my room, of the empty bunk beds, and my hands trembled a little.

"Oh, sorry. Nia is one of the protestors. We chatted earlier today," I said, and took a sip of soda.

"It is sad though, about the orca, taken from his family as a calf probably. Stuck here. Sort of like me, I guess," Maya said softly.

I gulped. I thought of her house just two blocks from mine, with all those kids in it. "The people you live with? What about them?" I prompted.

"Alicia and Mike, they're my foster parents. They're really nice. Nicer than others I've stayed with. I didn't have much family to begin with. My mom lost custody of me when I was a baby. My dad, he's a human question mark. I don't know a thing about him. My abuelita raised me. She was from Ecuador. She used to say she wished she could take me to see the place where she grew up. But she was old, you know, and old people, they, they . . ." Maya trailed off, and started lifting the tab on her soda can back and forth until it popped off.

"I get it," I said. I didn't want to talk about Tia Annie with anyone either. I didn't want to say "dead," even if it had already happened, even if uttering it didn't make a difference either way.

And I definitely didn't want to talk about dads who dropped out of your life when you needed them most.

Maya looked off toward the Penguin Encounter exhibit, with its faux glacier sticking up out of the earth, flanked by palm trees. Someone in a penguin costume was waddling around outside and kept waving at us with a fuzzy flipper.

"This place is nuts," I said, trying to break the tension.

"*So* nuts," Maya said, and we laughed a little. Maya sat thoughtfully, staring into the void of her soda can, as if she could see something inside other than carbonated sugar water. "The world is nuts. But I'm gonna make it better, Callie," she said, and when she looked at me, I saw a fierceness in her eyes that I hadn't seen before.

"I believe you," I said.

Maya and I spent the rest of the day together. Between us, we got four wax figures—two sea lions, a penguin, and a shark. We watched the dolphin show, rode a paddleboat, petted a tortoise, all the while sweating like crazy in the blazing heat. We didn't run into Max or Violet again, though I could tell Maya was looking for them, her eyes scanning the paths for a tall, handsome Haitian boy. I kept turning around myself, half expecting Thalia to be there, or Mela, or Nia, but each time, it was just my own shadow playing tricks on me.

My mom picked me and Maya up right on time. Ms. Rinse was there to check us off her list. I stole a glance at it and yep, no Thalia, Mela, or Nia anywhere on her roster. Clio had been very thorough indeed.

In the distance, Max and Violet were waiting for their ride. Max saw us, and he waved at Maya, grinning. Violet huffed and crossed her arms.

"I saw that," I said, pointing at Maya's blushing cheeks.

"Stop it," she whispered, smiling, and scooted into the backseat of my mom's van.

"Did you have fun?" my mom asked, handing us each a granola bar and a juice pouch. My mom was a big believer in what she called "getting ahead of the hangry beasts" she claimed lived inside all kids who missed a meal or snack time.

"Yep," I said, and stuffed my face. I really was hungry. Getting kicked out of a mythical super group can do that to a person.

Maya ate quietly. I knew I wasn't supposed to be doing muse business anymore, but since I had her with me, and since I might not get the chance again, I asked, "Has Max given you any gifts? Like, tokens of affection?"

"Oh my God, no," Maya said.

"No small boxes, yea big?" I asked, demonstrating with my hands.

Maya laughed. "I'd forgotten. Yeah, he totally did. Inside was a forty-carat diamond and we are getting married tomorrow. You're invited. Be my maid of honor, please?" Then she elbowed me lightly. "You're so weird, Callie," she said lovingly, still laughing. "Max is just a friend. And even if he wanted to be my boyfriend, which he doesn't, I am so not ready for that. Are you?"

I shook my head. Nope. Part of me still thought boys were gross. Part of me, at least. "I'm eleven. Ask me again when I'm fourteen or something," I said, and took another bite of my granola bar.

We walked Maya to her front door. My mom greeted Alicia, and then, in classic Trudy-style, invited herself in. "We are neighbors, no? And I can lend a hand with this one," she said, and lifted the wailing toddler out of Alicia's arms. Alicia, for her part, seemed sort of relieved.

"Maya, why don't you show Callie your room?" Alicia offered, and so we went.

Maya's room was actually in the center of the house, surrounded on all sides by French doors with glass inserts. "This used to be a dining room," she said, closing the doors. They had pink curtains on them, but didn't block out much of the noise from the rest of the house. Once she closed the doors, though, the effect was sort of magical, like living inside a genie bottle. I told her so.

"If only I could make wishes come true," she said with a small smile. One of the doors was permanently closed, and an overstuffed bookcase rested against it. Beside the bookcase was a dollhouse, exactly like the one I had at home. "My abuela gave it to me," Maya said.

"I have a dollhouse just like this. I mean, I don't play with it anymore, but yeah. Loved that toy," I said. I sat before it, and started arranging the plastic furniture inside. "I liked to put the fireplace in the bedroom. Felt like a cozy thing to do."

"Bad move," Maya said, sitting next to me. "Carbon monoxide poisoning—it'll kill you in your sleep," she said, and slid the little fireplace to the living room.

"Right," I said, and set out tiny dishes on a dining table.

Maya opened up the windows on the house, and birdsong piped through tiny speakers. The batteries on the little house were still good! Mine had corroded ages ago. "Does Raquel live nearby, too?" Maya asked as she moved things about. "I always figured she did, since you two are best friends."

"We aren't even regular friends anymore, forget 'best,'" I said, switching on the minuscule lamp in the nursery room with my thumbnail.

"No wonder you've been wanting to hang out with me," Maya said.

I stopped. Faced Maya. "It's not that."

"It is. I understand. You'll be friends again, I'll bet. Once all this *America's Next Star* stuff dies down."

"And if it doesn't?" I asked.

Maya nudged me. "I'm not going anywhere. Age eleven. I'm super hard to adopt, and Alicia and Mike said I could stay until I age out."

"Age out?" I asked.

"Turn eighteen. Then I'm on my own," she said, setting a tiny watering can on a teeny coffee table.

We stopped talking after that.

We played for an hour, like I used to do when I was little, and the world fell away around me until the only thing that was real was that dollhouse and the people in it. I played the dad and the little sister, and Maya played the mom and brother. We gave them disgusting names—Mr. and Mrs. Caca-head, and the siblings, Moco and Puke. We had them making Christmas Eve dinner and playing hide-and-seek, and putting the baby, Little Mildew, to bed in her fluffy pink crib.

It was really fun, I gotta say.

And when Alicia and my mom knocked on one of the glass panes and opened a door, Maya and I were both startled out of the world we had made, and my throat constricted.

"See you at school," I said, and gave Maya a hug.

"Bye, Callie. Don't forget. County science fair soon."

"I won't forget. I promise," I said, and Maya looked so relieved that I almost hugged her again.

My mom and I were silent on the way home. Her brow was furrowed, the way it always gets when she's thinking up something big. Inside the house, my brothers were playing video games, as usual. I said hi, but they ignored me, so I headed straight to my room.

The bunk beds were gone, as if they had never been there.

In its place was my old dollhouse.

I sat down in front of it, stretched my hands into the little kitchen.

And I played.

Chapter 27
LETTING GO

I had a hard time sleeping now that the others weren't there. Without Mela sniffling, and Thalia tossing and turning, and Nia messing with her astronomy app, which lit up my room in a blue glow, I couldn't seem to rest.

The county science fair was fast approaching, and if I had learned anything about the sirens, it was that they were bound to ruin Maya's chances of changing the world someday.

There were other things going on, too.

Like, Tomiko and Elnaz had shown up in school, posing as teachers-in-training from the University of Miami. Tomiko's hair was no longer orange. Elnaz didn't hide her strange blue and brown eyes, but her ponytail was gone, traded for loose waves and a demure headband that always matched her outfit. And what a coincidence, they were both in all my classes with Maya, keeping an eye on us.

I sidled up to Tomiko during lunch, carrying my tray with a bowl full of mac and cheese. "You should know," I whispered into her ear, "that there's a boy named Max, who I don't trust entirely, hanging around Maya a lot. And his friend, Violet. I think she's okay, but you might want to check on her anyway, just in case. And definitely, definitely check on Ms. Fovos. She has to be evil. *Has to be*." I said it all so fast that I was out of breath when I finished. Then I swallowed hard. "How's the Muse Squa— I mean, the other girls?"

Tomiko looked at me, her glittering eyes scanning my own for a full three seconds before she told me to go sit down, threatening detention so loudly that Violet snickered and stuck her tongue out at me.

"Tomiko," I pleaded.

"Ms. Miura to you," she said, loudly again. "Now sit."

Which I did, my hands balled up into fists. How were they supposed to protect Maya if they didn't know anything about life at Miami Palms Middle, about the people around Maya, about the county science fair or SAP? Did they even know she lived in a group home? That in just seven years, she'd have nowhere to go?

Another video of Raquel played at lunch. In the video, she and her fellow contestants were at a movie premiere. She wore a blue dress and silver heels, which sparkled against a red carpet. Someone put a mic in front of her face. "Hi!" she said to the camera, and a bunch of kids in the cafetorium said, "Hi!" back. I looked at her usual seat. Empty. I hadn't gotten a text from her in two weeks. I sighed and ate my cold mac and cheese alone.

As for Elnaz, I caught up with her in the teachers' parking lot one afternoon. "Listen, Elnaz," I said, holding on to her sleeve. "I know I'm in trouble. I'm suspended, got it. But I'm going to that science fair whether you like it or not, and I'm going to protect Maya." My knees almost buckled as I spoke, and I could hear my voice quivering. I don't know why I was so afraid. What did I have to lose anyway?

Elnaz cocked her head to the side, considering me. "Just don't get in the way, kiddo," she said, ruffled my hair, and walked off. My scalp tingled at her touch. I wanted nothing more than to make her stop, drop, and start writing haikus on the sidewalk with the chalk I spotted in her pocket.

But a muse never uses her magic against her sisters. Rule number three.

I could feel the hair on my head lifting a little with static electricity. Was I even a muse still? Did the rules apply to me? I thought of what Clio had said about the Lost Muses and my heart constricted. I took a deep breath and looked away from Elnaz's retreating back.

Ms. Rinse began the SAP meeting after school that day with some anagrams, like we did in class. "Just for fun," she said, "how many words can you make out of 'science fair'? I've got lollipops for the winner."

Maya came out on top again with some seven- and eight-letter words like "sacrifice," "misfire," "critics," and "arsenic."

"You're very good at this," I said, as Maya unwrapped her lollipop. "I can't ever work them out."

"Break them down in chunks, see?" she said, circling letters here and there. "Tackle small problems one at a time, Callie."

"Okay, okay," I said. Maya had said that to me before, but I still didn't understand it. "Those are some ominous terms, girl."

"I know, right?" Maya said proudly, and enjoying her candy. "Hey, can I bring my project to your house? Two of my foster siblings keep messing with it."

"Of course," I said.

Elnaz and Tomiko were sitting in the back of the room, "taking notes" for their college education course and totally eavesdropping.

Ms. Rinse reminded us about the county science fair, and how we had to be on our best behavior. We spent the rest of the club hour playing Scientist Twenty Questions. Maya guessed Marie Curie, Albert Einstein, and Ada Lovelace, and was declared the Twenty Questions champion within the first ten minutes of playing.

Ms. Rinse watched us, a smile on her face. She was wearing a beige dress with polka dots in every color. Her shoes were dotted, too. Halfway through the game, Ms. Fovos came in, and the two of them chatted for a while. I strained to listen, but it sounded like they were complaining about a faculty meeting, nothing more.

That's when I noticed Fovos's briefcase. It looked an awful lot like the one the birds on the Tube had stolen from the pink-suit lady. My heart started to race. I scribbled a note on a piece of paper, balled it up, and threw it at Tomiko and Elnaz. It hit Tomiko on the neck, and disappeared into her shirt.

Sorry, I mouthed. Tomiko dug out the paper, glaring at me the whole time. She opened it, and she and Elnaz read my note. They didn't meet my eyes, but when Ms. Fovos got up to leave, they followed her out the door.

Part of me wanted to race after them. But I knew I had to let it go, and let the real muses do their jobs.

I took a deep breath and rejoined the Twenty Questions game. I guessed Charles Darwin after seventeen questions and Maya gave me a high five.

"You knew the answer after the first three questions, didn't you?" I asked.

Maya was kind enough to lie to me. "No way. You had it the whole time," she said.

That afternoon, Maya came over, rolling her science project all the way to my house on a wobbly cart. The tank was empty, and so I helped her lift it up the porch steps and into my room. My mom hovered nearby.

"Will you need a ride to the science fair?" my mom asked. "That contraption fits in the van, no problem."

"Thank you, Ms. Martinez," Maya said, her smile big and wide.

"Call me Trudy," she said.

Once my mom left, I closed the door and we got to work. "Okay, pretend I'm a judge. I'll stand here all stern and mean-looking, and you give me your spiel about your project."

I draped a blanket over my shoulders and made an angry face.

Maya stared, then laughed. "Will the judges be evil wizards, or something? Should I learn a spell?" she asked after a moment.

"Who knows?" I said. I wasn't joking, but Maya didn't know that. "You've got to be confident. Bold. Persuasive."

"Okay, okay," Maya said, and started to talk about sea level rise. "Pretending it's not happening is not a solution," she said, and described the technology of her project. When she stopped, she took a long, trembling breath. "How was that?"

"Perfect!" I said, and meant it. She didn't need me at all. A part of me felt a little . . . disappointed? What was the point of having muse magic if your assigned Fated One didn't actually need you?

I threw off the blanket and helped Maya glue down the plastic tubing at the bottom of the tank, and straightened the tiny buildings on the second level. We circled her project a few times and determined it to be "Done and done." But when we rolled it toward the door, a bolt slid out of the pump and tumbled under my bed.

Maya crawled underneath the bedskirt. "Got it," she said, and then added, "and I found this!" She emerged with one of the V and A dress-up cloaks in her hands. "Here you go," she said.

"Wha—?" I started to say, then closed my mouth. "Thanks, Maya. I thought I'd lost it." My eyes prickled a little. I probably would never get to see headquarters again. I lifted the cloak to my nose and sniffed. Still gross-smelling.

"I'm always losing stuff like that. Once, I lost my left sneaker on the way to school. I don't even know how that happened."

I laughed out loud.

"Don't make fun," Maya said.

"I'm not!" I said quickly. "I'm so glad you found it."

Maya chuckled. "Can I say something?" she asked.

I nodded.

"It's weird that you're going to be at the science fair and not the *America's Next Star* finals. Like, I appreciate it. I do. But Raquel is your best friend. And she's totally making the finals." Maya said all this without looking up from her hands. I stared at my hands, too. It wasn't weird. It was sad. I didn't want to think about it too long because it made my throat hurt like I wanted to cry.

"I keep telling you. She was my best friend. *Was*."

Maya looked at me, her eyebrows raised near her hairline. She lifted one of her braids and laid it across her top lip, like a mustache, then dropped it. "What do I know?" Maya said at last. "I've never even really had friends, except for you and Max this year. But if I had a best friend, then I would fight to keep her." She considered me for a minute, and I looked away. "Are you even going to watch the semifinals?" she asked, but I didn't answer.

A car horn sounded outside. Maya stood up and looked out the window. "It's Alicia," she said. It was raining heavily. Alicia had come in the car so that Maya wouldn't have to walk home in the downpour. "Can I leave my experiment here?" she asked.

"Yep," I said. Maya gave me a little wave and left. I watched from my window as she got into the car with Alicia and the two of them drove off.

The next night, I summoned up the courage to text Raquel.

> Good luck on the semifinals tonight

I watched the little bubbles on the screen that told me she was texting something back. They popped up and down, up and down, and then disappeared.

She'd given up on typing.

I typed: I miss being us. Raquel and Callie, besties.

Then, before I could hit Send, I deleted it.

Mami made picadillo that night, and Mario, Fernando, and I cleaned our plates, as usual. After dinner, Fernando turned on the TV.

"I'm out," I said, heading to my room.

"Hey, your best friend is on TV. Don't you want to watch, weirdo?" Mario asked.

My heart pounded. Yes. No. I didn't know what I wanted. "I'm not a weirdo, jerkface," I said instead.

"Yo, chill," Mario said.

"Hormones," Fernando said.

"SHUT UP!" I shouted.

I heard the slam of a kitchen cabinet. Mami's footsteps followed. "¿Qué pasa aqui?" she demanded.

"Nothing," we all said at once.

My mother held a damp rag in her hands. There were shadows under her eyes. I suddenly felt very small, and very mean. Ever since Papi left, Mario, Fernando, and I tried our best to be good, to not make Mami look like she looked at that moment—dead tired and super sad.

We weren't always successful.

"Your daughter," Fernando said, and I heard the sneer in his voice without even looking at him, "is jealous of her cool best friend and is taking it out on us."

"YOU!" I shouted, and launched at my brother. He pushed me off easily, and I fell onto the floor with a thump.

"¡Para sus cuartos!" Mami yelled, sending us to our rooms with a roar. Fernando snarled at me as he walked past.

Outside my room, I heard the TV volume come up. Some long minutes after, I heard Raquel's voice, clear and lovely, fill our house. I heard the announcers name her as one of the finalists. I heard Mario and my mom whoop and cheer for my friend. My best friend. My *ex*-best friend.

I threw myself on my bed, burying my head under my pillow, and cried myself to sleep.

Chapter 28
FROSTY'S ENCHANTED FOREST

Since the night of the semifinals, when I'd turned on Fernando like that, Mami and my brothers had been surprisingly patient with me. I guess they had understood after all.

As for me, I didn't understand a thing. The county science fair was coming up in two days—and so were the *America's Next Star* finals, for that matter. I hadn't heard from any of the muses, and I was nowhere near figuring out what the sirens were up to, where the Cassandra Curse was, or how to protect Maya.

At school, Raquel-mania had hit its zenith. Banners and posters went up in every hallway, and between classes, her song, "Friends of a Feather," was piped over the PA system. Meanwhile, every afternoon, Maya came over to work on her project, tweaking it here and there, muttering to herself about stuff like "carbon capture" and "ice cores" and "salt filtration" and ugh. None of it made any sense to me. While she worked, I sat out on my front porch, scanning the skies for birds.

Mami noticed I wasn't myself, of course. She notices everything. One night after dinner, she held up five tickets in her hand like poker cards.

"No way!" Mario exclaimed, snatching the tickets from Mami's hands. "Frosty's Enchanted Forest!"

"Shut up!" Fernando said, and tore the tickets away from Mario.

"Maybe we can bring Maya," Mami suggested helpfully, taking the tickets from my brothers. "Do you think she'd like that?"

I shrugged. "Sure," I said. Normally, I'd be thrilled about going to Frosty's. But here's the thing about being sad and confused, which I was—it was like eating when you have a bad cold. Nothing tastes right, no matter how delicious.

Mami pulled me into a hug, and whispered into my hair, "It's going to be okay, mi niña." She meant Raquel, of course. I had no choice but to let her believe that was the only reason for my moping.

"No, it's not," I whispered back.

"Then that's okay, too," she said, and left it at that.

The night before the county science fair and the *America's Next Star* finals, the Martinez-Silva family, plus Maya

Rivero, went to Frosty's Enchanted Forest. Frosty's was actually just a local park that was transformed into a winter wonderland each year. Every December, millions of Christmas lights were strung from the pines. Carnival rides were put up throughout the park—there were funhouses and carousels, roller coasters, and one ride called Kick Booty, which was everyone's favorite.

Maya had agreed to come, even though the county science fair was the next day. "A perfect distraction," she'd said. When we picked her up, she was wearing a holiday tutu, which she paired with pigtails and a jingle bell necklace.

The place was packed with kids, and we recognized a bunch of them from school. I spotted Tinker and Drang, the video game boys from SAP, and Allie, Mia, and Diana, the volleyball players, lined up to throw pies at a guy dressed like Santa Claus. We saw Max up on the Zipper with Leo, a puke-inducing ride if there ever was one. They spotted us and waved weakly, before puffing up their cheeks as the ride flipped them upside down for the hundredth time. Letty and Lisa took video of them as the ride spun. Alain and Violet held hands as they waited in line for the Ferris Wheel.

"That's new," I said to Maya, and she glanced over at them, her eyebrows lifting in surprise.

"That, too," she said a moment later, looking off toward Kick Booty. Raquel stood in front of the ride with two very large men in unnecessary sunglasses, Raquel's parents, and a third hat-and-sunglasses-wearing guy that had to be Jordan Miguel.

And it looked like Jordan Miguel was trying hard to get Raquel to get on Kick Booty.

Maya and I watched as Raquel shook her head vigorously. She was really afraid of fast rides, always had been. We walked on until we were standing just a few feet away from her and her posse.

"Come on," Jordan Miguel seemed to be saying, tugging her arm while she pulled away.

A part of me felt really bad for her. It seemed like a small thing, but Raquel was sensitive about this particular fear. I made fun of her for it once when she refused to ride the Tilt-a-Whirl at a church fair one year, and I felt so bad afterward that I promised I would never make fun again. A fear of heights and speed was why she panicked so badly on the Metrorail that night, and why I didn't mind her crushing me in a hug while that door was open.

But that was the old Callie and the old Raquel.

Then Raquel looked at me. She froze for a second, while Jordan Miguel pulled at her arms, laughing and teasing.

I took a step forward. "Listen, Raquel, you don't have to do what he wants," I said. It was the first time I'd spoken to her in weeks. One of the men in sunglasses quickly stood in front of me, his thick arms crossed.

"Beat it," he growled.

I tried to look around him, and saw that Raquel was

shaking her head at me, her eyes full of fear. She whispered something to Jordan, and he laughed brightly.

"Scram, kid," the man snarled again.

"Fine. Scramming," I said to the bodyguard. Then, I turned toward Maya. "Hey, Maya," I said as loudly as I could. Raquel's eyes bounced to us. She'd heard me. Good. "Let's go on Kick Booty."

"No way," Maya said, looking up at Kick Booty. The aerial swings spun around a center tower. Everyone took a seat in a swing and paired up with a friend, one in front of the other, the person behind holding on to a metal handle on the back of their partner's swing seat. The tower lifted, and the swing went up too, spinning out, the whole thing flaring open like a flower. When the operator yelled, "Kick Booty!" the person in the back would kick their friend up front, sending them flying. Reconnecting wasn't easy, but the operator waited until everyone did before shouting, "Kick Booty!" again.

"Come on, Maya," I said quietly, stealing a glance at Raquel, who was now looking at us intently.

"No," Maya said.

I pouted, but she shook her head, her eyes searching for my mom, who had gone to get some cotton candy. Maya had sat in the front seat on the way to Frosty's, and she and my mom had talked the whole time. Once, I'd caught my mom ruffling her hair.

I heard the operator shout, "Kick Booty!" and heard the kids on the ride screaming. My brothers had already

- 283 -

gone on twice, and Fernando had flown so far out that I thought the chains holding up his swing would snap.

It was awesome.

I could feel Raquel watching. The old Callie would have figured out a way to get around that bodyguard. The old Callie would have suggested Raquel and I go eat something, or go take pictures in a photo booth. The old Callie would have led her best friend away from the ride, the source of her anxiety.

The new Callie wanted to prove a point.

Raquel, I thought, *you are replaceable.*

"Maya, please," I begged. I could feel my fingers going numb. I could stop it now, the muse magic. I could halt it in its tracks, I knew. And after what happened at Sea-a-Rama, I knew that I probably should.

"KICK BOOTYYYYYY!" shouted the operator.

A muse never uses her magic against her sisters, I thought.

But Maya wasn't my sister.

And maybe I wasn't even a muse anymore. Did the rules still apply to me?

I let the magic wash over me. Maya's eyes narrowed as she looked at the ride. She took a deep breath, straightened her shoulders, and said, "Let's do it."

I grabbed her hand and pulled her into the line. Mario got in line behind us and gave us the thumbs-up. Fernando had gone off with Mom to get cotton candy. I stood on tiptoe to catch a final glimpse of Raquel, but she was gone, and whatever little victory I had hoped to feel evaporated.

Feeling small and mean, I fell silent as Maya chattered bravely about the ride. Her eyes glittered. My muse magic had done its job.

When it was our turn, Maya slipped into the seat behind me. "I'm going to kick your bu—" she started to say when the tower lifted us up into the air.

"You wish!" I shouted back at her. Up we went, the warm air of the night whipping our faces. Frosty's Enchanted Forest became tiny beneath us. Everything felt like it was falling away—muse stuff, Raquel, Papi and the new baby—none of it mattered because the operator shouted, "Kick Booty!" and I felt a mighty shove and was flying!

I stretched out my feet and pointed my toes, pretending to be an arrow slicing through the sky. The people watching us from the ground were a blur, but I hoped Raquel could see me. I kicked my legs, felt the ride speeding up, felt my eyes watering in the wind. For the first time in a long time, I wasn't thinking about anything but having fun. I threw my arms up in the air and shouted, "Woo hoo!"

I reached behind me, trying to reconnect with Maya when I saw them—three shapes flitting around the chains that held up Maya's swing. Blue-black feathers rode the wind and flew away.

"No! Maya!" I shouted, stretching out as far as I could.

Maya was laughing, unaware of the birds now pecking at the chains. Her fingertips touched mine, then slipped away. I swung my legs, hoping it would slow me down somehow. Around us, other riders were already connecting, getting ready for the next shout of "Kick Booty!" But I couldn't manage to get hold of Maya's hands. I was sweaty, and wiped my palms on my shorts, thinking it might help. Once more, I reached out. We hooked pinkies, but Maya swung away from me again. "Maya!" I shouted, and I think I was crying by then, because Maya's face grew concerned, and I saw her ask, "Callie, are you okay?" before the first chain snapped.

She screamed, holding on to her seat. The other three chains stayed put, and the sirens flew off. But now her swing swayed wildly in the air. Maya's screams were drowned out by another shout of "Kick Booty!"

How had the operator not seen what was happening? I focused on him, finding him behind the machine that controlled the ride. As we whipped around, I saw him. He looked dazed. Sitting on the controls were the three birds.

Maya screamed.

Now people on the ground were beginning to notice. I spotted Mami. Her hands were covering her mouth. Others had yanked out their phones—some to take video, some to call 911. I kept trying to reach Maya, even as the operator called out "Kick Booty!" again, and people went soaring past us, unaware of what was happening.

That's when I saw Fernando run up to Mami. I remembered the time I sprained my ankle roller skating, how he had carried me home, and how gentle he had been. My hands reached out for Maya, but I couldn't feel them anymore. My arms were numb with magic, all the way to my shoulders. My eyes filled with tears. *Fernando!* I thought, sending magic his way. I forgave him everything. The "cool best friend" comment, the "weirdo" comment, everything. My brother, my hero! And then I saw him leap over the fence that kept the operator away from the people in line. I whipped my head to and fro as we spun to watch him grab the man by the collar and shake him awake.

The ride began to slow down at once, and we were all jolted in our seats.

Maya screamed again.

Please don't let her fall. Please don't let her fall, I prayed.

I thought of the hero file I had found in Clio's office. So many heroes. Anyone could be a hero. Remembering the Metrorail, I reached out again, let the magic course over me like a wind, the tendrils touching everyone on the ride now, the feeling of it so strong that I grew nauseous, and I sobbed as I turned around.

Maya, holding on to her swing, was now sandwiched between two other riders, who held her close. One of them was Mario, and Maya had buried her face into his neck. "I gotchu, I gotchu," I heard him say. The other was a girl I didn't know, who had locked her legs around Maya's like a wrestler, her expression fierce and determined.

Heroes all around me. Did I do that? Or did they?

Did it even matter?

We slowed down. We descended. And when my feet touched the ground, I realized I couldn't stand up right away.

Mami rushed over to Maya. "Mi niña, mi niña," she was saying, unbuckling her quickly, then reaching a hand out to me and helping me stand, and leading us both off the ride.

A policeman met us on the ground. "Are you okay?" he asked. We could hear an ambulance in the distance, the sirens getting louder.

Maya nodded. "Yeah. I'm fine actually," she said bravely, though her voice sounded shaky.

I pulled Maya into a hug. "I'm so sorry I made you go on that ride," I sputtered.

"You didn't make me, silly," she said.

Then I cried even harder.

Maya slept over that night. She was surprisingly unfazed.

"Grace under pressure," Mami had said to her, and Maya had smiled. We ate ice cream at the table, the five of us. Fernando, for once, was the only one without an appetite, and suddenly he seemed a lot older than he'd been when we first set out for Frosty's Enchanted Forest earlier that night.

We ate in silence, Maya humming to herself every so often. "Frosty's Enchanted Forest was pretty great," she said at last. We all gaped at her. "I mean, before it tried to kill me."

Mami was the first to laugh. "You're amazing," she said to Maya.

"You're crazy," Mario added.

"You fit right into this family," Fernando said, then Mami choked on her ice cream a little.

I patted her back and offered her my glass of water. "I'm fine, fine," Mami said, clearing her throat. "It's late. Big day tomorrow, girls. Time for bed."

While Maya showered, I thought about everything that had happened. If I never saw another bird again, I thought, it would be too soon. The events of the night replayed like a movie in my head. The lights, the operator shouting, the three birds pecking at one of the chains.

One of the chains. Why not all four? Why not three or two? Why did they just break one? As long as she held on, Maya probably wasn't in real danger of falling with just one chain broken, I thought.

Why even bother with the chains in the first place? If the sirens could shapeshift, be anything, wouldn't a bigger animal be more effective? A stray dog could bite. Wasps could sting. An alligator could kill a person. It was Florida, after all.

The sirens weren't trying to kill her. They were trying to scare her. Maybe scare her enough to keep her from going to the county science fair tomorrow. It made me angry to think of them out there, plotting against Maya, trying to make her afraid.

Maybe I wasn't a muse anymore, but my magic still worked, and if I had to use it to save Maya, I would.

Besides, the sirens didn't count on Maya's courage, did they?

Chapter 29
THE COUNTY SCIENCE FAIR AT LAST

Mario drove us to the county science fair while my mom rode shotgun, gripping the dashboard. He was practicing for his learner's permit. Fernando sat with us in the back, commenting on Mario's driving the whole time.

"What are you, a senior citizen? Hit the gas!" he said.

"NO HITTING THE GAS," my mother shouted. "We've had enough excitement." At breakfast, nobody had mentioned what had happened at Frosty's Enchanted Forest, how close we'd come to something truly terrible happening. Mami's outburst was the only sign that we were all still a little shaken.

All of us, that is, except for Maya.

Maya had put on a rainbow tulle skirt and a plain pink T-shirt. "She's quite the creative dresser," my mom commented to me with a smile, before opening up the van doors and helping Maya load her project in. Birds chirruped in the trees above us. They seemed normal enough. I tried not to look at them.

"Are you okay?" I asked quietly.

"About last night?"

"Yeah."

Maya shrugged. "Yeah. I am actually."

"Nervous about the science fair?" I asked her as we climbed into the van.

Maya nodded. "Extremely." She pulled her backpack onto her lap. Inside were notes, spare parts for her project, and a Rubik's Cube. Maya twisted the interlocking plastic sections back and forth. "It helps me focus," she said. "Does it bug you?"

"Twist away," I said. "I thought you gave it to Max. Your boyyyyyfriend," I teased.

Maya gave me a little shove. "I did. This is a new one. By new, I mean old. See?" she said. The red stickers were peeling a little on the corners, but otherwise, the toy was in good shape. "It was a gift. For luck."

Fernando plucked the cube out of Maya's hands. "Ah," he said, "the coolest toy of the 1980s. Back when dinosaurs roamed the earth." He tossed it to Maya.

My mom turned around. "I'll have you know that the '80s weren't so long ago, kiddo. And they *were* cool."

Plink. There went that penny dropping in my mind again, except I didn't know why.

"I could never figure that thing out," I said to Maya.

"And I've never met a puzzle I didn't like," she said. "Besides, it takes away the nerves. You can learn, Callie. There are tons of videos online about solving Rubik's Cubes. If you're really good, you can speed-solve them, set a record, get famous."

"Let me see it," I said, and Maya handed the toy over. "Just looking at it actually *makes* me nervous," I said, laughing. I gave it a single twist, then I thought I heard something. A murmur. Like a whisper saying my name. Slowly, I turned another layer of the cube. There it was again. *Callie.* Where was that coming from?

"D-did you hear that?" I asked.

"Hear what?" Maya was looking at me funny.

Mario called out, "You mean these sick beats?" and turned up the radio until my mom yelled at him to turn it down again.

"Never mind," I said, handing the Rubik's Cube back to Maya. I probably imagined it.

"Aw, Mom," Mario whined. "Here, I'll find an *oldies* station for you," he said, fiddling with the presets on the radio.

"An '80s station for *old* people," Fernando added from the back of the van.

"Niños atrevidos," my mom muttered, but she was smiling a little, like she actually enjoyed their teenage sass.

Maya twisted the Rubik's Cube back and forth. A

Prince song blared from the speakers. *Toys of the '80s*, I said to myself as I watched Maya. Then suddenly my heart started racing. The broken case at the Museum of Childhood. The curator didn't know exactly what the sirens took that day. A cube was a box basically, and inside . . .

Maya held the cube up. "I'd say I'm about thirty or so steps away from solving it." She clicked and twisted furiously.

"How do you open those things, anyway?" I asked.

"Open?" Maya looked at me like I'd grown a third eye. "They don't open. You just . . . solve them."

"Hey, Maya, can you stop?" I asked.

"Sure," she said, and slowly put the toy back into her backpack.

I really had heard something. A whisper that had made me shiver. What if the curse wasn't in a box that had to be opened? What if it was in a puzzle that had to be *solved*?

"Maya, who gave you the Rubik's Cu—?" I started to ask, when Mario slammed on the brakes.

"We're here!" he announced, pulling into the parking lot of the Miami Beach Convention Center. Hundreds of kids and their science projects crowded the front entrance.

"Make way for the nerds of the year," Fernando shouted ahead of us.

Beside me, Mario shook his head. "How are we even twins?" he muttered darkly.

We said goodbye to my brothers and mom, and Maya

and I pushed her project into the convention center. We found her assigned table and got the pump going. It gurgled water out from the tiny limestone base perfectly, keeping the "street" above it dry.

"It's like our dollhouses," I said, "only science-y."

Maya laughed. "That's not a word, but I'll take it."

All around us, projects were going up. Giant volcanos, electrical generators hooked up to a bicycle, a weather balloon made out of gym socks, a vertically growing pumpkin vine—it was all very cool.

Maya paled at the sight. She reached into her backpack for the Rubik's Cube. I looked around the convention center frantically. Where were Elnaz and Tomiko when you needed them, anyway?

Click, twist, click. Maya had solved the first two layers of the puzzle. I let out a squeak and snatched it from her. "Remember that movie, Dumbo, the flying elephant, and his magic feather? The one he thought he needed to fly?"

Maya nodded.

"This is your feather," I said, holding up the toy. "And you don't need it." I could feel it, the top of my head buzzed. My fingers, too. Muse magic coursed through my body. "All these other projects, they don't offer solutions. Not real ones. Everything you need is in here," I said, and pointed at her head. "Now remember. There are three judges. You can't leave until you've talked to all three. I'll just go . . ." I looked around me and found a table and some chairs in the distance, by the concessions booth. A perfect place to keep an eye on things. "I'll go right over there and get out of your way so you can do your magic."

"Magic?" Maya said.

"Science magic," I said. I started to walk away, but Maya took the Rubik's Cube out of my hand.

"I won't fiddle with it. Promise," Maya said. Then she gave me a big hug. For someone so tiny, she was really strong. "You're my best friend, Callie," she whispered.

Oh, I thought, my heart suddenly feeling very full. Before I could say anything, or ask her who gave her the cube, Maya was gone again, skipping over to her project.

I walked over to one of the tables and took a seat; swiveling around, I looked for Tomiko and Elnaz. *Where are they?* I thought.

A voice came over the PA system. "Welcome to the Miami-Dade County Science Fair! Boys and girls, the judging is about to commence. Three judges will visit each project. You must be present for the judges' reviews. If they come by your project and you are not there, you will be disqualified. Take all potty breaks now!"

I watched as one of the judges—a man in a tan suit with a clipboard—made his way to Maya's table. I couldn't hear what she was saying, but she was talking excitedly, her braids flipping back and forth. She demonstrated the machine without a single drop of water out of place. The judge wrote on his clipboard and patted Maya's shoulder.

"How's she doing?" I heard a voice behind me. I jumped a little in my seat. It was Max. He had two slices of pizza on a paper plate.

"Good, I think. One judge down. Two to go. I'm glad you're here," I said.

Max handed me a slice. "I like Maya."

I made a kissy face.

"Not like that. She's my friend. And the smartest kid in school. Besides me, anyway," he said, and took a monster bite from his pizza.

I bit into my slice, too.

"That was crazy last night, at Frosty's," Max said. He lowered his voice. "I was puking my head off after riding the Zipper. I missed the commotion."

"Well, it was scary, that's what. But Maya was so brave," I said.

"Did you know she lives in a group home?" Max said, his voice still low. I thought I was the only kid at school who knew. Maya really trusted Max after all.

"Yeah," I said.

"Yeah," Max said, too. "I was in foster care last year."

"Oh," I said. I tried to hide my surprise.

Max looked away, chewing his bottom lip. When he met my eyes again, he leaned forward a little and spoke quietly. "Don't tell anyone. It's hard sometimes. I live with my aunt and uncle now. They do movie nights for foster kids, and Maya and I hung out a lot at those last year.

Seriously, don't tell anyone, Callie," Max repeated.

"I won't," I said. It was strange sitting there with Max, talking like this. He was actually really nice, and I felt bad for doubting him. If Maya trusted him, then I probably should have, too. "Anyone else from SAP here?" I asked.

Max spoke with a mouth full of gooey cheese. "Yep, those gamer kids came after all. And the coffee-drinking kids. The triplets from Key West or wherever."

"Tampa," I corrected. "What about Violet?"

"She's at the *America's Next Star* finals, where everyone else is, too. Surprised you aren't there."

I stared at my hands on the table. "Raquel and I—"

"Hey, watch," Max said, interrupting.

A second judge approached Maya. This time it was an old woman, also in a suit, a clipboard in her hand, too. She'd pinned a fake flower to her clipboard, and had another one in her hair.

When the judge left, Maya looked over at us and gave us two thumbs up.

The third judge, a woman in a drab brown dress, peered into the project tank. She dipped her arm inside and touched one of the little houses. It fell over. Then she tipped over a bridge.

Maya's mouth dropped open.

Max and I were halfway there when I heard the judge say, "Not enough glue, my dear." Then she left.

"I guess that's all three," Maya said, and patted her

tank before righting the house and bridge again.

Max was staring hard at the last judge's back. "Rude," I heard him say.

"I'm sure you wowed the other two judges," I said.

"I hope so," Maya said. "Gonna check out the competition. Come with me?"

Max gave Maya a high five, or rather, a low five, seeing as she was so short and he was so tall. "Are you coming, Callie?"

My eyes slid over to the Rubik's Cube on the table. Now was my chance to get rid of it.

"I'll stay with your project, just in case. Besides, I don't need to see the competition when the winner is right here," I said, pointing to Maya with finger guns.

"And they call me a nerd," Maya said, laughing, as she and Max wandered away together.

I scanned the room once more for Tomiko and Elnaz but they were nowhere to be found. I picked up the Rubik's Cube. It felt totally normal. I sniffed it. Just old plastic. I fiddled with the colorful stickers, many of which were peeling off on the corners. I held it to my ear.

A voice was murmuring.

I yelped and dropped the toy, paced a bit. I was right. I *had* heard something earlier. This was it. It had to be. Rubik's Cubes didn't talk, and they certainly didn't whisper.

I don't want to touch it, I don't want to touch it, I thought.

I got down on my hands and knees and put my ear to it again.

Callie, pay attention, the voice was saying. It was familiar somehow, but still terrifying.

I fell backward. "Don't say my name," I hissed at the cube.

Taking a deep breath, I leaned forward and listened again.

Calliope, Muse of the epic poem, look up. Look up. Look up.

Frozen, I counted to three. Then, slowly, I lifted my head and looked to the rafters of the convention center. They were hard to see, but they were there—three blackbirds peering down at me. And beside each of them was a . . .

Coffee mug? How did those even get up there? One of the birds dipped its beak into the mug. Then it licked its beak with a dark, wet tongue.

The triplets! *They* were the sirens?

I took a deep breath, picked up the Rubik's Cube, and shoved it down my shirt.

I had to find Maya and get her out of here.

Ahead of me, I saw three people—grown-ups—each in a suit, each wearing a big badge that read JUDGE.

And these weren't the same people who had come by before. That mean judge who had messed up Maya's model hadn't even been *human*. I stole a glance at the sirens. All three were smiling at me, showing those uncanny teeth. If

Maya wasn't standing with her project when the *real* judges came by, she'd be disqualified.

I tore through the convention center calling out, "Maya! MAYA RIVERO!"

Up and down aisles filled with kids and their projects I went, out of breath, calling her name.

"Maya!" I called, near tears.

"Over here," I heard behind me.

"Thank goodness!" I said, grabbed her hand, and ran. "The judges. You saw. Were fakes. The real. Judges. Are. On. The way," I said, out of breath.

"What?" Maya said. "That makes no sense."

"I'm not kidding!" I said. "You need to get back to your project." Maya let go of my hand and took off. I saw Max zoom past me on the right, but he couldn't catch up with her.

For someone small, she was strong *and* fast.

I heard the commotion before rounding into the aisle where Maya's project was supposed to be.

Caw, caw, caw, I heard, and spotted some black feathers floating in the sky.

Of course they'd gone after the project. Around the corner I went, then stopped in my tracks. I watched as the three birds swept down, their large beaks closed and pointy, their goal Maya's project.

I watched as someone whacked at the birds with a glittery purse, swinging it wildly above her head.

"Raquel?" I asked, stunned. What was she doing here?

"Some help?" she said, without looking up.

Max, Maya, and I rushed forward. Everyone nearby had stopped to look. We waved our arms frantically, but the blackbirds kept diving, pecking at Maya's braids and the top of Max's head.

I looked around wildly. No muse help was on the way. We needed heroes.

I let the muse magic come—the tingle that started on my head, coursed through my body, made me cry. All around us, other kids from other schools began flinging pencils and shoes at the birds. I saw a whole pizza soaring above us like a Frisbee. The kid one table over held up what looked like a massive water gun. Plastic wrap shot out of it and opened like a beautiful jellyfish in the sky, enveloping one of the birds, which dropped to the ground one aisle over.

"Check out Spider-Man," Max said, and gave the kid a high five.

I felt them all, felt their righteous anger, felt what they felt as they *made a difference*. The muse magic made me cry like a baby.

Soon, the other two birds flew off out an open window. A moment later, the third followed the others, trailing plastic wrap from its claws.

Around us, everyone was talking at once. "What was that?" and "How did those birds get in here?" while Maya thanked everyone who had helped out.

Maya's project hadn't been damaged, and she greeted the judges with surprising poise, considering what had just happened.

Well, maybe not so surprising. The top of my head was utterly numb with muse magic at this point.

Meanwhile, I walked over to Raquel, who had her hands on her knees, catching her breath. She was wearing a sparkly white dress, and the sides of her head were now dyed purple.

"What are you doing here?" I asked.

Raquel had a determined look on her face. "It was too much, Callie. They wanted me to drop out of school. They said I needed to get a nose job and lose weight."

"You have a great nose," I said. "And you're so skinny."

Raquel shook her head. "I know my parents left Venezuela because they wanted something better for me, but Cal, this isn't better," she said. "Besides. Looks like you guys needed me here. Freaky birds, huh?"

Speechless, I threw my arms around her. "I'm so glad you're back, Raqui," I said, sobbing now.

"Me too," she whispered. Then said, "Ow. What's under your shirt?"

The Rubik's Cube tumbled to the floor.

The last judge walked away, smiling and writing in his clipboard. Maya had clasped her hands to her heart and was grinning so widely at Max that I thought her face might explode.

"They loved it!" she said.

"Called her exceptional," Max said, as the two of them walked over to us. "But what's up with those fake judges?"

Before I could come up with an answer for him, Maya pushed past me. "Hey, my Rubik's Cube," Maya said. She picked it up.

"Maya, please don't, you—"

"Watch this!" She gave the cube three deft twists. "One more twist in this direction and blammo, I've solved it," she said.

"Wait," I blurted.

"Why?" Maya asked.

"That kid over there just called your name," I said, buying time by pointing to a boy in jeans and a hockey jersey, who was standing in front of a homemade solar panel.

"Oh yeah? Cool project," Maya said, and put the cube down before making her way to him.

I didn't know what to do. If I snatched the Rubik's Cube away from Maya and tried to destroy it, would it release the curse? Would we *all* be cursed? There were lots of kids around, milling about. Could the curse even be destroyed? Wouldn't Cassandra have done that, long ago? Maybe destroying it wasn't the answer.

Absently, I shoved my hands into the pockets of my jeans. Inside my right pocket, I felt something. My fingers twirled around a metallic object, and when I drew it out, there was Tia Annie's bracelet! How did that get there? Did Clio send it?

More important, was I back on the Muse Squad again?

I put it on at once. Around and around I spun the bracelet.

Suddenly, the little golden book charm on the bracelet clicked open. I didn't know it could do that! A tiny piece of paper fluttered out and fell on the floor. Cautiously, I bent down to get it, and opened it up. It was the size of a stamp. In the smallest handwriting I'd ever seen, there was what appeared to be a short letter.

Dear Callie,

You made the whole world spin, sweet girl. I knew you would.

There is often a dark night before the light shines again. Seek me out when you need the light.

You'll know where to go.

Love,

Tia Annie

"There is often a dark night before the light shines again," I whispered to myself.

This was it. This was the dark night.

I watched as Maya chatted with the boy about the solar panels, pointing to places here and there on his project board. He was nodding, and it was obvious she was being helpful. Raquel was nearby. Her hair was a mess.

She'd given up her chance at stardom, and what had she done? She'd come to the convention center and ended up defending Maya and her project. Meanwhile, Max was straightening the tiny fallen trees inside Maya's project, his brow wrinkled in concentration. He chose to be here, supporting Maya, instead of hanging out with Violet and Alain. I thought of the other muses, how each of them had first used their powers by performing a selfless act for a stranger in trouble.

That's what love was, wasn't it? Selfless.

As long as the curse was in the cube, it was a threat to Maya. There was only one way of making sure she didn't get cursed. It was scary, but I knew what to do.

By now, Maya had wandered back, making a face at me. "That kid didn't call my name. Callie, you're hearing things."

"Tell me about it," I muttered.

Maya picked up the Rubik's Cube.

"Hey, Maya, can I solve it?" I asked.

Maya shrugged. "Sure. I've done it loads of times before with my old cube."

"Thanks," I said weakly. I held it up to my ear.

You can do it, Callie, the voices murmured.

I looked at everyone. "You guys are the best," I told them while they still believed me.

Closing my eyes, I twisted the last section clockwise.

Chapter 30
THE CASSANDRA CURSE

Click.

Nothing happened.

I didn't feel any different. I was still holding the cube, so I listened to it again. Silence.

"Why do you keep doing that?" Raquel asked.

No better time than the present to test this, I thought.

"Listening for the voices inside," I said seriously.

Raquel laughed and rolled her eyes.

Not a great test, I'll admit. I wouldn't have believed me either, curse or not. The judges, the real ones this time, circled back to Maya's table.

"Congratulations, Ms. Rivero. You've won first place," said the first judge.

The second judge pinned a blue ribbon onto Maya's pink shirt. "Onward to Washington, D.C., young lady.

There's a trophy waiting for you on the stage," she said with a wink. "We'll announce you and the runners-up in a brief ceremony, happening shortly." By now, a small crowd had surrounded Maya. A camera flashed. Maya grinned.

"You did it!" I shouted, and gave Maya a big hug.

Maya smiled so widely that one of the rubber bands on her braces popped off and hit me on the cheek. "Sorry. That was gross," she said.

I hugged her again. It really was gross, but it was also super okay.

Maya had won the county science fair! I'd figured out who the sirens were! Sure, I was cursed, but there had to be a way to get rid of it. Clio would know how.

That's when I saw her—Ms. Rinse walking over to us slowly.

I rushed toward her. "Ms. Rinse! Maya won!" I said. "Extra credit for everyone, right?" I joked. She clamped her hands on my shoulders and looked me hard in the eyes. Then she pushed me away and marched toward Maya, a grim look on her face. I ran behind her. She walked right up to the third judge and began whispering in her ear, pointing to Maya's project. The judge's brow furrowed.

I heard Ms. Rinse say "cheater," and "Maya," and "dishonest."

No, no, no, I thought. What was Ms. Rinse doing? Didn't she want Maya to win?

I let the muse magic come as I stared at Ms. Rinse's

back. Feeling it wash over me again and again, I willed her to fix this, to take back whatever she'd said to that judge.

"Wait," Ms. Rinse said. It was working! She opened her mouth to say something when she stopped, turned around, and imperceptibly shook her head at me. My knees buckled at once. Just like that, my magic turned off, as if she'd flipped a switch. Her blue eyes grew brighter, as if they were being lit from behind.

I'd felt my magic turn off before. At Sea-a-Rama, when I'd tried to use my magic and Ms. Rinse had looked at me like that . . .

"Hey Maya," I said, looping my arm around her. "You never did tell me who gave you the Rubik's Cube."

Maya's bottom lip was trembling as she watched the judges turn to her with angry eyes. "Ms. Rinse did," Maya said, her voice small.

A chirp sounded behind me, and I turned to see a trio of blackbirds pecking at some popcorn on the floor. The birds were back! They waddled closer to Ms. Rinse. She looked down and gazed at them lovingly.

Ms. Rinse was with the sirens. They answered to her!

"Whatever this creep is telling you is a lie," I said, jamming myself between Ms. Rinse and the judge.

Ms. Rinse's nostrils flared. "Callie Martinez-Silva, step away *now*."

"Don't believe her. Not a word," I said to the judge.

Ms. Rinse started laughing. Maya, Raquel, and Max

joined her. My heart dropped. Of course. The Cassandra Curse. Everything I said sounded like a lie to them.

"Guys," I pleaded. "Listen to me." But they weren't. They were giggling and pointing at me.

Ms. Rinse laid a cold hand on my shoulder. "It appears that you are the one nobody believes, Calliope." The way she said it told me all I needed to know.

Ms. Rinse knew I was a muse.

And she knew I had solved the Rubik's Cube and released the Cassandra Curse.

I felt something sharp on my ankle, looked down, and saw one of the blackbirds beside me, teeth bared. I kicked it hard, and heard Raquel say, "Hey, Cal. *Not cool.*"

My eyes pricked with tears at the sight of Raquel's furrowed brow. I'd just gotten her back in my life and now . . .

Hurrying away from them all, I ran out of the convention center and onto the street. "Hello? Hello?" I called into my bracelet. If I was a muse again, they would hear me and come help. I hoped. But nobody answered. I was still holding the Rubik's Cube. "Hello?"

"Are you expecting a response?" a voice answered.

I looked up and was face-to-face with Clio.

"You're here!" I said, and wrapped my arms around her waist.

Clio patted my head. "There, there," she said awkwardly, and I let her go.

"Um, sorry. It's just that—"

Clio was fanning herself with a map of Miami. "Is it always so hot here?" she asked.

"Pretty much, yeah," I said.

"It was much cooler in the fountain," she said, pointing to an enormous fountain across the street, surrounded by bright pink hibiscus plants. "Entrance point," she whispered.

"Clio, there's trouble. This is the Cassandra Curse," I said, holding up the Rubik's Cube.

Clio stared at it, her mouth pursed. "Don't be ridiculous," she said.

"It is. I've been cursed. That's why you don't believe me. Or you won't. But Ms. Rinse is *bad*. And the triplets from Tampa, or wherever they're really from, are sirens, but they're currently blackbirds. Maya won the county science fair, but she's in trouble and—"

Clio laid a warm hand on my head. "Do you know how preposterous you sound?"

"Clio, please."

She sighed. "It was a mistake to think you were ready to be reinstated as a muse. Give me the bracelet."

I shook my head, backing away from her. Clio reached out for me. Then a scream from inside the convention center resounded, and Clio turned toward it.

So I ran.

Fast as I could, I made for the fountain. I stepped inside, my sneakers squelching in the water. In the center, a stone mermaid sat on a rock, her tail coiled beneath her. I held the Rubik's Cube up to my ear one last time.

You know where to go, Callie, the voice said sadly.

"Tia Annie, is that you?" I asked. I hoped it was. I hoped she'd been trying to help me all along.

I don't know who Tia Annie is. I am she whom none believed, the voice answered.

"Are you Cassandra?" I whispered back.

I am sorry that my fate has befallen you, she said.

I thought of Cassandra, so long ago, trying to convince the people in her city of the horrors that awaited them. How they hadn't believed her. How everyone she loved had died.

"I'm sorry, too," I said back. "How do I break the curse?"

The truth. You must tell it, Cassandra answered so dimly that I barely heard her.

"Okay. Bye," I said, feeling confused and ridiculous.

I took a steadying breath, pinched my nose, and ducked under the warm water, staying there until I felt it grow cold around me.

I rose out of the water into a London night, in the center of the courtyard fountain at the V and A. Because I'd seen Thalia do it, I walked forward, and as I walked, my clothes dried out. It was a miracle that I had the courtyard to myself. Inside the café, guests were grabbing meals and settling down with trays. Signs around the courtyard advertised "A Night Under the Stars at the V and A."

Somewhere, soft music was playing.

At first I didn't know what to do. What did Maya always say? "Tackle small problems one at a time." The cube had told me I knew where to go. Every time I went back to headquarters, I learned something new, so that was an obvious choice. Now what? Tia Annie had left me clues, hadn't she? Like the poems in her book, and the note. What had the poem said again? Something about dog bones, a path, and secrets.

And her note? *Seek me out when you need the light*, it had read.

I went straight to Tycho's grave and knelt before it.

The bolts holding the plaque in place were loose, and I twisted them out, scraping my fingers against the brick wall. The plaque itself was heavy, and it fell onto the ground with a thud.

Inside the dark box was a pile of small white bones that had been pushed to the side. The little dog skull was perched on top. The bones weren't scary, just sad, really.

I reached in, thinking I might find another note, or some other instructions. "Come on, Tia Annie. What did you see in here?" I whispered.

An old spiderweb draped across one of the corners, and a glimmer of light shone behind it. Where was it coming from? My fingers grazed the back of the box, and when they did, the panel I had touched fell away, revealing a vast green space beyond it.

I knew that field.

I had dreamed about it.

Sitting back on my heels, I considered my options. I couldn't just sit here, slip into the fountain, or even go home. I was cursed. Nobody I knew would ever believe anything I ever said again. For the rest of my life, they would think to themselves, *There goes Callie, that liar.* The thought made a big fat lump grow in my throat.

I wasn't sure what to do. "Hello?" I called. The grass was flattened into a narrow path that led to water. The bones, the path. Just like the poem said. Beyond were secrets.

The box was just a little wider than my shoulders. I heaved myself in, closing my eyes when my arms brushed up against Tycho's bones. "Sorry, puppy," I said, and prayed that dog-haunting wasn't an actual thing. It was a tight fit, and for a moment, I thought I'd get stuck. A vision of my butt hanging out of the tomb for all the visitors of the V and A to see nearly made me back out.

Pushing forward, I popped out into the green field and slowly stood up.

It was dusk there, too, and a few stars were visible in the sky. The grassy field was dotted with little yellow flowers here and there, and they swayed in a light breeze. The statues I'd dreamed of were gone. The field gave way to the water, and on the water was a small boat, bobbing up and down. Far out in the distance, past the water, a column of light caught my eye.

Searchlights. Three beams of light swept the sky, back and forth. I walked toward them thinking I'd either have to swim or go around the pond.

That's when the boat headed for me, leaving soft, glossy ripples in its wake. As the boat approached, the shape of the figure sitting in it became clear.

Her hair was long. She was smiling. And when the boat finally touched the shore, the woman stood, opened her arms, and said, "Oh, Calliope, mi vida, you've come."

"Tia Annie!" I cried out. I stepped into the water and clambered into the little boat.

"You're so big," she said, wrapping her arms around me.

"And you're—you're *you*!" I mumbled against her shoulder. "And this isn't a dream!"

Tia Annie cupped my cheeks with her hands. "How I've missed you, my Callie-Mallie."

I'd forgotten that nickname. How could I have forgotten it? I started to cry, and Tia Annie said, "Shh, shh," until I stopped.

"It's all been a lot," I said, my voice choked up.

"Understatement of the century, mi niña," Tia Annie said. She dipped her hand into the water. "Look."

I looked. The searchlights were reflected on the surface, each beam of light wavy and refracted, and in the glow, a picture emerged.

"That's Ms. Rinse!" I said, as an image of my science teacher appeared in the water. She was younger. Really young. But there was no mistaking those round cheeks and those bright blue eyes and her polka-dot dress.

"My old friend. Wendy was her name. Muse of science. She was so proud," Tia Annie said, touching the water again. Another picture emerged. Now Ms. Rinse was older, standing in a laboratory, whispering into the ear of a man wearing a lab coat.

"She was both an excellent muse and a terrible one," Tia Annie said. "Talented. Powerful. But she felt as if she was inspiring lesser beings. *She* was the smart scientist. *She* had the ideas. Why couldn't she claim them for *herself*? Jealous, she suppressed the Fated Ones. Sabotaged their careers."

"And the searchlights?" I asked.

The picture in the water changed again. "Wendy sought them out. Our power comes from the light. You know how sometimes, when someone has an idea in a cartoon, the illustrator draws a lightbulb over that person's head?" Tia Annie asked. I nodded. "Light is inspiration. Muses are like light switches. We just turn on the light in those we inspire. Wendy wanted that inspiration for herself. So she discovered the Tycho portal, came here, and tried to steal the light for her own use. I followed her and stopped her from reaching the searchlights, claiming all inspiration for herself. I denied her entry." Tia Annie touched the water again, and there was Ms. Rinse in the boat, lying very still, as if she were sleeping. "Wendy was my best friend. I broke her heart," Tia Annie said very quietly.

"Then what happened?"

"I turned her in to Clio, and her muse magic was stripped from her and returned to the searchlights. She became a Lost Muse."

I watched the lights. They were soft, not glaring. When I looked at them, I felt peaceful, like whatever I did next would be the right thing to do.

"Seems unfair," I said.

Tia Annie's eyebrows scrunched together, the way they always had when she was trying to figure something out. "What do you mean?"

"The lights," I said. "Why can't everyone have them?"

Tia Annie smiled, drawing me into a hug. "Human inspiration is infinite, but inspiration derived from magic? That's a limited resource. There's enough to power the muses and then some. But if the lights burn out because someone has abused their power, then it's gone forever. That's the deal."

"Bum deal," I said.

Tia Annie nodded. Once more, she touched the water, and there was Ms. Rinse, standing on a beach somewhere at dusk, her arms raised to the sky. Hovering over her were three creatures—half human, half bird, with very familiar teeth.

"In vengeance, Wendy called up the sirens," Tia Annie said.

"How did she do that?" I asked.

"Her magic was gone, but not her knowledge. She knew the ways a person could summon the sirens, and she knew that the sirens couldn't resist. It's a game to them, to see how much chaos they can sow."

I remembered how Ms. Rinse had resisted my magic at Sea-a-Rama, and how she'd done it again at the county science fair.

"Tia Annie, I tried my magic on Ms. Rinse," I said, explaining what had happened when I'd tried to "inspire" her. "But it didn't work."

"You can't force a person to be good if they don't want to be, deep down. Plus, she knew what you were up to, so it gave her an advantage." Tia Annie seemed very sad. "She'll be coming here next to retrieve her magic." Tia Annie looked all around—at the sky, the water, the searchlights. "I'll protect the lights, but first, we have to take care of you," she said.

I felt the Rubik's Cube, still in my shirt. I pulled it out and showed Tia Annie. "Cassandra, she talked to me. She tried to help me." The cube felt light. I put it up to my ear, but heard nothing.

Tia Annie held the cube. "She isn't in here, if that's what you're wondering. She's there, past the water, where the heroes go when they die," she said, gesturing to a far-off point across the lake, one that I couldn't make out. "That's where the muses go too, when their time on earth is over."

"Then why aren't you there?" I asked.

"I struck a deal," she said.

"A deal? With who?" If there was a place for heroes, and Tia Annie wasn't there, then none of this made sense. She was the most heroic person I knew.

Tia Annie waved her hand about. "Oh. You know. The ones who make decisions around here." She tapped on the Rubik's Cube with her fingernail, her face settling thoughtfully. "Maybe a little bit of Cassandra survived within the curse. A part of her that stayed behind to try to help others." Tia Annie sighed. "She wasn't a muse. But she could have been. Cassandra was a brave girl. Like you are, Callie."

"Tia Annie, nobody believes me." Cassandra might have been brave, but I'll bet she was heartbroken, too. That's how I felt.

My aunt looked sad. She reached out and touched my hair. "I know," she whispered. "I can see that curse all over you. Like slime."

"Cassandra told me to tell the truth," I said. "But I don't know what she meant."

Tia Annie's brow furrowed. She swirled her hand in the dark water. "Cassandra had a hard time of it, if I recall," she said. She was gazing out over the water, off to some distant shore I couldn't see.

I remembered something Clio had said when she'd shown us the boxes of curses in the museum stores. "A truth she'd been afraid to tell even herself," I whispered. "That's what Cassandra spoke, and it's what trapped the curse again."

Tia Annie gave the Rubik's Cube back to me. Picking up the oars, she rowed for a while, getting closer to the searchlights. They warmed my face. "What are you thinking?" she asked.

"I don't know, Tia Annie. I'm afraid of a lot of things," I said, cradling the toy in my hands.

Tia Annie rowed the boat out a little farther. "Do you know what hubris is?"

I shook my head.

"It's pride. In all the old stories, it's the one thing the heroes mess up. They get too proud. Too stubborn," she said. "And because of it, they suffer a downfall."

"But I haven't been. I'm not," I said. My eyes stung a little. "I'm not a hero. And I don't have anything to be proud of anyway."

"Hm," Tia Annie said. She dipped her hand in the water, and an image of Raquel onstage appeared. Then I saw myself, holed away in my bedroom while my brothers watched Raquel on TV. She swirled the water again and there I was at Frosty's, turning away from Raquel just as Jordan Miguel was tugging her toward a ride she didn't want to go on.

"Oh," I said. Sure, Raquel had gotten swept up in *America's Next Star*, but I had gotten jealous, just like she'd said. "Hubris," I repeated. "Did I make Raquel . . . hubristic?"

"That is indeed the adjectival form of hubris!" Tia Annie said, clapping her hands together.

"Don't get excited," I said. "It was a lucky guess." Tia Annie pursed her lips, and I got serious again. "Did I do that to Raquel? Did I break her with my magic?" My heart was fluttering in my chest. It was one thing to help your best friend. It was another to be the cause of her downfall.

"No, querida. If Raquel was feeling a little full of herself, she did that on her own."

"But I made her taller, Tia Annie. I made Maya's teeth straighter. And I don't know how I do that sometimes, or why it doesn't happen other times. Sometimes, I look in the mirror and I wish . . . I just wish." I stopped.

Tia Annie pulled me into another hug, longer and fiercer this time. "Mi vida, you are perfect the way you are. I know it's hard to believe sometimes, but I know you will understand that someday." She gave me a loud kiss on the cheek, then said, "Do you know, the first time I tried to inspire a hero, she fell out of a tree and broke her leg? She climbed a big old banyan tree back home trying to rescue a baby raccoon stuck on a branch."

"That wasn't your fault," I said.

"It is when you also manage to change her bad eyesight to twenty-twenty. The world looked so crisp and clear for the first time that she got dizzy and lost her balance," Tia Annie said.

Tia Annie had done it, too! She'd used muse magic to change a person without meaning to. And she'd made a mess of it. "I shouldn't laugh. Broken leg, and all," I said, but I couldn't stop myself from giggling.

Tia Annie rubbed my back in small circles. "We all make mistakes. But perhaps there's one you haven't admitted to yet, huh? A truth you've been afraid to tell even yourself? It's not Raquel's excessive pride I'm worried about."

I nodded. I had wanted credit for Raquel's success, hadn't I? And I didn't stop to think that while I'd given her a nudge, she'd already had those gifts inside her. I lifted the Rubik's Cube to my lips and whispered, "I haven't been a good friend to Raquel. I was proud. I was jealous, and I was mean. And I'm sorry about that."

The cube trembled in my hand, then began reshuffling itself. I felt cold all over. Really cold. Colder than the museum in the wintertime when you are wearing are shorts and flip-flops. Colder than the blast of air from the freezer when I open it back home to pull out some ice cream. For a moment, it felt so cold that my skin hurt. I heard a whisper coming from the cube again, muttering in a language I didn't understand. Faster and faster the voice spoke. I recognized it from before. Cassandra!

"Is she okay, Tia Annie?" I asked, the cube still twitching

in my hand as the puzzle rearranged itself.

"I think so. A part of Cassandra stayed behind in the curse, remember? To help people like you. Another part of her crossed over," Tia Annie said. "I think she's probably glad you figured out how to shake the curse."

Finally, the cube went still and quiet.

"Slime's all gone," Tia Annie said.

I warmed up quickly and felt a little lighter, now that I'd faced the truth about how I'd handled things with my best friend.

"You are a bundle of love, mi niña. Rule number two, 'muse magic is just love, concentrated.' And I love you very much, Callie."

"I love you, too, Tia Annie. And I miss you," I said.

Tia Annie smiled, and then her smile grew sad. "Don't come looking for me again, Callie. This place is not for you. You belong out there, where they need you." I heard a shout as if very far away, then another, and another. "You'd better go," Tia Annie said, looking past me and toward Tycho's open tomb. "Remember, the sirens' power is in their song. You don't have to listen to it." She lifted my hands and put them over my heart. "You have your own song, in here. Focus on that."

I started to get out of the boat when I remembered something. "Clio said you went to Mount Olympus. She thought it might have something to do with me, with my powers. They aren't like the others'."

Tia Annie sat up very straight, and I could imagine her in front of a classroom, the whole room silent and in awe of her. "The world as it is needs the kinds of heroes it hasn't had in a long time. And it needs the muses to help them along. I knew my time was ending. And I knew you would be ready, Callie. So I asked."

"You . . . asked?"

"Yes. Like I said. I struck a deal. I went to the seat of the gods, and I asked. And the world received. You have been given a gift the world has not known in an age. You're stronger than I ever was. You don't know it yet, but you will. Oh, mi niña. The world is in good hands," she said, and cupped my cheeks.

I gave my aunt another hug, one so big I would never forget it.

"Mmm," Tia Annie said, relishing the embrace. Then she stopped and took hold of my wrist. "Where's our bracelet? Don't tell me you lost it," she said.

I looked down at my bare wrist. "Oh no!" I searched all around.

"Why didn't you put glue on the clasp?" Tia Annie asked, and I couldn't help it, I started to laugh.

"You're just like Mami," I said, chortling, and Tia Annie laughed.

"What can I say? It's a family thing," she said.

"I love our family," I said.

"Me too. Now go, Callie-Mallie." I stepped out of the

boat and took a few steps forward. I turned around for one more goodbye, but Tia Annie was gone and the boat was empty. The searchlights continued to sweep back and forth.

Ahead, Tycho's tomb stood open. I walked toward it.

But just before I climbed in, three angry faces appeared on the other side, blocking my way.

Chapter 31
BATTLE AT THE V AND A

"You discovered a portal to somewhere supercool and didn't tell us?" Nia asked.

"Some kind of friend you are," Thalia added.

Mela tsked and shook her head.

Laughing in relief, I crawled out of the little tomb. Nia and Mela each took one of my hands and pulled, and I plopped out onto the grass.

"How did you get here?" I asked.

One by one, the girls showed me their communications items. Each had a massive grin on her face.

"Found mine in my left sneaker," Nia said, dangling her globe necklace.

"Clio must have sent them back. I thought my pocket was on fire before I realized my ring was in it," Mela said.

Thalia rubbed her jaw like she had a toothache. "Why

did Clio have to sneak mine into the scone I was eating?" Then she winked to let us know she was only kidding.

"I'm glad we're back. I missed you so much," I said, trying to hug them all at once.

When I turned to look into the grave, it was dark again, the back panel in place.

"Rest in peace, Tycho," I whispered, and put the plaque in place again. I turned to the others and pulled the Rubik's Cube out from under my shirt. "Cassandra Curse. Locked and loaded."

"In there?" asked Thalia. She slapped her forehead.

"Yeah," I said. "I was cursed briefly, and then . . ." I faced Tycho's grave and gave silent thanks to Tia Annie. "Let's just say I was un-cursed."

We heard a loud crash coming from inside the museum. "Sounds like the party started without us," Mela put in.

"All right, Muse Squad. We've got three sirens and a Lost Muse to get rid of. Let's go," I said.

But Nia held up a hand. "Houston, we have a problem." Her eyes cut toward the fountain. I followed her gaze and saw Maya Rivero standing in the middle of the water, drenched and sobbing, her rainbow backpack on her back and her hands balled up into fists.

"Um, she's *not* supposed to be here. We just got our powers back, and now Clio is going to take them away again, isn't she?" Thalia asked, staring.

I ran toward Maya, sloshing through the water. "Maya?

How did you get here?" I asked quietly.

Slowly, Maya opened one of her fists. Inside was my bracelet.

"You dropped it in the fountain. I saw you disappear. I saw you do it in the slide at the Sea-a-Rama, too," Maya said, handing it to me.

Another shout.

"Hurry!" Nia yelled.

I had to send Maya back to Miami. I pinched my nose and dragged her down into the water with me. I held my breath as long as I could, then came up for air, Maya gasping next to me.

We were still very much in London. I kicked at the water, sending up a splash.

"You okay?" Maya asked.

"The Great Bed of Ware then," I said, not answering her. But we had to get up there first. And that meant fighting our way to the third floor.

"Callie, listen to me," Maya demanded before she would take a step out of the pond. "Ms. Rinse lied. She told the judges I cheated. And they disqualified me. Why would she do that?"

I squeezed my eyes shut in frustration. After everything we'd been through, Ms. Rinse was actually going to derail Maya's destiny? "You didn't win the county science fair," I said.

"That's what disqualified means, sort of."

So we already failed, I thought. I took a deep breath.

Whatever happened, Maya still needed me.

"That doesn't matter right now," I said. "We have to get you somewhere safe. Come with me."

Maya took a big step backward, her hands up. "Where am I? And why did you steal my Rubik's Cube?"

That's when I realized I was still holding it. "I didn't steal it. I'll explain it all later, I promise," I said. Maya didn't move. "Just, trust me. Please," I added.

Maya's eyes were wide, but she dropped her hands. "Fine. I trust you," she said, and followed me out of the water and toward the others.

"Game plan?" Nia asked. Everyone was looking at me.

Okay. I was Calliope, First of the Muses, Annie Martinez's niece. I could do this. I bounced a little on my feet. I looked across the pond and into the Tea Room, where museum guests were running to and fro, using their food trays to strike the walls, which were covered in intricate mosaics.

Chaos. Siren song. It had to be.

"First. Earplugs," I said, and we dug into our pockets and bags for them.

"What about Maya?" Nia asked.

"Got it," Mela said, giving her headphones to Maya, plugging them into her phone first. "Put these on, please," she said, and Maya did. Then Mela hit Play, and Maya jumped. We could all hear a loud, twangy voice through the headphones.

Mela beamed while Maya winced.

"You're into country music?" I shouted, and Mela grinned broadly.

"Listen, everyone. It's Ms. Rinse. Ms. Rinse is making this all happen," I yelled so that they could hear me.

"That nice teacher? I mean, she made us do all those anagrams but . . ." Thalia put in.

"Anagrams! Of course. 'Rinse' is an anagram for *siren*," Nia said.

"But she isn't one. She only summoned the sirens. Rinse is a Lost Muse, stripped of her powers because she thought she was better than the Fated Ones," I said.

Nia swallowed hard. The others looked away. I know what they were thinking. We all could have been lost, too.

"Okay, then," I said, speaking as loudly as I could. I took a deep breath. "Let's make things right. Mela, you head to the Tea Room. Give them something to do other than destroy the café."

Mela bounded away, and as she ran, we could already see some of the guests dropping their trays and blinking away sudden tears.

"The rest of us will go through the gift shop," I said. But first, I unzipped Maya's backpack and dropped the Rubik's Cube into it. The curse now secured, we ran, with Maya trailing behind us, headphones on. We reached the doors when a pair of tourists waltzed past us. A girl performed a perfect pirouette in the distance, while two little boys breakdanced in the center of the gift shop. The shop itself was in shambles—toys and souvenirs littered the floor, and art books sat splayed open, their pages torn. Tomiko and Elnaz stood in the center of it all.

"You brought a guest. How nice," Elnaz said, indicating Maya.

"Glad you could make it," Tomiko shouted.

"Glad *we* could make it?" I asked. "Why weren't you at the county science fair?"

Elnaz raised an eyebrow at Tomiko. "Go on. Tell them," she said.

Tomiko rolled her eyes. "We were there. Ended up chasing a trio of suspicious-looking ducks in the parking lot."

"Go on," Elnaz said.

"They turned out to be regular ducks," Tomiko admitted at last.

I would have laughed, except a couple of tourists were trying to reach a sword replica that was hanging over the cash register.

Tomiko turned her attention to them. Her forehead glistened with sweat, and her hair was damp. At a flick of her wrists, the sword-stealing tourists began to dance an awkward tango. Tomiko seemed to be conducting the dancers—all visitors to the museum and employees, too—distracting them from whatever the sirens had sung in their ears. For her part, Elnaz was playing a tin whistle, flitting about the gift shop, her fingers flying over the instrument as the people danced. I noticed it then—they were dancing with a purpose. Tomiko and Elnaz were sending them out-side, through the front doors, away from the siren song.

We left them to it, running through the gift shop and entering the foyer. There, standing amid the rubble of a broken statue, stood Max.

"Maya?" he asked, a bloody gash on his forehead. "Help me," he said.

Beside me, Maya began to remove her headphones.

"No," I said, and held them in place. "Nia, find out who he is."

Nia walked gracefully up to Max. "Smart Max," she said. "Smartest boy at Miami Palms Middle. If you are Max, then this should be irresistible. Let's talk, huh? Thermodynamics? Black holes?"

Max swiped his forehead with the sleeve of his shirt. "What?" he asked.

Nia pressed on. "Maybe it's geology that floats your boat. Or organic chemistry."

Max tried getting around Nia. "Maya, help me," he said.

Beside me, Maya began to back away. "Something's not right," she whispered.

Nia laughed. "Oh, I know," she said. "You're into *chaos* theory, aren't you?"

Max, or the thing in front of us pretending to be Max, bared its teeth. Then, in one fluid motion, as quick as bat-ting an eye, Max became Leo, one of the triplets.

Maya screamed and covered her face, and the siren rushed forward.

"Get him," Thalia said, making a grab for the siren, but the triplet shifted again. Now he was Violet Prado, sneering at us. Then he was Raquel. Each time, the siren opened his mouth to sing.

I tapped my ears. "Can't hear you. Sorry," I said. "And I can't let you have my friend here."

The siren seemed to consider us, realizing it was outnumbered. One minute he looked like Raquel, the next he was a tiny sparrow, flitting into the air and disappearing over the second-floor balcony.

"It's just you and me, bird," Nia shouted, and tore up the stairs after it.

"Be careful!" I yelled after her.

Thalia, Maya, and I made our way through the rubble of the sculpture gallery and up a different set of stairs. Everywhere, museum visitors were making a mess of things. We inspired them to change course along the way, reaching out with muse magic the best we could, so that here and there, someone would stop what they were doing and start laughing at a remembered joke, or pause to try to piece together something that had been broken. "I'm going to get you out of here," I reassured Maya. "The Great Bed is around the corner." She was pale with fear.

But when we rounded into the room where the Great Bed usually sat, we found that it had been upended, the bed's beautiful canopy splintered in two.

"Noooooo!" Thalia said. "Not the Great Bed of Ware. COME ON!" She stamped her foot, then caught sight of something under the bedsheets. Thalia yanked the sheet off to reveal a brown hen, her feathers fluffy, her legs tucked underneath her, as if she were sitting on an egg. "You," Thalia said. The hen revealed a row of teeth.

Thalia reached out and snatched the bird by the neck. "Why did the chicken cross the road?" Thalia asked it. The bird flapped and growled. Thalia unlatched one of the heavy leaded windows, and without thinking about it twice, tossed the bird out. "To get away from our headquarters, you horrid creature," she shouted after it. The hen flapped away, squawking the whole time.

Maya and I stared at her, speechless.

"Remind me to always laugh at your jokes," I said.

Thalia smiled. "I'm sorry about the bed. That was a great entrance point," she said, sighing.

"So I've been told," I said.

"Two sirens down," she added. "Where to now?"

I thought it over. "The library," I said. Up we went to level three. Things were quieter up there, the books untouched.

An enormous crash resounded above us and we all jumped.

"That would be the ceramics gallery," Thalia said, her brow furrowed. "It's my mum's favorite spot in the

- 334 -

museum." She bit her lip, then seemed to decide something. "I'm on it, Callie. Wish me luck. And Maya, be safe," she said.

"Fight the good fight," Maya told her.

With a wink, Thalia left us alone in the library. The door closed behind her and all went quiet.

Maya slipped her hand into mine. She pulled the headphones off her head. "Tell me what's going on, Callie," she implored.

And I did, leaving out the part where Maya was a Fated One. It seemed like a lot of pressure to know a thing like that. When she asked, "But why me?" I merely said:

"Because you inspired us, Maya," and she seemed to stand a little straighter after that. "But you can't tell anyone about the muses. I don't know for sure, but it's probably rule number fifteen or something: a muse's identity must be kept secret."

"It's rule number six, actually," came a voice by the door.

"Ms. Rinse!" Maya said.

"Wendy," I hissed.

She laughed. "You've done your homework. For once. Looking for help?" Ms. Rinse pointed toward the spiral staircase. "Go on. See what you find."

Now it was my turn to laugh. "Sure thing. Like we're going to do anything you tell us to," I said, without realizing that Maya was already halfway up the stairs, Mela's headphones dangling from her hands.

But how had she made Maya do it? Ms. Rinse's muse magic had been taken away, and I didn't see any sirens helping her out. Unless.

The searchlights.

She'd been to Tycho's grave. I rushed to a window that faced the courtyard below. There it was, the plaque to Tycho's tomb, lying on the ground. I could even see tiny white bones scattered on the lawn.

Again, Ms. Rinse laughed. "Lost Muse no longer," she said. "Callie, the lights are gone. Annie tried hard, poor thing. But I have powers now that you cannot imagine."

"You leave my aunt alone!" I said.

Ms. Rinse waved lazily at me. "Up you go. Find your 'Fated One.' Fat lot of good it will do you."

Shaking, I chased after Maya, all the way to Clio's office, the door of which was wide open. "Hey," I said to Maya, and she seemed to snap out of it.

"How did I get up here?" she asked, and I slipped the headphones back on her head, clicking Mela's country music back on.

"Thanks!" Maya shouted. We hadn't noticed yet what was happening in Clio's office.

There, frozen in time, were Clio, Paola, and Etoro.

I ran toward them. "Wake up!" I shouted. I grabbed the lapels of Clio's jacket and shook her hard. "Unfreeze them, Clio. Don't listen to Ms. Rinse! Don't do what she says!"

But it was no use. Rinse had caught them by surprise

and used muse magic and siren song against them, compelling Clio to turn on the others and herself.

"What do we do?" Maya shouted.

"Yoo-hoo? Girls?" Ms. Rinse called after us. I could hear her heels clicking on the marble floors.

I pulled open Clio's desk drawers, throwing papers and office supplies to the floor. "Where is it?" I muttered to myself. When I'd almost lost hope, my fingers brushed cold, rough metal.

The bronze key! It was the same one Clio had used to get into the museum's stores.

"Come on," I said, and led Maya down a corridor and through a wide door, leading her deep into the V and A storage rooms. I slipped the heavy key into the lock, pulled on the bat-shaped door handle, and heaved the door open. Maya stuck close by as I led her through the aisles.

"Where are they? Where are they?" I muttered as we checked each row.

Then I found them—the curses. Tiny boxes full of gods-knew-what. I couldn't use my magic against Ms. Rinse. She'd already resisted me more than once. But could she resist a curse? The Cassandra Curse had worked on me. One of these *had* to work on Ms. Rinse. "Your backpack?" I asked Maya, and she handed it over. I unzipped it, pulled out the Rubik's Cube, and handed it to Maya. Then I swept my arm along the shelf and dumped all the other curses into the bag.

Maya held the scrambled cube in her hands.

"Do your thing," I told her, and she started to work it out, her fingers flying over the toy like a blur. "But stop short of solving it, okay? Whatever you do, don't solve it until I say so!"

We went back down to the library, where Rinse now stood, flanked by two tall women and one man, who might be beautiful if they weren't completely covered by black feathers. Letty, Lisa, and Leo were grown now, and they narrowed their eyes at the same time. In sync, they bent at the knees, as if ready to pounce. They hissed, and I could smell their nasty coffee breath in the air. Even as I watched, more wings sprouted from their backs, the feathers there as red and bright as fresh blood.

And before them were Thalia, Mela, and Nia, their hands lifted in our direction, their lips curled in anger.

Rinse, still in her blue polka-dot dress, gave a little twirl.

"It's over, young ones. The age of the muses is done. I'll fix the world's problems alone, thank you very much. I am all the inspiration the world needs," she said.

Thalia cocked her head to the side and suddenly, everything seemed very funny—from Rinse's dumb dress, to Maya's silly braids. "Thalia, stop it," I said, giggling. I doubled over in laughter.

Then, all at once, I thought of Tia Annie. A wave of grief knocked me to my knees. My tia. I missed her so much. Was she okay? What if I just went down to Tycho's

- 338 -

tomb and stayed there, with her? What then? Maybe this awful feeling would go away.

A flash of understanding pierced the sadness. I never gave up *this* easily. This was muse magic. I lifted my eyes and caught Mela's hard stare.

"Mela," I said, sobbing, "don't. Please."

Maya was shaking my shoulder. "My backpack!" she was shouting. She held open her rainbow backpack. I could see the outline of the Rubik's Cube under her shirt, where she'd hidden it.

With trembling hands, I picked out a box encrusted in sapphires. I had no idea what was inside, and I didn't want to hurt my friends. If we could make sure the curse was aimed at Ms. Rinse, or the sirens, then maybe we could stop them, or at least slow them down.

"We have to be careful, Maya," I said through tears. "Those are my friends."

"What have you got there?" Ms. Rinse asked. She took a step forward. Before I could think of something to say, Maya ripped the box from my hands and lobbed it at Mela.

"No!" I shouted.

The box opened in the air. We heard a loud pop as the box fell to the floor. A tiny paw poked out of the box, and out came a fluffy kitten. Then another cat followed the first. Calicos, white cats, black cats, out they came, ten, twenty, thirty kittens. I grabbed onto Maya's shirt and started to pull her back, just in case the cats were actually tiny monsters of some kind. The cats surrounded Mela, rubbing their heads over her legs. "Kitties!" she cried out. I flinched and covered my face. But Mela just sat among the cats, picking them up one at a time and rubbing her nose into their fur. Soon, she was covered in kittens, and was smiling so hard I thought she might explode with happiness.

The sirens screeched and flapped their red wings, hovering a few feet off the floor, afraid of the cats. Ms. Rinse growled at them. "You cowards," she hissed. "Nia, darling. Your turn," she said. The room filled with a light so bright that it hurt to keep my eyes open.

"Look!" Maya said, and pointed out a window. The moon was close, closer than I'd ever seen it. It filled the sky, bleaching it white.

"Nia!" I shouted, but she was deep in concentration, her dark eyes turning to amber again.

"Who needs a telescope to see the moon when you can just bring it down to your level," Nia said, her voice different. Distant.

"Well done, young one!" Rinse cried out, cackling.

Had Nia really brought down the moon, or had she only put the thought of it in our heads? Either way, my eyes felt like they were burning. In the brightness, I fished for another box and blindly sent it flying, hoping it went Nia's way. It opened on the ground before Nia. The moon was back in place like a tiny slice in the sky, and we watched as

Nia started to rise into the air. "Wha—?" she yelped as she floated right to the top of the ceiling.

"Anti-gravity! Cool!" Maya said, running toward the box. I held her back.

"Now is not the time to geek out on me," I said, but Nia was, indeed, geeking out, doing somersaults in the air like a real astronaut, whooping and cheering as she flipped.

I peered into the bag again. These weren't curses. These were gifts!

"Thalia, catch!" I said, throwing a box at Thalia. She caught the box. It opened on its own, and music started to play.

"Oh, I know what this is! It's a classic. Cheers!" she shouted, as a jack-in-the-box popped up, startling the sirens and launching them skyward.

"Chickens," Thalia sneered at them, pushed the little clown back into the box, sat cross-legged on the floor, and waited for the music to start up again.

"Enough of this," Ms. Rinse said, her voice deep and quiet. She snapped her fingers and Thalia dropped the box. Mela pushed the kittens off her lap and rose to her feet, while Nia sank slowly down to the ground.

"How did you do that?" I asked.

"Like I said, the searchlights hold more power than you can know."

"Why are you doing this?" I asked, buying time. Again and again, I willed my magic to come, but it was like trying to start a stalled-out car. The engine revved and revved, but it just wouldn't start.

Ms. Rinse stalked around the room. She picked up a kitten by the scruff of the neck and started stroking its fur. "Why? Vengeance, obviously. Your sweet little tia really ruined things for me. And we were once best friends, if you can believe that," she said.

"You ruined your own life!" I shouted.

Ms. Rinse dropped the kitten. It landed on its paws and skittered away. "Hardly," she said. "I would have done good things in the world with that power." Ms. Rinse approached Maya, who trembled, but did not run. "And you, you unbelievable nerd. How you irritate me with your ideas and hope. You think you're a real scientist. I was the Muse of science. *Me!*"

"There are thousands of scientists in the world. Why Maya?" I felt like I'd been asking that question all along.

Ms. Rinse stopped. She grabbed hold of one of Maya's braids and pulled her down, so that she couldn't stand up straight anymore. "It's got nothing to do with Maya. It's you. Your aunt took a little trip to Mount Olympus and secured unimaginable powers for *you*. And then she made it so that my powers were *taken* from me," Ms. Rinse roared. "HOW. IS. THAT. FAIR?" she asked, pulling Maya down farther with each word.

"Let her go!" I shouted. The top of my head felt like it was on fire. Out of the corner of my eye, I could see Nia,

Mela, and Thalia blinking and holding their heads, as if they were waking up from a long nap. The sirens hissed and hovered over the floor.

"It's not fair, that's what," Ms. Rinse said. "Our powers are not infinite. They are zero-sum. Your nerdy Fated One here knows what that means. Our powers are divvied up from one source, and you have the lion's share. I deserve that share," she whispered, then finally let Maya go.

I took a deep breath. "Fine. You wanted my powers. Why not just come after me?" I asked. She might have in a million different ways, I thought. I would have followed her anywhere at school, into a supply closet, or up onto the third floor. She could have used any excuse, and I would have gone with her to a place where nobody could help me. I had trusted her, after all.

Ms. Rinse started pacing the room as she talked. "Did you think that what happened on the Metrorail was an accident? Are you that stupid?"

The train door! *Ms. Rinse* had done that?

"Don't act so surprised, Calliope. Think. Who did you give up your safe seats for? A nice old lady and her nice old husband."

At that, the sirens that had been Leo and Letty stepped forward and gave a little bow.

I could feel my hands clenching at my sides. Raquel and I *had* given up our safe seats to an elderly couple. They had been so sweet.

Ms. Rinse huffed in exasperation. "And I even had them offer you candy. Poisoned candy, naturally, but *you didn't even take it*."

Inside, I was shaking. We'd come really close to disaster that day. But I hadn't realized just how close a call it had been. "Honestly, nobody likes those strawberry candies," I said.

"SHUT UP!" Ms. Rinse shouted, so loudly that the glass in the bookcases tinkled against their frames. She kept on shouting, "I didn't expect your powers to be as strong as they were. Nobody makes heroes on their first try. But you did on that train. I'm no fool. If I couldn't get to you directly, if I couldn't stop you from becoming a muse, then I'd get to your Fated One. I'd ruin her. You'd be a failure from the start. Then Annie would know that her sacrifices were for *nothing*."

I opened my mouth to ask what she meant about sacrifices, but with another snap of Ms. Rinse's fingers, it was my turn to go up, up, up, until I was flattened against the ceiling, sliding slowly to an open upper window. I gripped the tin tiles of the ceiling with my fingertips, but it was no use. Ms. Rinse moved me around like a magnet on the surface of a refrigerator.

"Calliope, Muse of the epic poem, Maker of Heroes," Rinse said. "Enjoy your trip to Mount Olympus. One-way ticket, my dear. The air might get thin in the upper atmosphere. Hope you can hold your breath," she said.

I screamed, called out for Clio, for my mom, for the Muse Squad, for Tia Annie. But I kept sliding, as if dragged by invisible hands.

Ms. Rinse laughed, and the others all watched me go, just a few feet from the window now. "Maker of Heroes," Rinse taunted. "You didn't even turn in a science project. A big fat F for you," she said, smirking at her own joke.

"Hubris," I cried out, remembering what Tia Annie had said. "You won't win because of it!"

"Ah, so you were paying attention in *some* classes at least," Ms. Rinse said. "The opposite of pride is weakness. You are weak, Calliope."

Down below, Maya was busy solving the Rubik's Cube.

My feet touched the window casing. I locked my knees. My fingertips were bleeding now. I'd left red streaks on the ceiling as I tried to hold on.

Now Ms. Rinse was pacing the floor beneath me, her eyes on mine. "Haven't you ever wondered, Callie, what it might be like if you thought of yourself first for once? You could have the whole school in the palm of your hand. No one would ever call you 'fat' again. Your father would come home. You'd inspire them all to *love* you. Just you. Consider it. There is no rule against it. None of those precious muse rules says anything about making yourself the hero of the story," she said, and it sounded like a soothing purr in my ears. "Don't you want to be a hero, too?"

If I could turn my best friend into a pop star, imagine

what I could do for my mom, my brothers, for myself, I thought.

But that wasn't the deal, was it? Muses weren't heroes.

We were helpers.

We were makers.

We were mortal, but our powers were immortal.

We were goddesses.

I tried one last time to harness the magic I'd been given and sent it Maya's way. My skin tingled. I couldn't feel my fingers anymore. Below me, Maya's own fingers became a blur.

Click.

Click.

Nobody looked her way at all. They just stared at me.

"Do it, Maya!" I shouted.

Click.

Maya sent the cube twisting in the air, solving itself the moment it struck Ms. Rinse on the forehead.

Then I dropped from the ceiling like a stone.

The last thing I remembered were the faces of the Muse Squad hovering over me before the world turned black.

Chapter 32
MISSION ACCOMPLISHED

When I opened my eyes, my mother was there.

"How does this keep happening to you?" she asked, a tired smile on her face.

I blinked the sleep crust out of my eyes.

"I brought you a burger," Mario said. He was sitting in the corner of my hospital room.

"But I ate it. Sorry," Fernando added, wiping a bit of mustard off his chin.

Later, my dad and Laura called. "Kiddo, do I need to make you a bubble-wrap suit or what?" he asked.

"Chicken butt, Papi," I said, and he laughed, warmly and deeply. "I'm sending you a picture, okay?"

"Okay," I said. My phone buzzed, and I opened my messages app to see a photo of an ultrasound. It read "It's a Boy!" in tiny white letters. The black-and-white alien-looking baby seemed to be waving at me.

"Another brother," I sighed. I showed the twins, and they bumped chests and made gorilla sounds in triumph.

A voice cut through the commotion. "Pardon me."

We all turned to look.

In the doorway stood Clio, back in her doctor's scrubs. Her bright white hair was in a long braid, and her golden trumpet earrings glittered. "Just a nasty bump on the head," she said. "No stitches this time. Those convention center steps are treacherous. Off your feet for a few days, yes?"

She winked at me, and everyone froze in place.

"Clio!" I shouted, then winced. "Is Tia Annie okay?"

Clio smiled, and nodded. "That she is. And the search-lights are bright as they ever were." She sat on my bed. "You have our thanks, Calliope. The Lost Muse was neutralized. There are nine rules regarding the work of the muses. You uncovered the last two on your own," she said.

"I did?"

"Rule number eight. A muse is no better, or worse, than the heroes she inspires. The problem with Wendy, or Ms. Rinse, as you knew her, is that she never quite took that rule to heart. But you did," Clio said, and booped my nose. I was too stunned to respond. Clio went on, "Maya was saved, and you accomplished your mission. All is well. We have a meeting at headquarters next Tuesday. Three a.m. London time. We fixed the Great Bed for you."

Then Clio patted my cheek and I felt warm and happy. She rose to leave.

"Clio, wait," I said. "What was the ninth rule?"

"Oh yes. The ninth rule. Muses are goddesses. And don't ever forget it." Then, she slipped away, and my family was back in motion, loud as ever.

That evening, it was just me and my mom at the hospital again. She fell asleep as soon as her telenovela, *La Escandalosa*, was done.

I texted Raquel.

> Hey. The science fair was super weird.

> Your mom called me. Told me you fell down the stairs. How's your head?

> Okay. How are you?

> Okay. The science fair WAS weird. Like, how did those birds get in there? They said the birds escaped the aviary at the Miami Zoo and somehow got into the convention center.

> SO WEIRD.

Clio had done a lot of cleanup, I realized. I'd have to catch up on all of it next week.

Even weirder? I hardly remember it. It's all so foggy to me. I guess leaving America's Next Star affected me more than I thought it would. The internet . . . has not been very kind about me.

Don't read that stuff.

I won't. I'm NOT. Believe me. I just want to be regular Raquel again. Violet is going to have fun being mean to me, though.

Forget her. You'll always be a pop star to me.

Shut up.

Never.

Night, Cal. Let's talk for real soon, k?

K.

I put down my phone and fell fast asleep.

The dawn came, rosy and bright. My mom had gotten up early. I heard her in the bathroom, humming to herself.

"You're in a good mood," I said when she emerged. She sat on the edge of my bed.

"I had a wonderful dream. Your tia Annie and I were back in Cuba. We were little girls on the beach again, looking for seashells. She said, 'Say hello to my Callie-Mallie for me.' Then we found a conch shell *this big*," she said, holding her hands out to indicate something larger than my head.

I grinned and sat up straighter. My head hurt. My shoulders and tailbone did, too. But I was happy to be back in Miami, and glad I didn't have to worry about sirens or Lost Muses or curses for the time being.

My mom picked at some fluff on my blanket. "I have an idea, and I want to run it by you," she said then.

"Go ahead."

She took hold of my hand. "You know your friend Maya?"

I nodded.

"You know how she lives in a group home? What if she came to live with us? As in permanently?" my mom asked. "She'd have to agree to it. You too, of course. Your brothers are on board. They have been since that night at Frosty's Enchanted Forest," my mom went on. "Maya needs a family. And if a person is loved—"

"Then they'll be okay," I said.

Maya didn't need to win the county science fair. What she needed was a home. A real home. A family.

Mission accomplished.

"Better than okay," my mom said.

My sister, a Fated One, I thought.

"Bunk beds?" I asked, and my mom laughed.

"Whatever the two of you want," she said.

I had been out of school for a few days when Raquel came over one afternoon.

"Hey," she said, standing at the door to my room.

"Hey," I said back.

"You missed the last day of classes before Christmas break. A shaving-cream fight broke out in the courtyard," Raquel said, staring at her hands the whole time.

I shrugged, pointing at the bump on my head.

"You feeling okay?" she asked, and I nodded. She took a tentative step into my room. Her hair was growing out, the shaved parts a little longer now and sticking up out of the side of her head. The blue dye they'd put in for her last episode of *America's Next Star* was already fading to silver. Raquel must have caught me staring at it. "I don't know why they gave me this cheesy haircut," she said, touching the side of her head.

Then we were quiet, and I couldn't stand it for another second. Sure, we'd texted back and forth a few times, but we hadn't talked, really talked, yet.

Raquel had a determined look on her face, and I knew she'd come over to bury the hatchet.

"You made me feel left out of your life," I said, as plainly as I could.

Raquel pursed her lips. "I felt the same way. I mean, Maya is nice and everything, but you were hanging out with her a lot. Plus, you were doing this weird British accent thing."

"I WAS NOT!" I said, though I think I may have used "brilliant" to mean "great" one time, and maybe I did sound a little like Thalia when I said it. "You hung out with Violet. And Max. Though Max turned out all right," I put in.

"Because I missed you. And Violet wasn't a good replacement, by the way." Raquel was breathing hard, her brown eyes glossy and penetrating.

I took a deep breath of my own. Why was this so hard? I steadied myself. Then blurted, all at once, "I was jealous, okay. I was super jealous. Not of any specific thing. Just . . . all of it. I wasn't a good friend. I was totally hubristic, and I'm so sorry."

That did it. It was like tearing open a Christmas present, or turning on the water faucet all the way at once. Raquel rushed toward my bed, where I was sitting cross-legged. Crushing me in a hug, she mumbled into my shoulder. "I don't know what hubristic means. But I'm sorry, too! I was this *diva monster*. Do you know I chewed out one of the craft services people because the arepas they'd brought me were cold?"

"What's craft services?" I asked.

"Like, the caterers behind the scenes at a TV or movie

set," she said, and I realized she was crying. "People like my mom and dad," she added, her voice quivering. Raquel's parents owned a little Venezuelan café nearby. They worked hard every day, her mom always smelling like onions and garlic, and her dad forever wearing a T-shirt that read COMIDA FALCÓN no matter the occasion. "I yelled at them, Callie. The people nice enough to find arepas for me from who knows where. Then my parents yelled at me for being a malcriada, WHICH I WAS," Raquel wailed. I hugged her tighter. "I was a monster," she whispered.

"You weren't a monster," I said. "Trust me, I know monsters."

"The producers wanted me to be someone else. And I gave them what they wanted, until the day I just couldn't anymore," she whispered.

"I'm glad you came. I needed you like crazy that day."

Raquel released me, looked into my eyes, and lifted an eyebrow. "What exactly did I miss while we were in the bestie-break-up zone?"

"Nothing. A lot of nothing," I said, remembering muse rule number six about secret identities, though I didn't think it should apply to best friends. I'd have to take it up with Clio. There would probably be paperwork. But for now, I said, "Nothing at all except for Maya. My mom is adopting her. It's going to be good. Really good," I added.

"Well, that's huge news. If that's 'nothing,' I don't want to know what you think 'something' is," Raquel said, still suspicious.

My best friend was no dummy.

I laughed nervously. Then quickly changed the subject.

"Listen to me, Raquel Falcón. Don't be too hard on yourself. You're amazing," I said. "And you'll be a super-star someday, at your own pace, in your own way." I could feel the tingling start to happen, but I willed it to stop. This was Raquel's fate, not mine. She had to be her own hero. Like Clio said, sometimes you had to wait for the moment when you didn't need magic anymore and trust that the right time would come. Raquel didn't need me to help her discover her inner hero. She'd found it on her own.

Raquel sniffed and wiped her eyes. "Let's never fight again," she said.

"You got it," I told her.

I thought of how things would change from now on. There would soon be two dollhouses in my room—one messy, one neat. There would probably be science experiments on the dresser. And Maya would have to pretend not to notice whenever I popped over to headquarters. Most important, Maya would be family, and Raquel was my best friend again, which was all the magic we needed.

"The last month or so feels like a crazy dream, you know?" Raquel said.

"I know what you mean. But it's back to the real world, right?"

Raquel pulled her backpack onto my bed. "Yep. Oh, and did you hear? Ms. Rinse quit. Nobody's seen her since the county science fair," Raquel said.

"No kidding?" I said, trying to play it off.

Raquel shrugged, opened her backpack, and pulled out a notebook. "I've brought your science homework for the week. Thank me later. Our new teacher? She's a real harpy."

I laughed. I really hoped the new teacher was just regular mean, and *not* the magical kind. "Well," I said, putting aside the science homework, "she can bring it on. I'm ready."

MUSE RULES

1. A muse always trusts her instincts.
2. Muse magic is just love, concentrated.
3. A muse never uses her magic against her sisters.
4. Inspiration knows no borders.
5. All people and places are worthy of magic.
6. A muse must always keep her identity a secret.
7. A muse is a person on whom nothing is lost.
8. A muse is no better, or worse, than the heroes she inspires.
9. Muses are goddesses. And don't ever forget it.

Acknowledgments

To my readers, thank you for cracking open this book, and for joining the Muse Squad on their first adventure. The Muse Squad wants me to remind you all that there is always a hero within, even when stuff gets difficult (*especially* when stuff gets difficult, actually), that art, music, theater, science, history, poetry, faith in goodness, and a healthy sense of humor are all important and worthy things, and that they believe in you (as do I).

Exemplary editors know that asking the right questions can open up a story in the best ways. I am so grateful to Kristin Rens for her brilliant curiosity about this book, and for loving these characters so much. Maya especially loves you right back, Kristin. And to everyone at Balzer + Bray, thank you for being such a terrific team.

Stéphanie Abou, thank you for supporting this book, my writing, and my love of J-Lo. Like the muses, eres una divina, through and through. I am so glad you're in my life.

Thanks to Mary Pender at UTA for your support and guidance.

I am forever grateful to the community of writers and early readers who cheered this story on. To Chris Green, your feedback when this was just a baby book draft was energizing. To Hallie Johnston, I don't know what I did to deserve such a good friend. Here's to manta rays and Saturday drivers forever. To Diane Berkley, you know I'll be loving you forever you, Didi. Thank you for reading, and for explaining science fairs to me. To Neha Rajan—thank you for smart and enthusiastic feedback, and for kickass suggestions. To Rachel Hawkins and Ash Parsons, I'm so glad we got to celebrate books together where the magic happens. Let's put those tiaras on and do it again soon. Mil gracias to fellow Cubiche, Pablo Cartaya, for your excellent kidlit example. Una pila de gracias to Las Musas, a group of phenomenal Latinx kidlit writers who welcomed me in and who are changing the world, one story at a time.

Thanks to my dear sisters in the work, Evelina Galang and Patricia Engel—you wondrous women, I'm so glad I know you. And to my colleagues and students at the U, I am grateful for your cheerful support.

My daughters, Penelope and Mary-Blair, and my goddaughters, Jaina and Vanessa, urged me to write a story for them one sunny day not too long ago. This is it, younglings. I promise I'll put buried treasure in the next one.

Callie knows that familia es todo, and so do I. Orlando, Penny, and Embee—you are my everything. Thank you for your love and unending support. And kids, I'm sorry I yelled at you to get out of the room while Mommy is writing. (But seriously, get out of the room while Mommy is writing.)

Turn the page for a sneak peek of the sequel,

MUSE SQUAD
The Mystery of the Tenth

Chapter 1

ARACHNOPHOBIA

My room looked like it had imploded. There were items of clothing draped on every surface—my dresser, the doorknob, the door itself, my sister's new microscope (an adoption day gift from our twin brothers), and even on my sister.

"Callie, this is entirely unacceptable," Maya said, a long sock dangling over her face.

"Sorry!" I said, snatching it away. "I can't figure out what to pack for New York." I was out of breath and sweating. It was summer in Miami and the air-conditioning in our house had conked out that morning. Even my elbows were damp.

Maya glanced at her own suitcase, already packed and propped up by the door, ready for our flights tomorrow morning. She was heading to Space Camp in Huntsville, Alabama. Meanwhile, I was going to New York City to spend a month with my papi; my stepmom, Laura; and my new baby brother, Rafael Jr. My brothers were staying in Miami to earn money to buy a used car. At least, that was the excuse they gave. Papi had asked them to visit, too, but they'd said no right away. The truth is, when Mami and Papi broke up, the twins got really angry at Papi for leaving, and a part of them was still mad.

Maya's summer sounded infinitely cooler than mine. While she would be learning about space and gravity and actual *rocket science*, I would be stuck in a small walk-up apartment in Queens, staying in the baby's room while the baby slept with Papi and Laura in a cradle by their bed.

"I wish I was going to Space Camp," I grumbled.

"Since when do you want to be a scientist?" Maya said. "Because astronauts are scientists first, you know."

I didn't have to take long to consider it. Science was Maya's thing. Did I even *have* a thing? I thought of my best friend, Raquel, who just knew she wanted to be a performer. What did I want from life? I had no clue. Whenever anybody asked me, "What do you want to be when you grow up?" I nearly always just shrugged. Could a person make a career out of hanging out with friends, eating snacks, and watching television?

I don't think so.

"Why the face?" Maya asked me. "I'm sure you'll have

plenty of a-*muse*-ing adventures this summer."

"Stop it," I said, rolling my eyes. Maya was the only person in my family who knew I was one of the nine muses. It's supposed to be a secret, but *you* try keeping information from your genius sister!

There have always been nine muses, and usually, they're grown-ups. But now, for the first time ever, *four* of us are kids. We're the Muse Squad, which is a silly name, but we've gotten used to it. I'm the Muse of epic poetry. It sounds a little boring, but isn't as it turns out, because epic poems are about heroes, which means I am a hero-maker.

Maya was right. Something interesting would probably come up this summer. But the thing was, I hadn't heard from the other muses in ages. Nia was trying out for a gymnastics club team in Chicago. Mela's mother had bought her theater passes for the summer, and she was catching every tragic play she could, and Thalia had volunteered to be a junior librarian at the British Library. They were all pretty busy with non-muse activities.

As for the other muses, the grown-up ones, I hadn't heard from any of them either. Usually every few weeks our leader, Clio, would call us to headquarters—which was in London, England, at the Victoria and Albert Museum— either for training or missions. Maybe things were quiet in the summer. Did muses go on vacation? I didn't know. But the silence made me nervous. It made me feel as if something was *up*.

"Earth to Callie," Maya said, snapping me out of my thoughts.

"Sorry, Mission Control. We've got a problem. I'm panicking," I answered her, then slumped on the floor on top of a pile of a sweatshirts and tees. It was so hot, I couldn't concentrate.

Maya smiled. She liked it when I called her Mission Control, and I liked to imagine her there, behind panels full of technology, solving important scientific problems. Maybe she could solve my problem, too. Without asking, she started plucking different clothing items off the floor and the furniture, folding them deftly and sliding them into my suitcase for me.

"No need to panic," Maya said, cool as can be. "When I was in foster care, I had to pack up a lot. You don't really need to take too much. Plus, you'll want room in your bag for all the souvenirs you're going to buy me," she joked, rolling a pair of jeans like a burrito. Maya had started wearing her hair like Princess Leia—in two buns over her ears—and they bobbed a little as she packed, like a pair of loose headphones.

"Why aren't you sweating?" I asked. I was drenched. The ceiling fan was spinning, but it was really just moving the warm air around. It felt like a giant was blowing his hot breath on us.

Maya giggled, lifting the bottom of her T-shirt a little. There, duct-taped to her stomach, were three ice packs.

"You won't be laughing when it's time to pull those off," I said.

Maya's smile slipped a little. "Climate change. We all have to manage somehow." Last fall, before Mami adopted her, Maya had won the county science fair with her project—a plan to address sea-level rise in South Florida.

It hadn't been an easy win. The competition was tough. Plus, a rogue muse who happened to be our evil science teacher, Ms. Rinse, and her three siren minions, did their worst to try to stop Maya from succeeding. Maya doesn't know it, but she's a Fated One—meant for great things thanks to that massive brain of hers, which means she's under the protection of the muses.

Maya zipped up my suitcase and said, "Voilà! All packed. Now can we please go to the mall where the temperatures aren't trying to kill us?"

She'd done it. She'd packed my suitcase. Sometimes Maya saved *me*.

"Vamos," I said, "we'll ask Fernando and Mario to take us."

Maya crossed her fingers *and* her eyes. She was right. We'd need all the luck we could get if we wanted to convince the twins to be our ride to the mall.

"Bros. My bros. My wonderful brothers," I called down the hallway. Mario popped his head out of his bedroom.

"What do you want?" he asked.

"The answer is no," Fernando added from inside. The twins would be seventeen soon, but Maya and I usually had them beat when it came to maturity.

"Please?" Maya squeaked, her hands clasped under her chin and her eyes doing their best puppy dog impersonation.

Mario blinked. "Well—"

"Don't you give in," Fernando barked. I could hear their favorite video game, Underwatch, blaring away.

"It'll be nice and cool at the mall," I said. "We won't even bother you. You can spend the whole time at Gamer Place."

"Air-conditioning, air-condiiiiitioning," Maya sang, the perfect backup.

"Fine," Mario said.

"Ugh. You always fall for it," Fernando said, shutting off the game. The truth was, they *both* always fell for it. When we'd gone before the family court judge in May to make Maya an official member of the family, the judge had given my brothers a big speech about what it meant to have a new little sister. And though it kind of bugged me that he was giving them the whole "men of the house" talk (I mean, let's be real here. I'm in an all-girls-*with*-ancient-powers squad, and my mom is the head of the house, no question), my brothers had taken it to heart. That meant Maya got away with a lot when it came to them, the big softies.

As for me, unlike Maya, I was old news. Just last week, they'd covered my bed in a hundred sticky notes that read "dork." It took all my willpower to keep from "inspiring" them to drink a ketchup milkshake.

Because that's what muses do, we inspire people. If we wanted to, we could convince just about anyone to do something truly awful. But muses aren't about that villain life. Besides, we have a bunch of muse rules we follow:

1. A muse always trusts her instincts.
2. Muse magic is just love, concentrated.
3. A muse never uses her magic against her sisters.
4. Inspiration knows no borders.
5. All people and places are worthy of magic.
6. A muse must always keep her identity a secret.
7. A muse is a person on whom nothing is lost.
8. A muse is no better, or worse, than the heroes she inspires.
9. Muses are goddesses. And don't ever forget it.

They're good rules, but lately, I've been coming up with my own. Like Callie's Muse Rule #236: Your brothers are idiots, but you love them anyway.

Still, when I saw my bed covered in sticky notes, and Maya's pristine and untouched, it hurt my feelings. I almost said something to them, but then I just . . . didn't. That's been happening a lot lately, too. Whenever I try to tell somebody about my *feelings*, my eyes get all watery and stupid, and I absolutely hate crying. Mami always says, "All feelings are valid because you feel them. That's the point." But I don't know about that. Sometimes my feelings seem pretty ridiculous, even to me.

"I'm getting one of those food court cookies the size of my head," Fernando was saying as he tied his laces.

"For sure," Mario added.

"Mmm," I said, my sweet tooth coming alive.

"I hope you brought your own money, 'cause I'm not sharing," Fernando said. My pockets were empty and I let out a groan. Sweet tooth deactivated.

Maya pointed at her purse and gave me a wink. She'd gotten lots of adoption day gifts from our extended family, mainly in the form of spending money. Our great-aunt Carmen gave her a hundred bucks. All I ever got from her at Christmas and birthdays was socks.

Sometimes it pays to be the new kid. Literally.

Mario and Fernando had gotten permission to take Mami's van, and we piled in. The air-conditioning was working, and we blasted it into our faces while Mario turned the radio to the reggaeton station.

Maya and I sang along to song after song the whole way to the mall. It was our last day together in Miami, and I wanted to make the most of it. First, we'd go straight to the food court for some ice cream (pistachio for Maya, plain chocolate for me), then we would make our way to Pop! Mania and see if they had any *Zombie Beach* merch for sale. *Zombie Beach* was a new horror show set in Miami. We'd seen the first season twice already and were halfway through our third viewing. I watched most of it through my fingers, covering my face every time a zombie crashed into the room and ate someone's face. Maya was fearless, though. For some reason, the bloodier the scene, the more she laughed. Mario and Fernando were that way, too, and they teased me about being so chicken.

I was just thinking about how my brothers had always been brave about that kind of stuff when Mario let out a bloodcurdling scream.

The van swerved, tilting up onto two wheels before slamming back down and going into a spin. My seat belt cut into my shoulder, and I watched as Fernando's head smacked the passenger door window. Maya curled into a ball in her seat, her hands clamped onto her hair buns. I could feel myself trembling all over, and I think I was saying, "No, no, no, no, please," out loud, but I can't be sure. The steering wheel spun wildly on its own. Mario needed to get a grip . . . literally!

I tried to summon my muse magic, but the instant tingling on my skin that came with the magic? It didn't happen. Again, I willed my magic to come, but it just wouldn't. After what felt like a million years, the van rolled onto the grassy swale on the side of the road and finally stopped.

Mario was still screaming.

"What happened?" I shouted, clicking off my seat belt. Maya was already clambering toward the front of the van, while Fernando was holding Mario by the shoulders and shaking him.

"Sp-sp-spiders!" Mario spluttered, and then I saw them—hundreds of tiny, nearly transparent spiders, crawling on the dashboard.

Fernando made a strangled sound, slamming his baseball cap over the crawlers again and again until they were still. Then he swept them into his hat and threw the whole thing outside.

Mario whimpered, his hands covering his face, his shoulders shaking. It broke my heart.

"Hey, bro," I said softly, laying a hand on Mario's head. I tried to call my muse magic one more time, waiting to feel my fingers going numb, and my hair standing up at the root a little, like it always did.

Nothing happened. "Don't panic," I whispered to myself.

"Too late," Mario answered, hyperventilating now.

Thinking maybe I could nudge the magic along, I pictured Mario taking deep breaths, calm and brave, like he normally was. The picture in my mind grew sharper and more defined until Mario stopped shaking.

Had my magic worked? Or was Mario just back in control of himself?

"I don't know what happened. I've never been funny about spiders," Mario said after his breathing returned to normal. "But there were so many, and they started getting on my hands." His voice was firmer, and he was smacking his own cheeks a little, like a person trying to wake up from a dream.

"Good job," Maya whispered to me.

"Um, yeah," I said softly. I rubbed my hands together, and they felt normal. No tingling. It was definitely my turn to panic. Where had my magic gone?

"That was nuts," Fernando said, running his hands through his hair. He took a look at his cap on the ground outside and shivered.

"M-maybe we should go home," Mario said, and we didn't argue.

"Want me to drive?" Fernando asked, and Mario nodded, so the boys traded places. I watched as Mario checked the van for damage (there was none), then came over to the passenger side, his eyes darting back and forth over the grass, checking for more spiders.

That's when I saw a different spider in the distance. This one was very large, black, and furry. It had crawled onto a traffic cone, perched at the very top.

I nudged Maya with my elbow. "Do you see that?"

Maya squinted. "The traffic cone?"

"No, what's on it."

Maya squinted harder. "Nothing's on it, Callie."

When I looked again, I saw that Maya was right—the spider was gone. I rubbed my eyes and leaned back in my seat. Clio had once told me that muses saw the world a bit more magically than others did. In fact, I had once spotted a nymph in the River Thames. It was possible that the spiders that had scared my brother weren't just any old arachnids. But there was no way of being sure.

My brain was racing all the way home, thoughts pinging back and forth, but nothing feeling like it made any sense.

I looked at Mario, drumming his fingers on his thighs to music. He was his old, chillaxed self again, but we were all very quiet. Nobody was in the mood to talk about what had just happened. We stopped at a red light, and I watched as a man standing on the sidewalk spit his gum onto the ground.

"Ugh. Litterer," Maya said in disgust.

Narrowing my eyes and staring at him, I called my magic again.

Everything was still as the world seemed to slow down before my eyes, but still, my magic didn't come. The man didn't move. In fact, we watched as he dug into his pockets and threw some crumpled receipts on the ground.

"He's the worst," Fernando said from the front seat.

My breath started to hitch.

"You okay?" Maya asked.

I shook my head.

"That was pretty scary back there," she added, resting her head on my shoulder. "But I wouldn't worry anymore. The odds of that happening again are astronomical."

Maya may not have been a muse herself, but she had a way of making people feel better that was pretty magical.

Outside the van windows, the man on the sidewalk pressed the crosswalk button repeatedly. I steadied myself, remembering that I'd used my imagination when Mario was freaking out, and he'd calmed down. Maybe it was a coincidence, or maybe . . .

I pictured the litterer bending down, retrieving his gum, and throwing it into a trash can that was only six feet away from him.

Just as the picture finished forming in my head, the man licked his lips, dug into his pocket for yet another receipt, bent down for the gum, and sailed it into the trash can with an elegant toss. Then he picked up the other receipts he'd let drop.

I frowned. Had I done that? Was I summoning my magic differently now?

"Three points, bro," Fernando said.

"You're two for two," Maya whispered.

That had been easy. I hadn't had to *call* my magic so much as *imagine* it. Was that a thing all muses did eventually? Had I, like, leveled up or something?

I was just thinking about all that when my muse brace-let started to heat up, hotter and hotter, just as Fernando slid the van into our driveway back home.

Perfect timing. The muses were assembling and I hated being late.